Champagne Problems
A Cross Security Investigation

G.K. Parks

Copyright © 2025 G.K. Parks

A Modus Operandi imprint

All rights reserved.

ISBN: 194271050X
ISBN-13: 978-1-942710-50-9

For my mom and dad

BOOKS IN THE ALEXIS PARKER SERIES:

Likely Suspects
The Warhol Incident
Mimicry of Banshees
Suspicion of Murder
Racing Through Darkness
Camels and Corpses
Lack of Jurisdiction
Dying for a Fix
Intended Target
Muffled Echoes
Crisis of Conscience
Misplaced Trust
Whitewashed Lies
On Tilt
Purview of Flashbulbs
The Long Game
Burning Embers
Thick Fog
Warning Signs
Past Crimes
Sinister Secret
Zero Sum
Buried Alive
Trouble Brewing
Balance Due
Hostage Situation
Damage Control

BOOKS IN THE CROSS SECURITY INVESTIGATIONS SERIES:

Fallen Angel
Calculated Risk
Light Them Up
Champagne Problems
Knife's Edge

ONE

"Lucien, your ten o'clock is here," Justin called from his desk.

I pushed the button for the intercom. Maybe one of these days my assistant would take the hint. "Send him in."

Justin gestured to my open door. "Mr. Cross will see you now." He spun in his chair, exaggerating his eye roll so I wouldn't miss it. But since a potential client was standing between us, I did my best to ignore it.

"Mr. Kershaw, please have a seat." I waited for him to sit before dropping back into my chair. "Would you like a cup of coffee? Maybe a bagel? My assistant would be happy to run to the nearest bakery to get you whatever your heart desires. How about some caviar? I can book him on the first flight to Russia to ensure it's fresh."

Justin stuck his tongue out at me, and I scratched my brow with my middle finger. Thankfully, Mr. Kershaw didn't notice.

"I ate before I came." Kershaw took an envelope out of his pocket and placed it on my desk. "When I spoke to the lady on the phone, I told her what happened. She said she wasn't sure you'd be able to help."

"Gloria didn't want to get your hopes up. Matters like

yours aren't the easiest to resolve. It's unlikely I'll be able to recover the funds you lost." I opened the envelope. Inside was Alan Kershaw's latest bank statement. His account had been zeroed out. "Is this everything that was taken?"

"Uh-huh."

"The scammer didn't ask for other account information, property records, credit cards, anything like that?"

"That was it. I should have known better."

"How exactly did it happen?"

"I received a call, allegedly from an online casino where I like to play poker from time to time. The caller said I'd won the jackpot and needed to verify my account information to deposit my winnings."

I scanned the sheet. A few small deposits had been made from the casino, the last being almost a month before the incident. "Wouldn't you have known if you won a jackpot?"

The look on Kershaw's face told me that wasn't helpful. "It wasn't from a particular game of hold 'em. The jackpot I allegedly won was from the casino itself. Every time a bet is placed, the player receives one entry for the big prize."

"Like a sweepstakes?"

"Yes."

"That's what you thought you won?"

Kershaw nodded.

I put his bank statement down and went to the online casino's website. Information on the sweepstakes jackpot was listed right at the top. I scanned the fine print which stated winners would be notified via text, e-mail, or by phone call. If the chosen winner could not be reached or did not respond within forty-eight hours, another winner would be selected. "Did you receive any other communication prior to the call?"

"This." Kershaw held out his phone. "That's why I thought it was legit."

I read the e-mail. The logo matched. The images and wording were the same. There were no typos or obvious clues the sender was anyone other than who he claimed to be. The only thing missing was the verified symbol next to the sender's e-mail address, and those didn't always pop up.

The details within the e-mail said someone would phone to follow up on Kershaw's winnings within twenty-four hours and he should have his username and account information handy.

"Do you mind if I forward this to myself?" I asked.

"Whatever you need."

After I sent a copy of the message to a secure box, I handed Kershaw back his phone. "All right." Asking the next question was likely to cause physical discomfort, but I had to know. "Have you gone to the authorities?" Yep, I was right. That one hurt.

"The police took my statement, but they said there wasn't much they could do."

"That isn't surprising." Dear old dad had dropped the ball again. "Have you spoken to the FBI?"

"The FBI?"

"The police should have told you to go there. They have a division dedicated to fraud investigations. Their cybercrime unit is less of a joke than the police department's. From what I hear, they even know how to turn on their computers without consulting the instruction manual first."

Kershaw looked bewildered.

"I'm joking." Maybe. "They're your best bet for recovering your funds." I performed an internet search, but this particular scam hadn't been reported, meaning it wasn't widely used or whoever was behind it was just getting started.

"Are you saying Cross Security can't help me?"

I didn't want to say that, but I'd seen and heard enough to know the chances this was a person acting independently were slim to none. More than likely, this scam was part of a much larger operation, possibly with international ties to organizations that killed people on a regular basis. I'd already had one run-in with organized crime. It'd be best to avoid a repeat if possible.

"I can look into the matter for you and gather some information, but I can't make any guarantees beyond that."

Kershaw stared at my desk while he processed everything I'd said. "The FBI will want information and details about what happened. Whatever you learn could be used to help them, Mr. Cross."

"I guess." I didn't like where this was going. The last thing I needed was the Feds asking how I obtained my intel.

"All right," Kershaw said. "I'll follow up with them and see what they say. In the meantime, I'd like you to find out who scammed me. See if you can get a name or address, something concrete."

"I'm sure they could find that for you."

"The look on your face suggests otherwise. In fact, I'd be surprised if you thought they could navigate their way out of a paper bag."

"Even if I find the party responsible, by now, your money is long gone. It'd take a team of forensic accountants and a few supercomputers to track it down. The way these things work, funds get dispersed and cleaned. It'd be impossible to make a recovery. The only way to put a stop to this is to shut down the people behind it."

"Hence the Feds," Kershaw said.

I nodded. "Cross Security can handle a lot of issues. We specialize in security and investigations, but this situation is beyond us. I doubt you'll find another private security agency that could tackle it either. I'm sorry I can't make you whole again."

"But you can get information the Feds need?"

"Probably."

"Okay. Do that. I'll let you know my point of contact and case number as soon as I speak to the FBI. Whatever you find, pass off to them."

"You're my client. I'll pass it off to you, and you can do whatever you want with it. But I'd appreciate if you leave my name out of it."

Kershaw quirked an eyebrow. "You don't want the credit?"

"I don't want the added scrutiny."

He extended his hand. "That won't be a problem, Mr.

Cross."

"In that case, you won't mind signing a contract saying as much." Reaching into my bottom drawer, I pushed the boilerplate contracts to the side and found the special ones Almeada drafted to deal with sensitive clients and subjects. It wasn't exactly an NDA, but it was damn close.

After Kershaw signed, he left the information on my desk and walked out of my office. I stood in the doorway, wondering if I should have given him a flat-out no instead of agreeing to look into the matter. I'd barely gotten the police off my back about that homicide investigation. Cross Security didn't need the FBI looking into how we conducted business.

"Hey, Lucien," Justin peered up at me, "your friend's back."

"When will this guy take the hint?"

"Do you want me to have building security throw him out again?" Justin checked the notebook beside his desk. "This will make the fourth time this week. I could call Sgt. Rostokowski and ask if she can have a patrol car drive by. At this rate, we could have him picked up for harassment or stalking."

"I don't think that will stop him." I narrowed my eyes at the corner of the screen. "At least he's not dressed in a giant chicken suit today."

Justin's lip quirked in the corner. "That didn't really happen."

"You wanna bet?"

"Seriously?"

"Go downstairs and ask him yourself."

"I don't have to. It didn't happen." Justin pretended to be fascinated with something on the billing spreadsheet.

I wasn't sure he knew I'd made that up or if he just wanted to avoid a trip downstairs. Either way, I had to do something to deal with the problem.

I didn't have anyone on payroll who could handle this for me. My security teams were out of the office. Gloria, my recently promoted office manager, was fielding calls. Plus, I wouldn't want to subject her to the lunatic downstairs. And even if I ordered Justin to go, he wouldn't. Maybe we'd have a talk about that one of these days. But he'd probably ignore that too. He had selective hearing when it came to tasks he considered optional. If he wasn't my number one, I'd get rid of him.

"You're lucky you're pretty," I said.

"You can't say things like that. It's sexual harassment, boss."

"If you want to sue me, call Almeada. He'd be happy to help you out. He might even do it pro bono."

Justin laughed. "I'll add it to my list of things to do."

Gloria looked up from her desk. "Are you sure he wasn't talking to me?"

I smiled at her. "You deserve a much greater compliment than pretty."

"Hey." Justin gave me a pointed look. "Now I'm insulted."

I headed for the elevator. "You can't have it both ways."

Once the elevator doors closed, the smile fell from my face. I'd been avoiding the issue for a while, but Ace Darrow wasn't going anywhere. The rival investigator had been fired from his last gig, and for some reason, he thought I owed him. According to the way he told the story, he saved my life. That wasn't exactly how I remembered it.

He hadn't responded to threats. Instead, he showed up every day to beg for a job. Building security always grabbed him before he made it to the elevators, but this had to stop.

Before the doors opened, I buttoned my jacket and straightened my cuffs and tie. To command respect, I had to look the part, and given the lack of respect from my office staff, I could only assume I was failing to dress appropriately.

Building security nodded to me when I stepped out. "Mr. Cross, he's right over there." They indicated the chairs near the front desk.

"I thought you were going to rope off a section and make a special detention area for him."

"We thought about it, but we were afraid it'd only encourage him."

I strode toward Ace Darrow. "When are you going to give this up, Ace?"

The P.I. climbed to his feet. "Finally, a meeting with the man himself. I knew you'd have to show your face eventually."

"This isn't a meeting. This is your final warning. Next time, I will have you arrested."

"We both know that won't stick. Face it, Lucien, you owe me. I'm not going anywhere until you give me a chance to prove myself. We both know you're hurting for investigators. You can't operate an office that size with you being the only investigator. It'll never work. Your corporate clients alone require too much time and attention. You have no one to work other cases, to put together backgrounds, to conduct interviews, or to work surveillance."

"What do you know about my corporate clients?"

"Afraid I hacked into your system again?"

I gave him my best death glare, hoping he'd keel over. Fortunately for him, I had yet to perfect that trick. "If I find out you're stalking any of them, you'll be facing a lot worse than harassment charges." I lowered my voice. "They'll never find your body, at least not all of it. Maybe they'll find a couple of teeth or a femur, but that'll be it. I hope you don't have your heart set on an open casket."

"You won't hurt me. You need me. Come on, you've seen my work. I'm better than you when it comes to research. You could use me." He reached into his shirt pocket and pulled out a folded sheet of paper. "Here's my résumé. I'm not asking for much. All I'd like is the same as what I was getting before you got me canned from my last job."

"I didn't get you fired."

"You forced my boss into retirement. It's the same thing."

"So go back to D.C. and find another job digging up dirt on politicians. There's always a new scumbag looking to run for office. Go harass him instead." I ignored the paper he held in my direction. "You know you can't work here. You aren't licensed in the state."

"Yes, I am." He put the paper down and pulled out his wallet to show me his private investigator credentials.

"Did you get that from a Cracker Jack box?"

"You could benefit from my years of experience. I've been doing this a lot longer than you have. I could teach you a thing or two. C'mon. What's the worst that could happen?"

I could think of several apocalyptic events. "Cross Security isn't interested in opposition research or dealing with elected officials."

"It's the same skill set for every investigation. Political, corporate, private, it doesn't matter. I have what you need. Just say yes."

I hated to admit it, but Darrow was exceptional at research and his surveillance techniques were so off the wall, they occasionally worked. But everything else about the man left a lot to be desired. "I'll think about it if you agree to stay away from my office until I call you."

Darrow pointed a finger at me. "I know what you're doing. You think that will get rid of me, but it won't." He studied my expression, unable to tell if this was a ploy. "But on the off chance you're not screwing with me, I'll give you a week to decide. If I don't hear from you by Friday, I'll be back with bells on."

"If I see or hear a bell, I'll shoot you." Turning, I headed for the elevator.

"You forgot my résumé," Darrow called after me.

I exchanged a look with the nearby security guard. "You can escort him from the building now. If he shows up again, call the police."

TWO

Alan Kershaw's drained bank account led me to another bank account, which had been emptied and closed right after the transfer went through. I wasn't surprised, but banks were supposed to put holds on funds to prevent things like this from happening. A mandatory waiting period was meant to remedy these types of situations, but scammers were always one step ahead. They had ways of circumventing the system. I just had to figure out what that was. It might lead me to the mastermind behind the scam.

I reviewed my notes again. One question was glaringly obvious. Why wasn't Kershaw notified of suspicious account activity the moment it happened? Emptying an account should have triggered an automated warning. But Kershaw didn't receive anything. Why not?

I called the bank and spoke to the manager, who said the bank followed the usual protocols. Notification had been made and the transfer had been approved. When I asked for details on how that happened, I discovered the contact information on Kershaw's account had been changed. Someone received a notification and approved the transfer, but it wasn't Kershaw.

After scribbling down the new phone number that had

been added to the account, I tried calling. As predicted, it was disconnected. I performed every search and reverse lookup imaginable, but that didn't get me anywhere. This scammer was good. A little too good.

Professionals, I thought. That would indicate the scammer had a whole call center, farm situation set up. Most people who made scam calls and sent fraudulent e-mails were forced to do so. They were victims too, at least when it came to the larger operations.

Walk away, Cross. But digging a little deeper wouldn't hurt. As Kershaw pointed out, the FBI could use all the help they could get. And I didn't disagree.

I went back to checking the bank account information. The rest of Kershaw's details remained on the account—his name, address, e-mail. The only thing that had been altered was the phone number. That made multi-factor authentication pointless. How did the scammer gain access to the account to change the number?

The bank manager said he'd have to look into it and get back to me. That was code for 'I don't have a fucking clue and have to come up with some way of covering my ass.'

It would be days before I got a response, if I got a response. Instead, I called Kershaw and asked a few additional questions. He didn't remember divulging any personal details to anyone over the phone or online, but conversation topics and online quizzes could appear innocuous enough that he wouldn't have noticed or remembered. It wasn't that difficult to get answers to questions like the street where he grew up or his mother's maiden name from public records. The rest could be determined through casual conversation by any grifter or expert manipulator. And that didn't even factor in the bots collecting data from every keystroke.

I squeezed the bridge of my nose, hoping the pulsing headache behind my eyes would go away and not turn into a full-blown migraine. I didn't have time for such things.

"Justin, pull Kershaw's phone records. This wasn't a one and done. Whoever scammed him had to gather details to change his account information. There's a slight chance I'm wrong and the scammer is local or someone Kershaw considers a friend or acquaintance."

"You, wrong? Never," Justin replied.

"I don't need the sarcasm. I just need those records." I opened the e-mail Kershaw had received and noted the date. He received the e-mail the day before the phone call. The scammer may have needed that time to have the account information changed. But if he could do that, why didn't he take the money and forget the scam? Why bother with the charade?

"You think Kershaw was catfished?" Justin appeared in the doorway with a printout.

"More or less."

"Damn." He handed me the paper.

I put it down without looking at it and went to the online banking page. Kershaw's username was easy enough, but I didn't know his password. However, the forgot password page allowed several different log-in options, among them was answering a series of questions. I didn't know what Kershaw's first concert was or where he'd been on a particular date, but if I did, I could access his account.

"Why are you trying to hack into our client's bank account?" Justin asked.

"Business is slow. I'm exploring alternative revenue streams."

"Oh." Justin watched me work. "Do you want me to call Kershaw and ask him for the correct answers? It'd save you time."

"Please."

Justin reached for the phone. "That was uncharacteristically polite. Are you feeling okay, boss?"

"Not really."

He read the questions to Kershaw and repeated the answers for me to enter. Once I was in, I tried to access Kershaw's checking account, but that required a password or a password reset which only the bank could perform. There was no going around that. However, I could access his profile which gave me the option to change his mailing address and phone number.

"That explains that." I glanced at Justin who hadn't

hung up yet. "Ask Mr. Kershaw if he received notification his account was accessed."

Justin repeated what I said, holding up his finger while Kershaw checked. Once Justin shook his head, I knew I was right. That's how the money transfer eluded him. The notification preference was set to text and the number didn't belong to Kershaw. If only I knew who it belonged to.

"Mr. Cross will get back to you as soon as he knows something." Justin grabbed the pen out of the cup and scribbled something on the side of my notepad. "Okay, I will let him know." He put the phone back on the cradle.

"Let me know what?" I asked.

"Kershaw went straight to the FBI field office after he left here. He spoke to an agent about what happened. He was told someone would be following up with him soon."

"Why do I need to know that?"

"I'm guessing he wasn't paying attention when you said you wouldn't work directly with the Feds."

"He signed a contract."

"So?"

"So?" I shook my head a little, hoping it'd clear away the throbbing buzzing, but it only made it worse.

"What are you going to do, Lucien? You aren't going to sue a client for a breach like that."

"Whatever you do, don't tell Kershaw that. I need to have an ace in the hole in case he becomes unruly."

"Maybe he's hoping you'll change your mind. After all, I don't think he expected you to do anything with his case this quickly. You basically told him hiring you was pointless."

I rocked back in my chair and rubbed my temples. "I didn't want to overpromise and underdeliver."

Justin cocked his head to the side. "Do you have another headache?"

"It's called tension from dealing with an issue I can't resolve. Actually, two issues. One being this. The other being Ace Darrow."

"Hang on, boss." Justin returned a moment later with a pill bottle and water. "You've been getting a lot of headaches lately. Maybe you should get your eyes checked. Do you want me to make you an appointment?"

"My eyes are fine."

"What about a neurologist? They do brain scans. Maybe you need your brain scanned."

"My brain is fine."

Justin snorted. "That can't be true. Your mind has never been right."

"Just for that, I'm taking back my pretty comment from earlier."

He pointed a finger at me. "See, not right."

Ignoring him, I went back to the computer, wondering if I should waste more of my afternoon on Kershaw. I'd gotten this far. Conceivably, the Feds could take it from here. With their vast resources, they could figure out whose number had been added to Kershaw's bank account.

"Is there anything else I can do?" Justin asked.

"Do you think you can handle our two o'clock?"

"Seriously?"

He was right. That was a bad idea. Unfortunately, Darrow was right too. I needed another investigator on the payroll. Hiring someone had been on my list of priorities, but no one met my minimum requirements. Maybe I should hire Darrow to look into Kershaw's issue. That way, when the Feds decided to do something about our less than legal investigative measures, Darrow could take the fall. Two birds, one stone. That wouldn't be a bad idea. "No. That was a joke."

"It didn't sound like one." Justin waited for my response. "Lucien, if you're thinking what I think you are, you *should* see a neurologist."

"What am I thinking?"

"I'm not going to say it out loud because it's bonkers, but Darrow's screwed with our office enough. You shouldn't invite him to do it again."

"How in the world?"

"I've been anticipating your needs for years. The only way that works is by reading your mind."

"In that case, you should get a tent and join the carnival."

"Already on it." Justin winked and shut my door on his way out.

THREE

Alan Kershaw's problem wasn't unique. He wasn't special. People were scammed all the time. The elderly were the most targeted, but that didn't mean younger generations weren't preyed upon too. Kershaw was in his early fifties, so not the typical target. He had a diversified portfolio. His bank account didn't contain the bulk of his assets, but it was a nice payday for the thief.

Ever since I agreed to work on his case, I'd had feelers out for any reports of the same scam. So far, I hadn't gotten any hits. Amir Karam, my resident tech expert, hadn't found anything either. I had alerts set to notify me as soon as anyone posted anything related to an online casino scam.

Out of ideas, I reached out to the casino.

"We have security measures in place to protect our users' privacy and personal information. You can review those details on this page." The woman rambled off the url. "We encourage our users to contact us directly if they receive any suspicious messages. At present, we have not been alerted to any current threats, but these things pop up all the time."

"I know."

"That's right. You work for a security firm. You must

deal with these matters every day."

"We deal with a lot, but nothing like this." After thanking her for her time, I put the phone down. I had plenty of other things to keep me busy. This shouldn't command my time and attention, but something about it was making me itchy.

The intercom buzzed. "Mr. Cross," Gloria's voice came through the speaker, "your four o'clock is here."

"Set Mr. Crabtree up in the executive conference room. I'll be right with him."

After giving the notes I'd made on Kershaw's case a final dirty look, I shoved them into my drawer, cleared my desk, and opened my door. Justin wasn't at his desk, which explained why Gloria was on the intercom. She smiled at me as she exited the room across the hall. "I got Crabtee and Associates settled with refreshments. Is there anything else I can do?"

"That should be it." I pointed at Justin's desk. "Where'd he go?"

"He said something about a tent." She shrugged. "I've been manning the phones while he's gone. Janet's handling walk-ins downstairs."

"Have we had any walk-ins?"

"Not since the renovation."

"Do me a favor. Call Almeada and see if he wants to grab dinner or drinks tonight."

"The usual place and time?"

"My new usual place." I moved toward the conference room, mentally preparing myself for an hour of answering questions and going over the brokerage firm's latest security evaluation. "Hey, Gloria, did you put my tablet in the conference room?"

"Uh-huh."

"Thanks."

My meeting with Crabtree and Associates wasn't as painful or tedious as I thought it'd be. Crabtree didn't care too much about most of it. As long as I said things were handled, he was happy. The Associates were another story. Luckily, they paid attention, asked precise questions, and made a million notations. When they called tomorrow with more questions, I'd let Justin handle that.

"Lucien," Gloria said, less formal now that the office was empty, "Mr. Almeada said he'd meet you only after I assured him you weren't in trouble."

I checked the time. "I have five hours. I'll do my best not to turn you into a liar."

"I appreciate that."

I gave Justin's empty desk another look. "He really didn't tell you where he was going?"

"No."

"Does he disappear often?"

"Not usually. Depending on the day, we may take turns running errands, but he typically hangs around here, unless you ask him to do something."

I skimmed the call sheet and calendar, but I couldn't figure out where he went. It didn't matter. Today was a slow day. He'd done everything I could possibly need. I was just surprised he didn't mention it to me. "Did he seem okay when he left?"

"As far as I know, he was fine." She gave me an uncertain look. "Should we be worried?"

"Nah." I waved my hand in the air as if to banish the thought away. "If you'd like to head home early, feel free. We don't have any other appointments scheduled today."

"Are you sure you don't need me? What if we get a walk-in?"

"I'll manage somehow. Janet's downstairs, right?"

"Yes, but—"

"But nothing. If you want to hang out for a while, that's cool. Whatever you want to do is fine with me." I opened my office door.

"What are you doing?" she asked.

"Fuck if I know."

She chuckled. "This is when Justin joins you in your office and the two of you have those serious conversations."

"Mostly, we talk baseball."

"Baseball?"

"Yeah. What's wrong with baseball?"

"Do you know anything about it?"

"There are bases and balls. What else is there to know?"

She wasn't buying that either. "All right. Go do whatever. If you want someone to talk to about baseball, let me know. I'd be happy to talk RBIs and player stats, unless you prefer talking starting salaries and team ownership. I can do that too."

"More than pretty," I said.

"Damn right."

Returning to my office, I checked the schedule. Tomorrow shouldn't come with any surprises, unless we had a walk-in. I wasn't sure how I felt about that. Jade had been a walk-in, and while that had turned into a disaster, it had been the most fulfilling case I'd had.

The corporate security work kept the lights on. It paid everyone's salary, including mine. But I wanted more. Not money. Though, that was always the goal. But I wanted to help more. To do more. To...I wasn't even sure. But it wasn't this. Well, only this.

I reached for the phone. *Don't do it,* my inner voice warned. I invited Almeada out to discuss matters. He could serve as the voice of reason. He'd tell me the ins and outs of why this was a terrible idea, and we'd find a way to mitigate the damage when things inevitably blew up in my face. After discussing it with him tonight, I could make the call. Not before. That's why I kept my lawyer on retainer. It'd be a waste to pay him and not bother consulting him.

I tapped my fingers against the desk a few times. Amir had hired additional techs to assist. They had run backgrounds and performed the digital security assessments for Crabtree and Associates and our other corporate clients who had meetings on the books this week. That left me with some free time, which meant I had no idea what to do with myself. Free time—the concept was completely foreign.

After checking my messages, I found an e-mail from Justin. He'd gone to the car dealership to check out the fleet of sedans I'd ordered. The cars weren't supposed to be ready yet, but a few of them had come in early. That explained his absence.

I'd have to discuss parking options with the building manager, but since buying three floors of the building ensured adequate spaces for my employees inside the garage and these were company cars, I should be able to leave the cars in those spots until I filled out my employee roster.

Pressing the intercom, I said, "Gloria, are you still here?"

She appeared in my doorway a moment later. "Yankees or Mets?"

"Neither."

"Dodgers?"

"No."

She looked very serious. "Don't say Red Sox or I'm walking."

"What about White Sox?"

"Why would you root for Chicago?"

"I wouldn't." I shook my head, nearly forgetting what I wanted to ask. "Do we still have job listings posted online?"

"As far as I know."

"Have we gotten any hits?"

"A few. I forwarded the ones worth your time. The others I filed in the shredder."

"Nothing new has come in since?"

"Sorry." She quirked her head to the side. "I thought you were planning on poaching potential candidates away from their respective agencies and departments."

"That's easier said than done."

"Do you want me to update the listing?"

"Yeah. Make sure you mention the perks—signing bonus, company car, hazard pay."

"It may be best to leave out that last one."

"How about flexible hours?"

"That's more like it." She gave me a look. "For my own clarification, by flexible hours, you mean they'd have to be flexible to work whatever hours were necessary."

"Yep, flexible hours."

"I'll get right on that."

"Thank you."

Once she was gone, I checked in with the security teams currently in the field. Miranda had taken several with her, but an absence of clients requiring protection meant that didn't matter. The rest of the security personnel would be ready for their next assignment once I called. Unfortunately, it didn't look like they'd be needed anytime soon. The only case I had was Kershaw's, and that belonged to the FBI.

FOUR

"Are you serious, Lucien? The last I heard, you wanted Ace Darrow thrown in jail. Now you're considering giving him a job. Justin's right. You should get your head examined," Almeada said.

"What's the saying? Keep your friends close and your enemies closer. If he works for me, I'll know exactly where he is and what he's doing."

"So you think."

"I don't think. I know."

"He hacked your system once. What's to stop him from doing it again?"

"Me."

Almeada rolled his eyes and gestured to the server for another. "Since you've already made up your mind, what do you want me to do? Do you want me to arrange a competency hearing? Having you committed should be enough to stop you from hiring the enemy. As your attorney, you pay me to act in your best interest. I believe that may be the only way to save you from yourself."

"Draft an employment contract. Temporary."

"Assignment based?"

"Yeah, let's do that. I only want Darrow working on

Kershaw's case. Nothing else. And I want to be able to fire him whenever I want."

"Yeah, yeah. I know. Everything he works on and discovers is your property. Do you want to tack on a noncompete?"

"No. I want him gone, by any means necessary, but I don't want him to take any of my clients, research, or information when he goes."

"Do you understand what the term noncompete means? I can get you a dictionary," Almeada said.

"Let me rephrase. He can work for a competitor or he can start his own P.I. firm. I don't care. All I want to make sure is he doesn't poach or harass my clients."

"You shouldn't hire him."

"He'll find a way to sabotage me if I don't. He's been staking out the building. He knows which clients I've recently met with. I don't want him going near any of them, but he will if I don't give him a chance. I have to do something to stop him. It's either this or buy a machete and shovel."

"Do you really believe that?"

I wasn't sure what I believed. All I knew was Ace Darrow would continue to show up at my office and annoy me until I hired him. And whenever he got bored or realized I was ignoring him, he'd go a step further, and he'd keep on until I reacted. "He's a dog that rips up the carpet to get attention. If I keep ignoring him, he'll move on to the furniture, then the walls. I just had the office built. I don't want to redecorate."

"What kind of dogs have you been around?"

"Retired drug dogs my father would bring home."

"That explains the wall comment."

Shaking it off, I picked up my gin and tonic. It had been sitting untouched for so long beads of condensation dripped down the sides, causing the cocktail napkin to stick to the bottom of the glass. "Put something together, airtight, so we can be done with this."

"It's your funeral."

I gave him a look, hoping he was wrong. "On to other matters. Alan Kershaw. He's one of your clients."

Almeada smiled. "You know I can't answer that."

"He said you recommended me. What do I need to know about him?"

"He's a decent fellow."

"With a top defense attorney as his general counsel?"

"You know my firm specializes in more than criminal defense."

"Do you have any idea why someone would target Alan Kershaw? Does he have enemies? People to which he owes money? Anything like that?"

"I thought you ran background checks on your clients."

"I didn't find anything, but background checks only tell part of the story." Darrow's words came back to me. He was better at research. Maybe I could learn a few things from him. In exchange, I could teach him not to wear a giant chicken suit to a place with an industrial fryer.

"Are you sure Kershaw was specifically targeted? Most of these scammers put out wide nets. It's a numbers game. They hit anyone and everyone who takes the bait," Almeada said, "like online dating."

"That's what I told Kershaw. Based on the e-mail he received, I assume the scammer set up a redirect that caught people trying to access the online casino. Tracking software would have provided the details necessary for the scammer to make contact, and you know the rest. But no one else reported an issue."

"That you're aware of."

"There's that." I shrugged. "If I'm wrong, if this scam isn't widespread and Kershaw was the only target, it'd be best to find out sooner instead of later."

"You think someone went to all that trouble to steal a relatively small sum from an otherwise rich man?"

"That's how personal vendettas work."

Almeada didn't look convinced. I wasn't either, but I didn't want to dismiss the possibility. "I don't know of anyone with a personal vendetta against Alan Kershaw. His legal issues aren't personal in nature."

"Good to know, but I can't rule out the possibility. The woman I spoke to from the online casino said they hadn't received any other reports of such things happening.

However, Kershaw could be the first victim or no one else has come forward yet."

"You could talk to the Feds. They'd know how often this scam is used."

"I would, but I don't want to trigger my allergies."

"It's federal law enforcement, Lucien. You went to that symposium. You should have gotten a few names and numbers. Call one of your friends."

"Friends?"

"Didn't you make any friends?"

"Things at that event didn't turn out exactly as I'd hoped."

"You need to work on making friends."

"So I've been told." I signaled for the check. "Are you up for some poker?"

"I know better than to play with you. I've always made our relationship very clear. You pay me. I don't pay you."

"You're no fun."

"That's not what your mom says."

"Really? You're making mom jokes? How old are you?"

"If I made a reference to your girlfriend, you'd punch me in the mouth."

"I don't have a girlfriend."

Almeada gave me a look.

"Jade isn't my girlfriend. We haven't even spoken this week." I eyed him. "But you're right. I would have punched you in the mouth."

"It's that self-destructive nature of yours. That will get you in trouble, especially when it comes to this Darrow business." Almeada sighed. "I'll send the contract to your office tomorrow afternoon, but sleep on it. Hiring Darrow is asking for trouble, and you know better than that."

"High risk, high reward."

"Poker or Darrow?"

"Both."

FIVE

As promised, the contract arrived the next day. Justin placed it on my desk, took a seat, and stared at me while I read it.

"Come on, boss. Tell me this is a joke. Where's the punchline?"

"Do you have any better ideas?" I asked.

"If you hire Darrow, I'll walk."

"Well, in that case, I should have done this weeks ago."

"Lucien—"

"I haven't made up my mind yet. I'm exploring my options. In the meantime, take care of the parking situation. The building manager is expecting you."

"Fine, but if Darrow's going to be working here, he's getting the spot farthest from the elevator."

"I wouldn't have it any other way."

"Yeah, well, if you hire him, I'll make sure your space is moved next to his so he can ding your door every morning."

"Now you're just being nasty."

Justin got out of the chair. "This is a bad idea."

"Story of my life." Putting the contract aside, I checked my messages, replied to my e-mails, read the reports Amir had sent regarding the tech department's analyses and reviews, wrote several reports of my own, and gave them to Gloria to proofread before sending them to our clients.

The folder containing my notes on Alan Kershaw's case sat on the corner of my desk, nagging at me, begging me to pick it up, to look at it, to do something. "Not your job, Cross." Except it was. Kershaw paid for my services. I didn't feel right leaving things the way they were.

When I opened my office door, I found Justin at his desk. He turned to look at me. "Do I need to tell the security office to have an ID made for Darrow?"

"Not yet." I grabbed my jacket off the hook and put it on.

"Where are you going?" Justin asked.

"I have a meeting with your tent salesman friend. Since you said you planned to quit, I thought I'd get your new career off to the proper start. Maybe I'll even splurge and get you a double-wide or whatever the tent equivalent of a double-wide is."

"New career? You're leaving?" Gloria asked Justin from across the room.

"Yes," I said.

Justin glared at me. "No. Lucien's doing a bit. He thinks he's funny."

I smiled. "I'll be at the federal building if anyone needs me. Feel free to forward my calls. I may need an excuse to leave."

"Whatever you say, boss." Justin didn't believe me, which may have been for the best. If he realized I was serious, he would have scheduled that brain scan.

Mid-day traffic was a beast. I could have walked to the federal building faster, but sitting alone in my car gave me time to work on my pro/con list for hiring Ace Darrow. The pros were limited. Giving in would stop him from harassing building security, my employees, and potentially my clients. However, working for Cross Security would give him access to a lot of sensitive information with one major caveat. I'd have legal recourse.

Lawsuits and criminal charges would only work as damage control. That's how I'd clean up the mess he made, but it wouldn't stop him from making the mess in the first place. That's why Justin and Almeada were adamantly opposed to adding Ace Darrow to Cross Security's employee roster. My gut said regardless of what I did or didn't do, Darrow would find a way to screw with me and my business. The only way I could see to stop that was by keeping an eye on him.

"Hey, Amir," I said once the call connected, "I have a massive favor to ask. This is a project for your entire department. On the bright side, everyone's getting a bonus."

"What can we do for you?"

After explaining how I wanted a separate network set up that would give Darrow limited access to non-sensitive materials and the relevant research and law enforcement databases without allowing him to see any of our data, I hung up. That project would take a couple of days to complete, which would put us close to Darrow's deadline.

I wasn't concerned. I didn't want him to think I was giving in to his threats. I wanted him to think I needed him. The more focused he was on the project, the less time he'd have to poke around in my business.

Finally, I arrived at the federal building. Finding a place to park that wasn't reserved or in a red zone took almost as long as the drive. Next time, I would walk. Maybe I should hire car service. I'd used it before for client meetings. It'd be good to have the option for everything.

On my way inside, I shot a text to Justin and asked him to look into several of the services and private drivers and get some quotes. The lack of an immediate response or snarky comment told me my executive assistant was still miffed about the Darrow situation. I'd have to find a way to smooth things over, starting with picking up lunch on my way back to the office.

"I'd like to speak to Agent Olsen," I said. I told Kershaw I didn't want to involve myself with the Feds, yet here I was.

The man behind the desk, either a civilian employee or a probationary agent, the logistics were lost on me, eyed me curiously. "What is this regarding, sir?"

"I'd rather not say."

"Sir—"

"This is in regards to a fraud investigation."

"What's your name?"

"This is about Alan Kershaw's fraud investigation."

The agent assessed me carefully. "Are you law enforcement?"

I tried not to laugh. "No."

"Your identification says Lucien Cross. It doesn't say Alan Kershaw. What business do you have asking about his case?"

I was pleasantly surprised that Kershaw had respected my wishes. Unfortunately, it was for nought, seeing as how I was going back on my word that I wouldn't get involved. "I'm a private investigator. I have information Agent Olsen may find useful. I also have some questions that I hope he can answer."

The man at the desk punched something into the computer, mouthing my name a second time while he typed and clicked. "Take a seat." He pointed to a row of benches against the wall. "Agent Olsen will be down to see you."

The lobby was as I expected. Metal detectors, gothic architecture, benches, greenery, and not a lot of personality. Most of the people who came and went wore the uniform—cheap suit, ugly shoes, gun at the hip. I'd been smart enough to leave mine in the car.

A few people were being questioned or assisted by agents at desks or behind the large counter, which reminded me more of a bank than a law enforcement agency. Maybe I had banks on my mind.

"Mr. Cross?" A man stood in front of me, similar dark suit to the ones I'd seen a dozen times today.

"Agent Olsen?" I asked.

He nodded. "I hear you have information on one of my fraud investigations." He gestured to the elevator. "How about we go upstairs and chat?"

"Great."

Olsen didn't wait for us to get to his office. Instead, he started grilling me the moment the elevator doors closed.

He wanted to know how I knew Kershaw and what I'd done involving the investigation.

Normally, I wouldn't be nearly as forthcoming, but instinctively, I knew this wasn't a situation I wanted to handle on my own. I'd told Kershaw as much. "The bank never got back in touch. I chalk that up to a security oversight on their part that they don't want to admit."

The elevator opened. Olsen led me to the first office on our left. It was small, a fraction of the size of my own. Even the offices I had carved out for future investigators were three times as large. I'd have to add that as another selling point to the job listing.

Olsen grabbed the pad of sticky notes and wrote something down. He put it on the table behind him, so I couldn't see it. "What about the online casino?"

"They didn't know anything about the scam."

"Do you believe them?" Olsen asked.

"Do you have reason to believe they're responsible?"

"You're a professional investigator, Mr. Cross. I thought it'd be pertinent to ask for a second opinion."

That was a first. Was Olsen patronizing me? I couldn't be certain, but my gut said he was sincere. "I hadn't considered that."

"Did you conduct an assessment of their site and app? Have you heard of any other complaints or rumors?"

"I haven't found any other scammed customers, but I have limited access and resources. Cross Security is a tiny operation. I don't have the power of the federal government behind me."

"We haven't found anything either, but private security companies such as yours travel in different circles and have access to different things. Since you showed up, claiming to have intel, I thought I should ask. I want to cover all my bases."

"Consider them covered."

Olsen opened the file on his computer and rocked back in his seat so he could read the screen and look at me without having to shift sideways to see over the monitor. "Was that all you had for me? The limited intel on the bank and casino?"

"I've looked into Alan Kershaw. I have yet to determine if he was specifically targeted."

"In other words, you came here with questions rather than answers."

"I wanted to offer what I had. Kershaw asked me to get a name or address of the party responsible." I pointed to the pen on his desk. "Do you mind?"

Olsen gestured to the writing implement.

I wrote down the phone number. "This number isn't Kershaw's. Whoever it belongs to emptied his bank account." I slid the note across the desk. "I couldn't attach a name to it. Maybe you can."

"That number's a dead end."

"Even to the federal government? Don't you have friends at the NSA who could zero in on whoever had the phone and their exact location when the notification on the account was made?"

"You watch too much TV."

"I don't have time for TV."

"Then stop reading thriller novels. That's not a thing. The government has better things to do than spy on its citizens."

I didn't want to sound like a conspiracy nut, but I also knew the kind of technology that existed or was rumored to exist. The issue wasn't if we had the capabilities; it was if using those resources for a case like this would be considered a waste or an abuse of power.

"I don't have time to read much either," I said. "So how about you give me the bare bones breakdown of this situation? Was Kershaw another statistic, or was he the target? That's all I want to know."

"We're still investigating."

I ran a hand through my hair. "How many other incidents have been reported with a similar MO?"

"All online scams share certain traits."

"Sure, but how many involved a call and an e-mail message?"

Olsen went to the filing cabinet in the corner, unlocked the middle drawer, and reached in, scooping out the stack of files. He put them on top of his desk. "All of them."

"You think Kershaw's a statistic?"

"It's hard to say. Tell your client we're doing the best we can. But he won't see that money again."

"He knows." I gave the stack another look. "Any idea who's responsible for this?"

"We don't even know if it's the same party. Most of these originated overseas. That's the first thing we have to determine when it comes to Kershaw's case. The bad actors who operate locally are easier to shut down. Everything else involves multiple governments, multiple agencies, and a lot of luck."

"In that case, I'll let you get back to it."

I was almost out the door when Olsen called, "You find a lead or any indication this was a targeted attack, let me know. Otherwise, it'd be best if you stay away from this. These scammers are often organized, dangerous, and well beyond your reach."

"Thanks for the tip. I told Kershaw the same thing."

SIX

When the elevator doors opened, a face I hadn't seen since the symposium stared back at me. SSA Mark Jablonsky. Blond hair, mustache, and the beginnings of a beer gut. His suit always looked wrinkled. He fit the law enforcement cliché perfectly.

Unlike me, Jablonsky didn't look surprised to see me. In fact, he expected to see me. "I heard you were in the building, kid."

"I'm not your kid," I said.

Jablonsky stepped to the side, waiting for me to enter the elevator. "What are you doing in the federal building, Mr. Cross? From what I recall, you thought FBI agents were nothing but prehistoric nincompoops."

"Not all FBI agents."

Jablonsky looked like he wanted to hit me but refrained. We would have come to blows at that symposium except I had a rule about hitting the elderly. Jablonsky insisted he was in his late-forties, which would have exempted him from my rule, but I wasn't convinced. Either the stress from the job had aged him, or he was a liar.

"I'm guessing you got yourself in trouble and need the FBI's help. What did you step in this time?"

"I've never stepped in anything."

"Your record says otherwise." Jablonsky hit the emergency stop once the doors closed. "I was told you showed up with information concerning a fraud investigation."

"I had a client with an issue. I said I couldn't help but told him the FBI could. I wanted to see how quicky your people could turn me into a liar."

Jablonsky smiled. It was that perverse, know-it-all look that drove me insane the whole week we were stuck together in that hotel. "We both know you don't need any help with that."

I tucked my hands into my pockets and cleared my throat. "Are we done? This could be construed as an unlawful arrest."

"You're not under arrest."

"You have me trapped in a metal box."

"Do I?" Jablonsky hit the emergency stop, allowing the elevator to resume. "I must have hit that button by mistake."

"That'd be the senility kicking in."

The elevator opened in the lobby, but Jablonsky didn't take the hint. Instead, he followed me out and fell into step beside me.

"In all seriousness, Cross, the whispers I'm hearing about your client's case aren't good. Online scams are designed to fund large-scale criminal activities. Your client's money is probably being used by a cartel or worse. Do us all a favor, and stay away from this. It's above your paygrade. You don't need the headache, and I don't want to add a homicide to the list of known offenses when we take the party responsible down."

"I never knew you cared."

"I don't, but I hate paperwork."

I gave him a final look and continued out of the federal building, the itch stronger than ever. Being told not to do something always made me want to do it. I suspected that had something to do with my father, but I didn't feel like psychoanalyzing myself. I had enough on my plate. Or maybe not. If it hadn't been for that damn free time, I wouldn't have bothered with Kershaw. But now that I'd sunk several hours into it, I didn't want to back off. I just didn't want to get killed either.

"Pick your battles," I mumbled. I was already waging a cold war with Darrow. And that's when I decided this would be the perfect case for him. I'd already said as much to Almeada and Justin, but now I was sure. Darrow didn't put himself in danger. He didn't take unnecessary risks. He would get answers and stay out of the line of fire.

Before starting the engine, I called Darrow. He answered on the first ring. *Too anxious,* I thought. *You should never let them see you sweat.* Things like this made me wonder if he actually was a professional or if he just had an inordinate amount of dumb luck.

"I have a job for you. One case. Consider it an audition. You do a good job, and I'll think about offering you a permanent position at Cross Security."

Darrow didn't bother to ask what the assignment was, which was another amateur mistake. Instead, he said, "I'll take it."

* * *

"Stop looking at me like that," I said.

Justin held the unwavering glare. He hadn't said a word since I told him the news, believing a silent protest would change my mind. It wouldn't. But it was creeping me out.

"I could fire you," I reminded him.

"You can't. I told you I quit."

I pointed at him. "Ha! You spoke."

He rolled his eyes. "Lucien, you know better than to invite the fox into the henhouse."

"Amir is installing barbed wire. Nothing will go wrong."

"Famous last words."

"I thought those would be *what could go wrong.*"

"Stop being cute. This is serious."

"Now who's bordering on inappropriate sexual comments in the workplace?"

"Screw you." He walked out of my office.

"I consider that an inappropriate advance," I called to

his retreating back. So much for smoothing things over.

Once I finished everything I had to do for the day, spoke to the VP at Crabtree and Associates, and answered whatever remaining questions their security team and public relations people had come up with since our last meeting, I grabbed the Kershaw files and the research I'd put together and tucked them safely into my bag.

"I don't plan on returning to the office after I get Darrow squared away. You can call it a night."

Justin stared at the solitaire game on the screen as if it were of the utmost importance. "Uh-huh."

"Will you be here in the morning?"

"Will you?"

I gave him a confused look. "Why wouldn't I be? Do you think Darrow plans to kill me?"

"I wouldn't discount the possibility."

Crossing my arms over my chest, I rested my hips on the edge of the desk and faced him. "Are you serious right now?"

"You don't know this guy, Lucien. You don't know the lengths he'll go. For all you know, he could have been involved in that other private eye's murder. You don't know all the details. All you know is he has an axe to grind since you got him fired."

"He wants me to rectify that by rehiring him."

"That's it? Really? It's that simple?" Justin tore his eyes from the screen. "You can't be that naïve."

"Hiring him is damage control."

"No. It's taking out house insurance before hiring a demolition expert to blow up your kitchen."

"Darrow isn't blowing up the kitchen."

Justin stared at me. "This could literally end up being your funeral. If it is, I'm not going. I'm not planning it. I'm not lifting a fucking finger."

"Hey," I said, realizing his anger was due to genuine concern, "I got this."

"That's the problem, Lucien. You don't. You never have. I don't want to get a call saying you're lying dead in a ditch or shot to pieces at the hospital."

"That's not happening. Not this time."

"You can't promise that."

"You have my word."

Justin went back to his game. "Fine. I'll check with Amir and see how much progress he's made. Darrow isn't setting foot in any of our offices until everything else is locked up tight. I may even see about upgrading that barbed wire to razor wire."

"That's why you're my executive assistant."

"Yet, Darrow, your arch-enemy gets an office and I don't."

"You have this entire floor. You don't need an office."

"I need an office. And a raise. And an emotional support animal."

"Okay." I turned my attention to Gloria, who'd been doing her best to appear busy to avoid the awkward conversation. "Can you see about getting Justin an emotional support animal?"

"Sure. I'll take care of it." She winked.

"Thank you, Gloria," I said. "In that case, you can have a raise too."

Justin gave me a funny look. "Are you serious?"

"Wait 'til payday. I want you to be surprised."

On my way to the lobby, I realized I'd need to have a few mental health professionals on staff in addition to the medic I had hired. Dangerous jobs took a toll. To be fair, all jobs took a toll. I knew that firsthand. So did my previous boss. I didn't need Justin throwing my chair through the window. I hoped it'd never come to that.

In fact, I was touched by his level of concern. My sanity may have been the only thing in question, given that he was right about everything. However, I had no intention of telling him that.

Darrow's apartment wasn't in a nice neighborhood. The dent and paint transfer on the back of his SUV deterred the area criminal element from wasting their time stealing it. They had better taste, but a local graffiti artist had tagged the side.

Depending on how quickly things went south, maybe I'd come back with some spray paint to take out my frustration. Again, I wondered about my sanity.

I parked beneath a street light, locked my car, and hoped to find it where I left it when I returned. The anti-theft system was top of the line, but that didn't mean anything to an expert car thief. But an expert wouldn't be slumming it around here. He'd have his sights set on some place nicer, which meant I'd get a brick through my windshield and holes in my tires.

After the brief trek to Darrow's doorstep, I rang the bell. I kept one eye on my car and the other on the metal door in front of me. Thoughts of revenge and murder popped into my head, thanks to what I hoped was Justin's paranoia. I'd really hate for him to be right about this.

When the door creaked, I stepped to the side, my hand moving toward my weapon. Darrow yawned and scratched his chest. He had on a white t-shirt which had neon orange cheese puff dust stuck to it.

"Let me guess," I said, "you're trying to blend in."

Darrow peered behind me. "I'm doing a better job than you." He pulled the door wide. "Come on in."

"This is business. Let's discuss terms over dinner and drinks, like civilized humans. My treat."

"That's called a business expense."

"It is." I remained on the stoop. From what I could see of his place, it matched its owner. "But it's still a free meal."

"You don't think I can afford food?"

I indicated his shirt. "Clearly, you can. Come on. I'll drive."

"Are you afraid someone's going to jack your car?"

"Dress like a normal person, not like an escapee from a disco, or I'll rescind my offer."

Darrow grumbled to himself, leaving his front door open while he went in search of something to wear. I leaned into the doorway. I didn't see any contraband. The walls weren't plastered with surveillance photos of Cross Security clients. He didn't have a shrine dedicated to me either. But Darrow wouldn't leave that out in the open. He'd hide it away in a locked room. Part of me wanted to search, but car repairs were expensive.

"I'll meet you at the car." I pulled his door closed since I didn't want him to get robbed or assaulted. Having to provide a witness statement to the police would waste most of my evening.

Fifteen minutes later, Darrow joined me in the car. He wore an oversized blue suit that hadn't been seen since the original airing of *Miami Vice*.

"Where are you taking me to eat?" Darrow asked.

"Where I take all my prospective new hires."

"You mean you've had more than one?"

"I've had plenty."

Darrow stared at me for a long time, but he couldn't read me. "What place would that be?"

"It's a steakhouse," I said.

"With entertainment?"

"I don't conduct business like that."

"You need to lighten up, Lucien. That's part of your problem. It's why you do all that corporate work. Though, people like that know how to party. You were a trader. I'm sure you have stories. Why don't you let that guy out to play? I bet the old you was a lot more fun than this present incarnation."

"Being around the old me isn't safe."

The smile on Darrow's face bothered me. "Oh, I know. Remember, I looked into you. I know all your dirty little secrets. It's a good thing you finally came to the conclusion it'd be better to work together."

"This is temporary, unless you prove yourself a vital asset."

"I will." He spotted the files in my back seat. "Are those for me?"

"It depends. We have to negotiate the terms of your contract first."

"We already discussed it on the phone."

"I want it in writing."

"You don't trust me?"

"Not even a little bit."

"We're going to have to fix that."

SEVEN

By the time we finished our salads but before the main course arrived, Darrow had signed on the dotted line. He understood the terms, the repercussions, and that his body would never be found if he did anything to screw with me or my business. There was a fifty-fifty chance he'd listen. Okay, sixty-forty, not in my favor. But he hadn't shot me or stabbed me with his steak knife, so we were off to a good start.

"Tell me about the client," Darrow said around a mouthful of bread. He reached for the butter. Instead of using his knife, he dunked his roll into the cup and shoved more of it into his mouth.

I had called Kershaw on my way to Darrow's to ask if he was okay with me hiring another private eye to consult. Kershaw had been thrilled.

Since I'd been given permission, I filled Darrow in on everything. Pushing the bread plate closer to him, I picked up my gin and tonic, took a measured sip, and waited. Darrow chewed while he thought about what I said. A question formed on his face. He leafed through the file and skimmed the lines of text with his middle finger, leaving a greasy butter trail down the page.

"You're missing something," he said.

My better judgement. "What?"

Darrow tapped the page. "I'm not sure. This only tells us what Kershaw wants us to see. He dabbled in online gambling at this one casino. He didn't wager a lot, and he didn't win a lot. Everything got paid off, nice and easy. He only ever used this bank account, which is tiny compared to the rest of his assets. Doesn't that seem convenient to you?"

"It's smart."

"It's a plant. This makes him look like an upstanding guy. No skeletons. No dirt. His one vice is tiny, inconsequential. It's endearing. It doesn't make him look sleazy or sketchy. It makes him relatable."

"That's because he is an upstanding guy."

"The innocent victim?" Darrow asked.

"He is innocent. He didn't steal his own money."

Darrow licked a crumb from the corner of his mouth. "Now that would be brilliant."

"Kershaw lost mid-five figures. That's nothing to him. It wouldn't be worth his time or trouble. He didn't steal his own money. He doesn't have any known enemies. He got scammed. Plain and simple."

"He let himself get scammed."

"That's not how this works. We do not blame the victim."

"Yeah, yeah. I got it. Cross Security's mission statement. Help the helpless. Protect the downtrodden. Blah, blah. Woof, woof. Meow, meow." Darrow wiped his mouth with a napkin. "That's how your other client screwed you over. You can't assume these people are innocent little lambs, Lucien. That will bite you in the ass every time. Always assume the worst of people."

"I always do, but Kershaw's clean."

"Put your money where your mouth is." Darrow reached for his silverware when the server placed his dinner in front of him. "After we eat, let's conduct recon. It'll give me a better grasp of this situation, and maybe you'll learn a thing or two."

"I don't—"

"Unless you want me to handle this on my own."

"That's why I hired you," I spat.

"So I get free range?" Darrow pointed to the contract. "It didn't read like that to me. Did I miss a clause somewhere in this mess?"

"I have ultimate oversight and say in what you do and how you conduct yourself. That is nonnegotiable."

"I guess that means you're coming with me."

Dinner dragged. Darrow gorged himself. Watching him made me lose my appetite. When the server returned to ask if we wanted dessert, I answered before Darrow could order the chocolate lava cake he'd been eyeing for the last twenty minutes.

"You're getting anxious, huh?" Darrow snickered. "Maybe we'll make you into a decent investigator after all."

"I am a decent investigator."

"Could have fooled me."

Once the check was paid, we returned to my car. I made sure we weren't followed and no one was paying an inordinate amount of attention to us. I'd adopted Justin's paranoia as my own and wondered if Darrow hired guys to rough me up or worse.

That's ludicrous, I reminded myself.

"Stop here." Darrow pointed to a dark place beneath some trees on the other side of the street from Kershaw's apartment.

"You can't see anything from here," I said.

Darrow pointed more emphatically. "Pull over."

I hadn't even turned off the engine when Darrow got out of the car and scurried over to Kershaw's vehicle. Resisting the urge to drive away, I peered down the street. No one was out. I couldn't see what Darrow was doing, but I was familiar with his tactics.

Five minutes later, he returned. "I thought you'd help."

"I'm not going to bug my client's vehicle. We don't do that."

"Right, like you've never done anything like this before. For the record, I planted a tracker. I didn't bug his car. You saw me. I didn't go inside his vehicle."

"Not for lack of trying," I muttered.

"Are you planning to help with the rest? This is your case."

"Which I offered to you. Do we need to go over the ethics clause of your contract again? You seem fuzzy on what you're supposed to be doing."

Darrow sighed. "Lucien, you can't expect results if you're going to hamstring me."

"Talk me through your process. Why do you want to surveil our client? We've been over this. He didn't steal his own money. He doesn't stand to gain anything by doing that."

"You're right. I gave it some thought at the restaurant, and I agree with you. However," Darrow waved his finger in my direction as if having an ah-ha moment only without the ah-ha, "I'm not convinced this was a crime of convenience. You're not sure about that either. It's why you did the research and why you asked for my help."

My headache was back with a vengeance. "That's not the reason. I wanted to give you a fair shake."

Darrow wasn't buying it. "No, you had a reason. It has to be this."

"Actually, I hoped you'd blunder into the cartel's way and they'd off you."

"Yeah, sure. Whatever you say, buddy. Even if that were true, you went to the FBI. They told you the same thing your research suggests. No one else has been hit by this scam. Our guy can't be that unlucky. He was targeted."

"The FBI didn't tell me that. They didn't tell me anything."

Darrow pointed to the window. "Why him? Everyone in this neighborhood's in the same economic boat. Any one of them would make the perfect payday. No one else was robbed. The scammer can't be basing this on geography. That's out. I didn't see much research into Kershaw's place of employment, so I'll get started on that once I finish looking into him, but my gut says no one else at his office was scammed either. You looked into the casino angle. Like I said, we're missing something. Kershaw looks good. He looks clean. He doesn't want you to see the dirt. That's why we have to look for it. Once we find it, we'll find the scammer."

"You aren't saying anything I don't know, but nothing backs that theory. Do you have a shred of evidence to support it?"

"Do you have anything to refute it?"

"That's not how this works."

"We're not cops, Lucien. I know you had that police training during your formative years. Clearly, it screwed with your sense of things. This isn't a court of law. There is no innocent until proven guilty. We're private detectives. We go into situations assuming guilt, and we dig until we find it."

"Our client isn't guilty. He's the victim." At this point, I should record that and play it on a loop.

"That's not my point."

"That's what you just said."

"What I said—" Darrow looked at me. "I'll wait for you to get a pen so you can write this down."

The look I gave him should have killed him.

"Kershaw's dirty little secret is why he was targeted. We have to figure out what he's hiding before we can do anything else. That will lead us to possible motives, which should lead to suspects, which should lead to the scammer," Darrow said.

"Unless Kershaw isn't hiding anything."

"There's only one way to find out." Darrow grinned. "And we've come full circle. In case you forgot, we already had this conversation. Really, you should take notes. It'd save us both a lot of time."

I squeezed the steering wheel. "How exactly do you plan to look into our client? There are lines, boundaries."

Darrow jerked his chin toward the apartment building. "You could take me upstairs and introduce me. That would be the fastest and easiest way of doing things. If not, we can sit here all night and have more of these conversations."

"Did you notice that drainage ditch we passed?"

"The worst you'd do is have me arrested. You'd never hurt me, Lucien. I kept you from getting killed."

"You ran as soon as you could."

"I went for help. That's the rational thing to do."

"Like planting a tracker on our client's car?"

Darrow folded his arms over his chest and sank into the seat. "Fine. We'll sit here all night. Did you bring snacks?"

I opened my door. Tomorrow, I'd stop making asinine decisions. Until then, I wanted to make things as painless as possible, at least for me. Alan Kershaw probably wouldn't agree this was painless, but I had warned him. Hopefully, he was prepared.

EIGHT

"Do you have a different take on this situation?" Kershaw asked.

Darrow glanced at me. If he repeated what he said in the car, I'd fire him on the spot. To my relief, Darrow wasn't as stupid as he looked. Instead, he launched into a long-winded account of how he used to conduct research for political campaigns. That didn't answer Kershaw's question, but it satisfied him nonetheless.

"You must have seen and heard just about everything," Kershaw said. "Work like that must have provided a lot of connections."

"You have no idea," Darrow replied.

Kershaw nodded to me. "I appreciate this, Mr. Cross."

I wasn't sure how much he'd appreciate being spied on, but I held my tongue, the pit in my stomach turning into a full-on ache. *Guilt.* I'd never done well with that.

"Do you mind if I use your bathroom?" Darrow asked.

"Your place isn't far," I said. "We're leaving now. You can wait."

"I really can't." Darrow gave Kershaw a pleading look and wiggled back and forth a little.

Kershaw pointed to the first open doorway. "It's right through there."

"Thanks." Darrow got up.

"You'll have to excuse him," I said. "In fact, I hope you'll forgive tonight's intrusion. Had I known Ace wanted a meeting, I would have asked him to schedule one during normal business hours."

Kershaw shook away my apology. "He seems anxious to get started. Rumor is you've been pretty active on this too. That wasn't the impression you gave me in your office. Do you mind if I ask what changed your mind?"

"I had some free time. But what I said holds true. I don't believe we'll be able to help. I've spoken to the FBI and shared what I found. They told me what I told you. They're your best bet."

"But you hired Darrow anyway."

"We've crossed paths before. He's hoping to secure a permanent position at my firm. I thought your situation warranted another set of eyes from someone eager and with plenty of time to dedicate to the problem."

Kershaw didn't look convinced that's all it was. He hoped Cross Security would get to the bottom of this.

"Is the money that important to you?" I asked. "Is that why you're adamant we find the party responsible?"

"It's not about the cash. It's about my dignity. I was made a fool. I don't like that. I'd like payback on the people who did this to me. Justice would be nice."

"I can't guarantee anything."

"I know."

I wondered if Kershaw was telling me the whole story. "Are you sure you haven't made any recent enemies?"

"No."

"What about legal situations? You said Almeada sent you to see me. His firm handles a lot of different things. Maybe someone was annoyed with a deal you made or a contract you signed."

"I haven't had any issues publicly, and my personal life is humdrum."

"What about dating?"

"As you know, I'm divorced with three beautiful children. They're away at college now, but I haven't had much desire to get back out there."

"What about your ex? Is there any reason she would want to scam you?"

"No."

"Is she seeing anyone?"

"I don't think so, but I can't be sure. My kids usually keep me updated on what's going on with their mother. Occasionally, we're all together—holidays, sporting events, plays, anything the kids are into. She hasn't brought anyone with her."

I hadn't looked into his ex beyond a preliminary background check. Kershaw didn't pay alimony. They hadn't comingled their assets when they married. They kept everything separate, except a joint account they paid into equally for household expenses and raising their children. When they dissolved their marriage, they split that account in half. They both came from money and had good jobs. Neither was struggling. Everything indicated they were evenly matched.

"Do you think she'd want to make you feel foolish or stupid?" I asked. "Divorces can get messy."

He shook his head. "We grew apart. We had one fight and called it quits. We didn't hate each other. We simply realized we didn't love each other anymore. It happens. There's no animosity. No tension. There's nothing."

That may have been the most depressing thing I'd heard all night.

Darrow returned. I didn't recall hearing the toilet flush, but I was sure he hadn't been using the facilities. I didn't want to know what he'd been doing instead. But since he was working for me in a limited capacity, I'd have to ask. Perhaps I should call Almeada first and inquire as to plausible deniability, but given the givens, I doubted anyone would buy that.

"Lucien, are we ready to go? We don't want to take up too much of Mr. Kershaw's time," Darrow said, as if he were the voice of reason.

I eyed Darrow, who communicated with his eyes that we should take off.

"It is getting late," Kershaw said.

"Again, I want to say how sorry I am for the intrusion.

We appreciate you taking the time." I shook Kershaw's hand. "If we hear anything, we'll let you know."

"I'll do the same if I hear from Agent Olsen." Kershaw walked us to the door and shook Darrow's hand. "It was nice to meet you."

"That was fun," Darrow said as we headed back to the car. "We make a good team."

"We aren't a team."

"You distracted Kershaw while I—"

"Bup-bup-bup," I interrupted, holding up a finger to silence him. "Kershaw is our client. You wanted to meet him. I was not distracting him. I was asking questions, like a responsible investigator."

"Yeah, but while you were yapping, I stuck a few bugs around his place. We'll know what's what soon enough."

"Drainage ditch," I repeated over and over as we made our way back to the car. It was the only happy thought I had. Justin was right. When would I learn to listen to him? Maybe I would schedule that brain scan, after all.

* * *

While Darrow kept an eye on our client and dug deeper into Kershaw's personal life, I kept an eye on Darrow. The office I assigned him was on the floor below, closest to the reception desk and the elevator. I had the rest of the hallway roped off with construction signs, even though the project had been completed over a month ago. However, the less access he had, the better.

Gloria and Janet took turns manning that desk. They knew not to leave Darrow unsupervised. My office staff didn't realize they'd be assigned babysitting duties, but I couldn't be everywhere at once, not with client meetings and reports due.

Justin appeared in my doorway. "Darrow phoned. He wants to have a chat with you. He called it a progress report. He likes making these things sound super official."

"Good for him."

"He's wearing a suit today."

"Does the flower in his lapel spray water?"

Justin grinned. "I told him you'd meet him in his office in half an hour. You can find out for yourself."

"I take it you're still mad at me."

"No, but I am enjoying this."

"Do you still think this was a terrible idea?"

"Do you?"

"That depends on what updates Darrow has for me, but so far, this has been a waste." I indicated the three-inch binder Darrow had put together. "This is everything on our client through his college years. I'll say one thing, Darrow is thorough."

"Yeah, but isn't that a huge waste of time and paper?"

"I don't trust him to send e-mails or use our dropbox system without inserting some sort of malware, so this is the only feasible alternative. Make sure we donate to reforestation efforts."

"Okay."

"Great."

Justin jerked his chin at the paperwork. "Still, don't you think that's a waste?"

"This case is a waste."

"Why did you contract the work out to Darrow? Why did you invest all the time and effort you put into it? What was the point?"

"I don't know."

"You really think Ace Darrow could be valuable to Cross Security?" Justin picked up the binder and flipped the pages. "He is meticulous. I'll give him that."

"I don't know how he finds the things he does. I'm no slouch, and Amir is a highly regarded expert in several fields. Even combined, our research doesn't come close to this."

"Maybe it's bullshit," Justin suggested.

"It isn't. Remember what Darrow found on me?"

"That wasn't substantiated. He didn't have proof."

"He doesn't worry about such things." Saying the words out loud triggered an uneasiness in my brain, a sense of impending doom, like a precursor to a panic attack or a foreboding before violence breaks out.

"Legally speaking, evidence is a crucial element in most

cases."

The feeling wasn't going away. It was only getting worse. Needing to change the subject, I asked, "Where are we on the company cars?"

"The first six are being delivered by end of business today."

"That's all we need for now. One for each of us. Is the rest of the fleet delayed?"

"You should have all twenty cars within the next few weeks," Justin said. "Are you giving one to Darrow?"

"I will after our techs have the cars properly outfitted with security measures."

"You mean trackers."

"Hey, if Darrow thinks it's okay to track a client, there's no reason why I shouldn't keep track of company property, regardless of who is inside it."

"Are you sure you and Darrow aren't two-sides of the same coin?"

I handed Justin the binder. "Read through this in your spare time and let me know if I'm missing anything. In the meantime, I'll let Ace update me on the investigation."

"Ace." Justin rolled his eyes. "Are we sure he didn't change his name?"

"Not that I'm aware."

"Well, you're not that good at research." Justin took the binder and returned to his desk. "That's why I'm always stuck doing your homework."

NINE

I leaned against the doorjamb. Darrow didn't look up. The computer screen in front of him had his attention. For an investigator who could end up in dangerous predicaments, the guy had zero tactical awareness.

I crossed my arms over my chest and waited. He didn't notice. Would my posture suggest I was closed off or afraid of him?

Rethinking my stance, I tucked my hands into my pockets. Maybe he was fucking with me. Surely, he couldn't be that oblivious to my presence. He should have felt my eyes on him. But he continued to type on the keyboard.

I had given him one of the interior rooms. No outside windows. There was only one way in and out. Gloria was at the reception desk. We'd angled it to face Darrow's office so he couldn't slip out without her noticing. But he hadn't even tried. He liked his cage. Maybe he'd done time and was used to nothing but bare walls, or he didn't do well with distractions and this made for ideal working conditions.

Gloria caught my eye and quirked an eyebrow. I shrugged, so she made a 'go on' gesture with her hand, hoping to shoo me into the room.

I let my eyes grow wider. *No.*

She sighed dramatically and pointed to the phone on the desk beside her. I didn't need her to announce my presence. This may have been one of Darrow's games. I wasn't in the mood to play.

After another thirty seconds, I cleared my throat.

Darrow jumped. He hadn't been pretending not to notice me. He wasn't that good of an actor.

"Justin said you had something for me," I said.

Darrow clicked a few more keys, closing whatever tab he had opened and indicating the chair in front of his desk. "Take a seat, so I can give you an update."

I peered around the room. Security had been checking every night to make sure Darrow wasn't doing anything dangerous in here, and I had techs scanning for hidden surveillance devices and searching his computer for suspicious activity. As far as I knew, Darrow had been behaving himself, which surprised me. Maybe he really did want this job.

"How long were you standing there?" he asked.

"Not long."

"I didn't hear the elevator."

"You must have been engrossed in whatever it is you're doing."

Darrow looked like he didn't believe me. "As you know, I've been pulling everything I can find on our client."

"Including identifying his kindergarten bullies," I said.

"The bugs I placed in his apartment haven't gotten much of anything. The guy's a hermit. He goes to work. He comes home. He watches boring TV and goes to bed. His phone conversations tend to be brief. Work conversations are specific to the job. No deviations. No mention of extracurricular activities. The only time Kershaw shows any real personality is when he's speaking to his children. Those conversations have given me a lot more to work on. I've created dossiers for all three of them, including—"

"Stop." I didn't want to hear this for so many reasons. "Does anything indicate the casino scam connects to them?"

"Not exactly. But it's too soon to dismiss the possibility.

All three are in college. His oldest is in graduate school. She seems the most stable in terms of relationships. Not a lot of parties. Not a lot of crazy activities at the present, but that wasn't always the case. His youngest is about the same. A bit of a wallflower, really. The middle kid, well, you know what they say about middle children."

"What?"

"It's that whole Jan Brady thing."

"What's wrong with Kershaw's middle child?"

"He's an attention hog. For starters, he's in a frat. He drinks. He parties. He has several vices which he has posted all over the internet for everyone on the planet to see." Darrow showed me several screenshots he'd taken of the kid's social media pages. "Drinking. Strippers."

"Those aren't strippers," I said. "That's spring break."

"That doesn't mean they aren't strippers." Darrow clicked to another screenshot he had saved. "Those are definitely strippers."

I couldn't disagree. "What's your point?"

"Maybe the kid got in trouble or needed a quick payday. Maybe he scammed his father or told one of his buddies to do it for him." Darrow grabbed a stack of sheets off the printer and handed them to me. "Careful. Those are hot off the presses."

Surprisingly, they were a little warm. "Matthew Kershaw. Twenty-one." I scanned the rest of the details. Darrow had everything from the kid's address and phone number, to intel on the fraternity, when he pledged, a list of reports made to the authorities and campus police regarding that frat house over the course of the last fifteen years, long before Matthew Kershaw ever stepped foot inside the building, his class schedule, his classmates, hangouts, and everything else imaginable.

"I'm looking into his known associates now," Darrow said. "Several people he's crossed paths with are technologically savvy."

"Everyone that age is technologically savvy."

"Feeling old?"

"Do any of them have experience running scams?"

"Not that I've found, but I'm still looking. As you can

see, this is a comprehensive list. We're looking at weeks, if not months, of research." Darrow glanced toward the open doorway. "Rumor is you have an entire tech department at your disposal. I wouldn't know since I haven't seen or heard from any of them, but if you'd allow me—"

"No."

"It'd be faster."

"No."

"Fine." Darrow settled into the chair. "I can do this without any help. This is part of proving myself capable, isn't it?"

"That's exactly what it is."

Darrow sighed. "Fine. I'll prove to you that I'm a team player."

I ran a hand through my hair, uncomfortable with the thought that he was spying on dozens or hundreds of college students. Hopefully, none of them were minors. I didn't even want to think how that would look if this got out. My reputation and my company's rep had taken a few hits. I wasn't sure we'd bounce back from the optics of spying on children. Depending on the types of things Darrow found, we could be bordering on child pornography.

"No more saving screenshots of questionable photos," I said. "And if anyone is underage and in a compromising position, report it."

Darrow gave me a sideways look. "Are you really this squeamish, or are you trying to prove something to me?"

"I don't have to prove anything to you." I leafed through the printed pages. "Besides his son's questionable ties, have you found anything else to indicate Alan Kershaw was specifically targeted?"

"Not a thing."

"Do you have any reason to think Matthew Kershaw owes someone money?" I held up the kid's bank account information. "He looks solvent. His tuition is covered, along with room and board. His account is adequately funded. His parents set him up with a trust fund. Don't you think if the kid needed a quick infusion of cash, he could ask mom or dad for it?"

"Maybe he wouldn't." Doubt resided in Darrow's eyes. He realized where he miscalculated, but he was too stubborn to give up on the possibility. "It could be a pride thing or he didn't want to answer his parents' prying questions as to why he needs the money."

I pointed to Matthew Kershaw's phone records. "He speaks to his parents a few times a week. I don't think that would be an issue. The kid isn't doing anything harmful. He's a stereotypical frat guy." I skimmed the rest of the pages. "Possibly on the tamer side if the stories I've heard from Ivy Leaguer friends are to be believed about the types of things that go on inside those hallowed halls."

"You wouldn't know?" Darrow asked.

"I didn't grow up with money." *Stupid,* my internal voice berated. Feeding Darrow intel on my upbringing wasn't part of our deal.

"You did exceptionally well for yourself. Your father's the police commissioner. How did that come about without funding and political support?"

I ignored it, but now I wondered if Darrow had pestered me for this job to dig up dirt on me. Maybe he realized he needed proof and that's the real reason he was here. "Have Alan Kershaw and his son been fighting when they've spoken on the phone?"

"No. They're on good terms."

"Then Matthew didn't set up his old man. This is a waste of time." I put the pages down. "Have you found anything else? Anything at all?"

"No."

"What does that tell you?"

Darrow glared at me. "You may be right. Kershaw was randomly chosen. Is that what you want me to say?"

"Do you believe it's a possibility?"

"Yes, but it's not the only one."

"All right. Stay the course for now, but remember what I said."

"Don't fill up the hard drive with porn. Got it, Lucien."

I took the printed pages. "I'm glad you were paying attention."

"Whenever I find something, and I will find something,

you'll learn to respect me," Darrow said.

"It's not about respect." I knew it was stupid to engage, but I couldn't stop myself. "It's about logic and deduction."

"Oh, so you're trying to teach me something." Darrow winked. "I'll be the first to admit you are better at that intuition thing, except when it comes to walking into traps. It looks to me like this is the start of a perfect partnership."

Holding my tongue, I headed out of the office and waited for the elevator. "Keep an eye on him."

Gloria nodded. "Yes, sir."

TEN

I wasn't sure what possessed me to return to the federal building. Agent Olsen was under no obligation to assist me. If anything, he thought I should assist him, but I didn't have anything new for him. Maybe I just wanted to find out if Darrow had been poking around or asking questions about me. If Darrow wanted to take me down, he wouldn't go to the local cops. He'd go to the Feds. That's where his connections were.

"An associate is considering the possibility someone close to the family could have targeted Alan Kershaw," I said. "Have you heard anything from him?"

"I haven't heard anything from anyone." Olsen stared at me. "Do you have a person of interest in mind?"

"No."

"No? So you came all the way here to share this theory with me, but you have nothing to back it and no one in mind for me to investigate?"

"That would be correct."

"Jablonsky said you were a ballbuster."

"I'm sure that's not all he said." Jablonsky would know if I was under investigation, but he would have confronted me about it. He'd want to gloat.

My paranoia was reaching new levels. I needed to relax

and focus on the task at hand, except I had nothing.

"This is a federal investigation, Mr. Cross. We do not require or want your assistance in this matter. I thought I made that clear the last time we spoke."

"In that case, I'll make myself scarce." I eyed the filing cabinet behind Olsen's desk. "Before I go, at least tell me if you've made any progress."

"Investigations take time."

"So you don't know who is behind this either."

"We are investigating several possibilities."

"Like family and friends?"

"No, Mr. Cross, like overseas click farms, organizations with suspected ties to terrorist organizations, and several domestic hackers."

"Mr. Kershaw would like the person who did this identified," I said.

"We all want something. Rest assured, we are doing the best we can. With any luck, we'll identify the party responsible and build a solid case. You can tell that to Mr. Kershaw. However, this," he indicated the space between us, "is wasting my time and yours. Now if you don't mind."

Speaking to law enforcement and exchanging information wasn't something I ever thought I'd do voluntarily, but having Darrow at the office made me change my tune. It wouldn't hurt to improve relations with law enforcement before things took a turn, and I knew they'd take a turn. It was only a matter of time.

The elevator in the federal building was smaller than in my office building, and it had a smell. Sweat? Desperation? Fear? I couldn't quite place it, but I didn't like it.

Before the doors closed, a man slipped inside. He glanced at the buttons to make sure the lobby was illuminated before leaning against the handrail. "Excuse me."

I looked in his direction. He wasn't a federal agent. He looked like a guy who should have been feeding pigeons in the park. He had on a checkered brown jacket over khaki pants. His button-up shirt was done all the way to his chin. His tie was a little too short, but given how diminutive he was, at most 5'4, I suspected he had gotten it from the boys' section.

"Were you speaking to Agent Olsen just now?" he asked.

"Briefly." Could this guy be a reporter?

"I couldn't help but overhear. You mentioned something about a client being caught up in a casino scam."

"It's complicated."

"Client?"

"Lucien Cross, Cross Security and Investigations," I said.

"Nathan Boter." He nodded curtly. "I came to speak to Agent Olsen about a casino scam too. I was hoping you could spare a few minutes."

"I have an appointment after this." Almeada was waiting for me.

"I'll make it quick." Boter watched the numbers above the door count down. "I got ripped off a few days ago. They cleaned out my entire checking account. They took everything."

"From that one account?"

Boter nodded.

"Nothing else?" I asked.

"Isn't that enough?"

"What about savings, property, other investments?"

"The rest was untouched. I'm trying to safeguard everything. I don't even know where to begin."

"How did they take it?"

"How should I know? All I know is it's gone. The last time I accessed that account was when money was supposed to be wired into it after I won a jackpot."

"Where did you win this jackpot?" That twitchy feeling was back. I had been on to something. But I let it go for many reasons, which was why I put Darrow on it. But he'd been looking at this all wrong, unless Nathan Boter connected to Alan Kershaw, and I didn't think that was possible. My money was on the casino.

"A local place."

"Not online?"

"No."

"What local place?"

"Chelsea's. Are you familiar?"

"Yeah." I pulled out my card. "Call that number and set up a meeting at your earliest convenience."

"You can get my money back?"

"No, but I would like to hear more about how this happened."

Boter didn't look happy with my response. "I'll think about it. I'm not really looking to hire anyone."

"That's great because I'm not looking for new clients, but sharing intel could benefit us both. My assistant will be expecting your call," I said, hoping that would sway him to cooperate.

Either Agent Olsen knew more than he let on, or he was as incompetent as I suspected. My money was on the latter. I had a list of reasons not to poke around in this. I also had Ace Darrow doing exactly that. Did I want to point him in a new direction, possibly toward his own demise? Or should I take over the investigation? We could work it from two different angles and meet in the middle. However, the thought of working closely with Darrow made me a little queasy. For all I knew, Darrow wanted to bury me.

At least I'd have a few new hypotheticals to discuss with Almeada over dinner.

* * *

"Do you know how this sounds?" Almeada asked.

"Crazy," I said. "And before you say anything else, I know. I wasn't supposed to hire Darrow. I was supposed to keep my distance."

"You were afraid. Acting out of fear has never worked out for you."

"I wasn't afraid."

He cocked an eyebrow. "No?"

"No."

"What about now?"

"I'm considering the possibility."

Almeada sipped his Old Fashioned. "I haven't heard anything. The police department wouldn't be in favor of you getting taken down, so I doubt Darrow would go to them with whatever suspicions he has about you."

"Even if he did, they wouldn't listen to him."

"Thanks to your father."

"It's not out of family obligation, if that's what you're thinking."

"If you go down, things would come to light about the settlement you took. They wouldn't want that," Almeada said.

"God forbid the public finds out not all cops are good guys. The city would be plunged into chaos. I mean, it's not like there aren't a million videos online depicting just that."

"Lucien."

I picked up my drink, waving it around as I said, "Yeah, I know. Mouth shut. Got it."

Almeada studied me closely while I drank my gin and tonic. "Do you have any basis for thinking Darrow's in your house to look for skeletons?"

"No."

"Do you think Justin's paranoia has rubbed off on you?"

"I think it combined with mine."

"That would explain why you've gone a little batshit. This situation with Kershaw isn't helping matters."

I fished a dollar out of my pocket and handed it to him. "You're hired. I need confidentiality."

Almeada put the dollar down. "You're a client. I'm on retainer. And my fees are a hell of a lot higher than that." He scooted his chair closer. "What's going on?"

"This could be a conflict, if you represent Kershaw."

"It's okay. Go on."

That answered one question. Alan Kershaw wasn't Almeada's client, but he was a client of their firm. Or Almeada liked me better. I provided more billables. "Darrow's spying on him."

"Spying?"

"Trackers, surveillance devices, the whole nine. As if that wasn't bad enough, he's doing the same to Kershaw's kids."

"Wow."

"Yeah."

"That explains that strange call you made to me the other night. Did you see him plant any of these devices?"

"No."

"Stick with that."

"That's not why I bring it up. I'm bringing it up because Darrow was convinced Kershaw was hiding something and that would lead to the scammer. But he hasn't found anything. I told him Kershaw's clean."

"I told you the same thing. And I told you first," Almeada said.

"Right, which means this was a random act. A crime of opportunity." I filled him in on Nathan Boter. "He didn't tell me much, but there's a clear connection. The MO sounds almost identical. Same with the payday."

"A local casino and an online casino don't share a lot of similarities. It could be a coincidence."

"Usually, I'd agree with you, but this feels like it fits together."

"You don't know enough yet to jump to that conclusion. Does Kershaw have any ties to Chelsea's?" Almeada asked. "From what I know of the man, underground casinos aren't his thing. He'd be mortified to get caught in a raid."

"Which is why I called and asked. Kershaw said he's never been to Chelsea's. He said he never even heard of it. I don't doubt that."

"An underground gambling establishment and a legit, highly advertised online casino are worlds apart. I'm sticking with coincidence."

"Look at the victims. These two men are roughly the same age and scammed under the same pretense. That's a hell of a coincidence."

"Except you know next to nothing about Nathan Boter. Frankly, Lucien, I'm surprised you didn't think he was an undercover FBI agent planted there to weasel his way into your security firm and assist Darrow in taking you down."

"I hadn't thought of that."

"On the bright side, we know your paranoia hasn't crossed over into delusional."

"Why do you say these things? Do you want to torture me? You know I'm going to be considering that insane possibility until I get back to the office and run a background on Boter." I pointed at him. "You and Justin are bad for my mental health."

Almeada nearly choked on his drink, far too amused for my liking. "Well, whatever it is you plan on doing, I suggest you don't. Darrow is a thorn in your side. Give him a few more days to gather whatever info he can, look it over, and thank him for his services. As far as Nathan Boter, dig a little, but I'm sure you'll come to the realization the two aren't connected, and call it a day. You have plenty of corporate clients to keep you busy."

"Not that many."

"Business isn't booming?"

"Not really. Not since all that stuff went down with the prosecutor's office and Darrow. His former employer traveled in specific circles with specific people who heard a version of what happened that didn't paint me in the best light. Those people were urged to stay away from me, and unfortunately, they have friends who travel in the same circles as most of my prospective clients. And no, that isn't the paranoia speaking. That's pragmatism. I didn't lose any clients, but I haven't been hired by anyone new either."

"Are you sure it isn't because of your political leanings? It's a well-known fact you've been backing Miranda's social equality campaign."

"I've always been a women's rights advocate. That shouldn't be political. It should be considered humanitarian, just like wanting to protect the rights of all humans."

"Yeah, well, not everyone sees things like that."

"My involvement and donations weren't publicized. I doubt anyone even noticed."

"Do you think Darrow's screwing with your business, or do you think this is coming entirely from his former boss?"

"I'm not sure."

"Is that why you hired Darrow?"

"I like to know who my enemies are and how they plan on coming for me," I said.

"Here's some professional advice. Stay away from Chelsea's. The FBI will be looking into it now that they received a new report from another victim. You don't want to make yourself a bigger target in case you're already a blip on their radar."

"There are other casinos. Chelsea's isn't the only underground establishment."

"The kinds of people who run them won't take kindly to your questions."

"I could send Darrow."

"Since he's a private contractor, he's not on your company's healthcare plan, so you don't have to worry about your deductibles going through the roof when his kneecaps get broken. But I would still advise against it, at least until you find out more from Mr. Boter."

"Do you think he'll call?"

"You could always call him."

"I wouldn't want to seem desperate."

Almeada chuckled. "I'm pretty sure that ship has sailed."

ELEVEN

I got up from my desk and took a seat across from the sofa, indicating that's where Nathan Boter should sit. "Thanks for agreeing to meet. I appreciate you taking the time."

Boter peered around my office, turning to give Justin an uncertain look. My assistant smiled. Today, he was on his best behavior. He must have realized how skittish Boter seemed and didn't want to add to the man's nervousness.

"Would you like a cup of coffee or tea? Maybe a sandwich or bagel?" Justin asked.

"I don't know." Boter wiped his palms on his pants. The lack of sweat stains told me he wasn't scared, but he was uncomfortable.

"Bring the usual selection," I said to Justin. We didn't have a usual selection, but Justin understood.

"Right away, Mr. Cross." My assistant practically clicked his heels together before closing the door. Maybe he'd gone a little too far in the other direction.

"Yeah, I, uh," Boter looked around the room again, "had no idea this was the kind of place you operated."

"It's new," I said. "I used to have a little hole-in-the-wall for an office. The closet doubled as a break room. Winter was hell. We couldn't get to the coffeemaker without putting our coats back on, and once we had our coats on, it was too hot to drink coffee."

Boter nodded, as if that made sense. I'd have to work on my material. "I wasn't looking to hire you. Frankly, I can't afford you."

"I wasn't looking to be hired. I thought I made that clear in the elevator. However, I'd still like to hear your story."

"There's not much to tell. I don't have a lot in the way of assets. I manage a grocery store. My salary barely covers my rent and utilities. My daughter sends me money to help out when she can. I don't want to mooch off her or be a burden. That's why I gamble every now and again. If I hit it big, I'll be set."

After dinner and drinks with Almeada, I'd returned to the office, relieved to find it Darrow-free. I'd pulled up Nathan Boter's financials and criminal history. He didn't have a record of which to speak. But he did have a tiny gambling problem. Not enough to owe anyone a substantial amount of money, but enough that his daughter had to cover his rent on many occasions.

"How long have you been going to Chelsea's?" I asked.

"As long as it's been in business. Seven years, I guess."

"Where else do you gamble?"

Boter didn't bother to look indignant. "I bet on the horses whenever I can get down to the track."

"Do you have a bookie?"

"No."

"What about online betting?"

"No."

I narrowed my eyes, but Boter didn't crack. None of my research indicated he was lying, but I liked to be sure. "What about this place?" I picked up the tablet and held it out for him to see. The page was to the online casino Kershaw used.

Boter shook his head. "I told you I don't bet online. It'd be too easy for things to get out of control. I don't do that. I like to have clearly defined limits. It helps. That's why I don't have my bank account linked to any of that. At least, I didn't until the other night."

"Tell me what happened."

"I'd been playing cards in the back. Chelsea's has a few games going after hours. There were four of us at the table, I think. We were playing five-card. I was down to my last chip. I had a pair of sevens. It wasn't going to happen, so I walked away."

"You folded?"

"Not officially. I went to use the bathroom. I'd already bet, but I knew it wouldn't matter. Someone else could flip my cards over if they cared enough to see what a loser I was."

"How many other players were still in the game?"

"Two."

"Go on."

"After I finished in the bathroom, I didn't think there was any reason to return to the table. I had nothing left."

"You had a pair of sevens."

"I take it you don't play cards."

I did, but I didn't want him to know that because then it would turn into a debate on why he didn't fold sooner. "The chances may have been slim, but you could have won."

"I doubted it. Luck hadn't been on my side all night, so I stopped by the bar to have one last beer before heading home. While I was drowning my sorrows, a woman came over to me. She'd been at the table and told me I won the hand."

"And you believed her?"

Boter's cheeks turned crimson. "I may have had more than one beer at that point."

"Chelsea's serves its players at the table at no additional charge."

He looked up at me again. "I guess you do play."

"Not for a while," I said. At least not at Chelsea's.

Justin knocked before pushing open the door and putting down a serving tray with two coffee cups, creamers, sugar packets, and a plate of assorted breakfast items. He left without a word, closing the door behind him.

Boter reached for the sugar packet, shook it a few times, and ripped off the top before pouring it into the closest mug. "The doctors say I should cut back, but these are trying times."

"Doctors?" I wondered if he wasn't well.

"Y'know, the usual. Don't drink. Don't eat fried foods. Cut out sugar."

"Right." I eased back in the chair, watching as he selected an egg and cheese croissant from the platter. "I can see if we have any healthier options."

"Please don't." Boter winked before taking a bite. "As I was saying, this woman told me I won. I figured she was yanking my chain. But she wouldn't give it up. She said we both won, that the pot split. She wanted me to have my share of the winnings."

"Why didn't she give you the cash then and there?"

"That's where things get even more convoluted. I should have stuck with my gut, but she was so insistent and I wasn't thinking clearly. She said after that hand, she didn't cash out. She played with my chips too and went all in on the next hand. She had trip jacks. She should have won, but another player had a flush. She insisted she'd pay me back. I wasn't sure I believed her, but she was pretty and nice. I thought what's the harm in sharing my contact information with her. If nothing else, maybe I'd have a pleasant conversation."

"She called?"

"The next day. We only spoke on the phone that one time. She wanted to wire me the money. I don't use any of those fancy apps, so I gave her my checking account information. I didn't think she could use that to take everything from me."

"Did you go to the police?"

"I gave them her information, her phone number and name, but they said those were dead ends. Everything was fake."

"May I see your phone?"

Boter handed it to me. "Her number didn't come up. She had it blocked. When I tried calling her back with the info she gave me, the call wouldn't connect."

"I can see that." It'd take some work, but I could get the number. However, if the police already looked, I didn't need to waste my time. "Do they know how she managed to empty your account without authorization?"

"The detective I spoke to suggested she could have spoofed my number when she contacted the bank."

"Even if she did, she'd still have to answer security questions. Does anyone else have access to your account?"

"My daughter." The light bulb turned on over Boter's head. "Do you think she impersonated her?"

"I wouldn't doubt it. Did you mention your daughter to her?"

"I think so."

I opened the notes tab on the tablet. "What's your daughter's name?"

"Eloise Boter."

I'd already looked into his family, but I didn't want him to know that. Part of it was for show and the rest was to see if someone put him up to this. Maybe I was paranoid, but that didn't mean people weren't coming for me. After all, I had invited the fox into my henhouse. I needed to find a better comparison.

"Have you spoken to Eloise since this happened?" I asked.

"I didn't want to tell her about any of this. She already acts like I'm an old fool. This will only make it worse."

"She needs to know. If this woman scammed you by pretending to be her, she may try the same thing with your daughter's accounts."

"All right." Boter sighed and finished his breakfast sandwich. "This is why it doesn't pay to gamble. Did your client encounter a similar situation?"

"He didn't meet his scammer in person which makes it harder." I wondered if Boter had sat with a sketch artist, but memory was a fickle thing, especially after a night of drinking. "What day did this happen?"

"Thursday. The money went missing Monday."

"But you were at Chelsea's Thursday night."

"No, Wednesday night into Thursday morning. It was after midnight, so that made it Thursday."

Despite running an illegal game in the back, Chelsea's operated as a restaurant the rest of the time. The legit business cleaned the money that came in from the underground casino which meant they had security cameras in the front. Once I found the scammer on the footage, I could go from there.

"What did this woman say her name was?"

"Claudia Bellman."

I made a note and asked Boter to describe her. "Is there anything else? Any other interactions or oddities that occurred? Phone calls? E-mails? Random online quizzes you may have taken?"

"Online quizzes?"

"Yeah, like *Which superhero are you?* or *What flavor potato chip would you be?* Y'know, the quizzes where they ask a bunch of random questions and spout out ridiculous nonsense as a way to kill time."

"I don't waste my time with stuff like that."

"Does gambling take up that much of your free time?"

"I don't gamble that much. Just every now and again."

"You've been going to Chelsea's for seven years. I'd say that's more than every now and again."

"I know my limits."

I held up my palms. "I never said you didn't. I'm just trying to figure out how this woman was able to override your bank's security measures."

"We talked for a while that night at Chelsea's. I don't remember much about the conversation, but maybe that's how."

"Yeah," I said, "maybe."

TWELVE

Claudia Bellman didn't exist. Correction, several existed, but none of them matched the description Nathan Boter provided. The few who lived in the city hadn't been anywhere near Chelsea's on Wednesday or Thursday. Things couldn't be that easy. If they were, the police would have already made an arrest and told Nathan Boter to be more careful.

"Lucien," Amir waved a hand in front of my face, forcing me to stop eyeballing the monitor in front of him, "facial rec will take a while, but this woman doesn't match any of the ID photos we've pulled for Claudia Bellman."

"I didn't expect her to." The woman on the screen was middle-aged with frosted blonde hair. Her hair didn't look quite right. She could have grayed prematurely or had a bad dye job. My cosmetology skills were limited, but something about her appearance seemed off.

"Since you paid Chelsea's management for the footage, why didn't you ask them for a name to go with it?" Amir asked.

"I did."

Amir waited, fingers poised over the keys. "Okay."

"They didn't know."

"Do you believe them?"

"It's a cash business. They have regulars, but no one I spoke to recognized her. They figured she was a newcomer. I tracked down the dealer from the card game, but he didn't get a name either. He also didn't recall the pot being split. As far as he was concerned, Boter lost that hand."

"So the story Boter told you was bullshit."

"Yeah," I said, "but he believed it."

"Or so he says."

I rubbed a hand over my lips to hide the smirk. "When did you become so cynical?"

Amir gave me the side-eye. "I spent decades working for federal law enforcement."

"That would explain it, but you mean to tell me the private sector hasn't renewed your faith in humanity?"

"Working here?"

"Point taken." I went back to staring at the footage, but it didn't tell me much of anything. From what I could see, things went down exactly as Boter described. "Send a clean shot of her face to Kershaw and ask him if he recognizes her."

Amir cut a still from the footage. "Done."

I looked behind me, paranoid that Darrow had snuck out of his office and was spying on me. But he wasn't. "Has Cross Security's latest contracted hire been causing problems?"

"Problems?" Amir shook his head. "He's made a few requests for intel, which I already told you about."

"That's it?"

"That's it."

"You haven't caught him trying to hack into our servers or sneak into the labs?"

"No."

"That's good. I'm glad to hear it." I checked my phone. Since I didn't contact Kershaw directly, I doubted he'd send his response to me. He'd respond to Amir, eventually. "Let me know what Kershaw says or if anything shakes loose."

"Lucien," Amir stopped me before I could leave, "are you going to share this lead with Darrow?"

"It's not a lead, yet."

* * *

The precinct was always at the top of my least favorite places list. It was this, the hospital, and the cemetery. Those three places meant you were going in the ground or could be put in the ground. Come to think of it, prisons weren't a lot of fun either. The same was true of the dentist's office.

Usually, I'd call Sgt. Sara Rostokowski with whatever requests I had. But I didn't need access to a report or dirt on someone in uniform. I wasn't sure what I needed, but talking to the detectives who'd spoken to Alan Kershaw and Nathan Boter would be a good place to start.

"What are you doing here, Lucien?" the familiar voice asked from behind the front desk.

"Hey, Sara."

"Don't 'hey, Sara,' me," she said. "Are you here to file a report? Or did you decide to stop by because you were having a slow afternoon and thought you should cause trouble?"

"I'm thinking about getting a dog and needed your opinion."

She stared at me. "No one from the K-9 unit wants to speak to you."

"I didn't say anything about a drug dog or a bomb-sniffing dog. I just said a dog."

"You shouldn't have pets."

"Why not?"

"No."

"I could be a dog guy. We could go for walks."

"You'd get mugged or shot, especially if you're walking around late at night in that suit."

"Not if I have a big, scary dog with me." I tugged on my lapels. "Do you like the suit?"

"You look like a stockbroker."

"Maybe in a different life."

She gave me a bittersweet smile before coming around the desk and giving me a hug. "Lucien, why are you here?

What's wrong now?"

"Nothing's wrong. I thought I'd stop by and see how you are before performing my due diligence." I told her about Kershaw and Boter. "The FBI is looking into it since the police dropped the ball."

Sara settled behind the computer. "Who did they speak to?"

"Kershaw spoke to someone in cybercrimes. He didn't remember the guy's name. Boter spoke to Howard. I think he works for the grand larceny unit."

"That would make sense." She entered something and studied the screen, creases appearing around her mouth as she read. Her lips pursed and her eyes narrowed. "Howard's report has been uploaded to the database. Boter told him the same thing he told you. Howard looked into the name and number Boter provided. The phone number was out of service. The name didn't match the description. Howard was supposed to follow up with the restaurant where this woman made her approach, but I'm not seeing anything here."

"I'm not surprised."

Sara gave me a sharp look. "Be nice."

"That was nice."

"Try harder."

"If you knew what I was really thinking, you'd commend me for my restraint."

"Lucien, I know damn well what you're thinking. Now be nice."

"Yes, ma'am."

She reached for the phone and dialed an extension. While she waited, she said, "Since it happened at Chelsea's Bar and Grill, maybe Boter should have spoken to someone in vice."

"Detective Howard should have suggested it."

She held up a finger when someone answered. After a few questions and several uh-huhs, she hung up. "Howard asked vice what they thought. They had nothing for him. People get scammed all the time. Your client lost his savings, but it was less than five grand. It sucks, but it's not a top priority around here."

"This is why I want to privatize security and policing. That's a lot of money to most people."

"I agree, but dozens of crimes are reported. Someone getting scammed like that, there's not much we can do. The chances of making a recovery are damn near impossible. It's easier to investigate home invasions and robberies. Items can be tracked. Cash is a lot harder, especially when it's ones and zeroes."

"Did Howard follow up with the bank to find out how it happened?"

"The bank didn't notice anything suspicious."

"A guy's account was zeroed out."

"Yeah, a guy's account which is usually zeroed out when it's not overdrawn. The fact he had any money in there to take was a miracle."

That gave me pause. I hadn't looked too deeply into Boter's financials, only far enough to make sure he wasn't a plant or decoy. Once I knew he was legit, I turned my attention to comparing and contrasting. But since he didn't normally have a ton of money in his account, Claudia Bellman or whatever the scammer's name was, must have had perfect timing or gotten lucky.

"The bank said Eloise deposited a few grand into the account the week before," Sara said.

"That was for Boter's rent, but he's a gambler. He took his rent money to Chelsea's."

"Or he took his paycheck to Chelsea's since his rent was covered," Sara said, "or there is the other far more obvious and much more likely possibility."

"You think Boter's making this up."

"You said he has a gambling problem he's not ready to face. Wouldn't it be easier to blame some mystery woman for stealing his money than admitting he lost it at the poker table?"

I ran a hand through my hair, ignoring the tickle in my brain. Sure, that was the easiest explanation. It made logical sense. And it meant Detective Howard didn't have to put in very much work to wash his hands of the mess. "The FBI disagrees."

"Are you sure about that?"

"Do you want me to go to the federal building and have this conversation with Agent Olsen?"

"You could call," she suggested.

"He doesn't want me poking my nose into this."

"Can't imagine why." She picked up the phone a second time. "You have his number handy?"

I gave her the card I'd taken from Olsen's desk, which included his extension. "Please and thank you."

Sara pointed to the staircase. "While I do this, talk to cybercrimes. They're waiting for you."

"They are?"

She pointed more emphatically. "Go before I change my mind."

THIRTEEN

Cybercrimes didn't tell me anything Alan Kershaw hadn't already said, so I detoured to see Detective Howard. He wasn't in.

Based on the ringing phones and overcrowded corkboards, grand larceny had a lot going on. Thefts were up. That may have explained why Howard hadn't been that interested in helping or investigating. Either that, or he was a lazy bastard. Since he wasn't here, I had no way of knowing which was accurate. The cynical part of me figured it'd be a safer bet to assume the worst, but Sara told me to be nice. Maybe I'd give him the benefit of the doubt, if I ever met him in person.

Unsure how to proceed, I considered my options and made a second detour to vice. As their name suggested, they handled a lot of dirty little secrets, namely prostitution and gambling. On occasion, their cases overlapped with narcotics.

"Underground casinos, that's what you want to know about?" Detective Taylor rocked back in her chair. "I figured a guy like you would be looking for high-end escorts instead."

"I already know where to find them."

"Why am I not surprised?"

"The casinos," I repeated.

"There are plenty. Chinatown's got dozens of places. Ask around. I'm sure a guy like you can find a game."

"I don't need to find a game." I wasn't planning on playing this card, but I couldn't make heads or tails out of her responses. "Do you know who I am?"

Taylor looked me up and down. "That's a nice watch."

"Thanks." I tugged on my cuff, finding myself growing increasingly uncomfortable.

She leaned over, crooking her finger so I'd scoot closer. Before she spoke, she peered from left to right. Then she lowered her voice. "It'll cost you five hundred, but I'll make sure wherever you're going tonight won't be raided. What do you say?"

Was this woman serious? "You're asking for a bribe?"

She straightened, a loud barking laugh escaping her lips. "God, you should see your face, Lucien. Everyone in this place knows you're the commish's kid." She laughed again. "I thought you'd be smarter."

"I'm smart enough not to insult my boss's son."

She shrugged, the smile as bright as ever. "Look, I get you're investigating a theft on your own. But there are a lot of places that operate under the radar. We don't have the resources to deal with most of them, so we pick and choose our battles. Chelsea's is at the bottom of that list. Do you know why?"

"Money talks."

"Bingo." She eyed me again. "I'm surprised you'd take on a client who gambles there. Word is you handle large accounts." Her eyes traveled again. Was she flirting or crazy?

"This is the second case I've encountered. One victim was scammed online, the other in person."

"You think this is a grift?" she asked.

"Possibly, but it's a short game. A quick in and out. Make an intro, take the cash, and move on. Not a lot of backstory or effort needed. Definitely not a long con."

"The payday would be minimal. Pros would want more, given the risk."

"Risk is minimal too."

"Word is you're more of a high risk kind of guy."

"Where are you hearing these things about me?"

"Watercooler."

I wasn't buying it. "Uh-huh."

She studied me for another few seconds. Somehow, I managed not to fidget. "Hang here a sec." She headed across the room. Her gait was more of a glide, very smooth, very seductive. When she returned, she tucked the printouts into an empty folder. "You want this?" She held it in my direction.

I reached for the folder, but she jerked it away.

"Not so fast. There are conditions. I give you this, you give me whatever intel you gather. I could use the collar."

"Tired of working undercover?"

"I'm tired of every arrest I make being directly connected to that. I am capable of conducting an investigation with my clothes on."

"Then why aren't you?"

She gave me a withering look and shoved the folder at me. "You find any evidence that points to a single grifter or a group of scammers targeting gamblers, you bring it to me. If I find out you didn't, I'll arrest you for interfering in a police investigation."

"But you aren't investigating." I smiled. "You need to work on that carrot and stick routine. Most cops know you can't play good cop and bad cop by yourself. The only way that works is with multiple personalities."

"I'm doing you a favor here. You could say thank you."

"There are a lot of things I could do." I flipped through the pages. It didn't look like there was anything in here I hadn't already seen. "You should talk to Agent Olsen at the FBI. He's my point of contact on this. The two of you can fight over me. I would have come to you first, but when Mr. Kershaw reported the crime, he was sent away. Seems like the PD dropped the ball. You can't expect me to pick it up and run with it, at least not for your team." I put the folder down. "Thanks, but no thanks. In case you didn't get the memo, I work private. I'm not a cop, and I have no intention of doing your work for you."

Taylor waited until I was halfway out the door before she said, "Kershaw wasn't the first."

Don't turn around. Keep walking. But curiosity would kill me. Hopefully, it wouldn't be because of this case.

I stopped in the doorway, unsure if I should turn back around or ask my question while facing the stairs. However, the acoustics in this place meant she wouldn't be able to hear me, which would lead to me having to turn around and repeat the question, thus ruining my attempt to appear indifferent.

"Who was?" I asked, facing her. To my relief, she had already crossed the bullpen, which meant she planned to chase me down to hand me this information.

"Eric Greene." She thrust another folder at me. "The report is in there, along with his account and my notes. Look it over. Maybe it's connected. Maybe it isn't."

"Why do you care so much about a collar?"

"It's my job."

"That's usually my line. Are you stalking me, Detective Taylor?"

She groaned. "Get over yourself. You were just as pompous in the academy. But you spoke up when it mattered. You wanted to do what was right. You wanted things to change, to be better. I hope I'm not wrong thinking you haven't changed. From my experience, people are fundamentally who they are and that never goes away. And you were always a good guy, despite what anyone said to the contrary."

Shit. "We came up together?" I didn't remember her. There had been hundreds of us, which might explain why I didn't recognize her.

"I was in the class behind yours. We didn't have much overlap, but I saw a few things and heard a lot more. You were the only thing anyone talked about for quite some time after your dismissal. The instructors forbid any discussion about you, but there were always whispers." She stared at me. "Am I wrong?"

"That depends on who you ask." I took the folder. "I'll look into this, but I'm not doing it for you. I'm doing it for them. Whatever my client wants to do is what we'll do."

"You'll do the right thing," she said. "I know it."

*   *   *

After Sgt. Rostokowski reassured me Detective Taylor was on the level, she told me that her call with Agent Olsen hadn't resulted in much of anything. Olsen had spoken to Nathan Boter, but he had reached the same conclusions the police had. Boter lost the money and blamed it on someone else.

"I don't buy it," I said. "The bank manager said a woman had the money transferred out of the account. Boter doesn't sound that feminine to me."

"Maybe his daughter got fed up with him gambling away his rent money month after month. Maybe she realized by giving him the cash, she was enabling him, feeding into his addiction. Have you spoken to her?"

"Has anyone who was tasked with investigating?"

"Lucien, you know things slip through the cracks."

"I'll take that as a no." I ran my finger against the edge of the folder. "You said Taylor's on the level. Why hasn't she done more than this?"

"She works vice. None of these cases crossed her desk. Honestly, even if they had, she deals mostly with undercover operations."

"She works as a decoy." I found that a little deplorable, especially since the police department had tried to entrap me a time or two. Except, I wasn't the type to hire sex workers.

"She'd like to do more."

"Tell her to transfer to a different unit. Hell, maybe when all is said and done, I should offer her a job at Cross Security."

Sara gave me a funny look. "How come you haven't made me an offer?"

"Because you'd break my heart by saying no."

She gave my cheek a firm pat. "You got what you wanted. Now get the hell outta here."

FOURTEEN

The file Det. Taylor gave me didn't contain much of anything, which I had immediately realized. The only thing I hadn't seen or heard had to do with this alleged first victim, Eric Greene. But those facts and details left a lot to be desired.

According to Greene, he'd been playing mahjong. There had been a raid and some confusion. One thing led to another, and he got swept up with everyone else. Several mahjong parlors operated in the area. Whenever vice got bored or narcotics got a tip that the same people running the betting houses were also trafficking, they'd make wide-scale arrests and try to convince someone to talk.

Once Greene had been released, he assumed his winnings had been forfeited. The police would have confiscated whatever they found. Even if they couldn't hold the cash in evidence, he doubted the mahjong parlor would pay out. The rules were the same, be it mahjong, poker, or any other betting activity. The house always wins.

However, two days later, someone reached out to Greene. He received a call from a blocked number with the offer to transfer his winnings into his account. Happily, he gave the caller his account number. The next thing he knew, his checking account was zeroed out.

I tried calling Eric Greene, but he didn't answer. Since I didn't feel like making a house call until I had more information, I did some research. Darrow may have been better, but I was no slouch either.

Greene's story sounded similar enough to Kershaw's and Boter's that I believed they could be connected, but the details were different enough that one could argue these men had been targeted by three separate parties for any number of reasons. No one in the police department had made the connection, except Detective Taylor. But she hadn't done anything with the information. What would she have done if I hadn't shown up with questions? That thought made me a little itchy, almost as if this could be some sort of ploy.

"Hey, boss," Justin said from the doorway, "do you want me to order dinner?"

"What time is it?"

"Late." Justin nodded to my window. "The sun set three hours ago. Didn't you notice?"

"I was busy."

"Working on the proposal for Miller Industries?"

"Shit. When is that meeting?"

"Tomorrow at eight."

"Shit," I said again. "I thought there wasn't anything pressing on the schedule. We haven't had any new clients in a while."

"Miller isn't exactly new."

"We've never worked with them. We just jumped through all the damn hoops so they could go with a different security firm."

"One that screwed them over, which is why they're coming back to us," Justin said.

"Shit."

"You mentioned that a time or two. Or is there an echo in here?"

"Justin—"

"Don't worry, boss. I have the old proposal saved. I already plugged in the updated numbers and projections and changed the timeline. You may want to reread it so you can make whatever changes you want. I forwarded it to your inbox." Justin moved closer, so he could see what I was working on. "You're still digging into Kershaw's case. I thought you hired Darrow for that."

"I did."

"Then shouldn't he be working on this?"

"Tell me he's not still here."

"He left before the sun went down."

"Good."

"Boss, you told Kershaw this wasn't a priority, that it wouldn't have a resolution. Is this still about Darrow or proving something to yourself?"

I rubbed my eyes. "The police aren't doing anything. The FBI has dropped the ball. They say this is a big investigation involving dangerous organizations, but that's a line. No one is doing a damn thing."

"So you are."

I ran a hand through my hair. "I know. This is insane."

"Do you want pizza or Chinese?"

"How do you feel about Indian?"

"Extra rice and naan?"

"Always."

After placing our dinner order, my assistant returned to my office and sat in my client chair. He put his laptop on my desk. "Tell me what I can do to help."

"You don't have to. If I remember correctly, you didn't want me to involve myself in this, so that means you're exempt from assisting."

"You didn't listen, so we're here now. And since this keeps happening on a small-scale, I'm hoping our early assessments were incorrect, that some faceless terrorist cell isn't behind this and we aren't going to get murdered because of it."

"To be on the safe side, if you make any calls or do any research, make sure you use Darrow's name."

Justin glanced at me, an amused glint in his eye. "Is that what you've been doing this entire time?"

"Maybe."

But he knew me better than that. "You know you will have to hand this over to him at some point."

"I will, but I want to find everything I can first. Once I know what the facts are, I'll give it to him and he can tell me what facts he's found."

"You're testing him. And here I thought you were incapable of multitasking."

"Only some of the time." I finished pulling up everything I could on Eric Greene. "Run Greene and Boter. Get everything you can on them, Chelsea's, and the mahjong parlor. While you do that, I will go over the Miller Industries proposal and see if we need to make any more tweaks."

"We? You mean me."

"I can tweak," I said.

"That'll be the day."

I gave him an odd look. "Is that some kind of slang term I haven't heard?"

"You are getting old and out of touch, boss."

"Tweak you," I said.

"If only you could."

We worked in amicable silence until the food arrived. Working through dinner came with light conversation. Justin filled me in on everything that had been happening with the office, our security teams, and the parking situation now that the first delivery of our company cars had arrived.

"I don't pay you enough," I said.

"Agreed." Justin nodded to the glass of scotch I put on the table beside him. "I'll take care of it the next time I go over payroll."

"I handle payroll."

"You're so busy. I can take that over for you."

"Keep dreaming."

Justin spun the computer around. "I haven't found anything you missed. Greene's a delivery driver. That's probably how he learned about the mahjong games and got involved in the betting. Most of those places are invite only, and he's not the typical player."

"Do you think that's why he got scammed?"

"How would that fit with Boter? Boter checks the stereotypical gambler boxes."

"Not all of them. Boter doesn't owe anyone a large sum of money, and he doesn't have a bookie."

"Okay, but he checks the other boxes." A thought crossed Justin's mind. "Do you think he's ever been to a meeting?"

"Boter doesn't believe he has a problem. Why would he go?"

"Maybe his daughter made him."

I made a note to call her in the morning. I had wanted to do it earlier, but time had gotten away from me. "Even if he had, Greene and Kershaw have never been to meetings."

"You know that for a fact?" Justin asked.

"Not with Greene, but definitely with Kershaw. He doesn't check any of the gambler boxes. He doesn't even play locally. Gambling is a recreational activity for him, not an addiction."

"So he says."

I'd gone over everything related to Kershaw. Darrow had done a much deeper dive. In fact, I'd say Darrow had gone off the deep end when it came to research. "Darrow would have mentioned it." I checked my email to see if there had been any updates. Amir had finally heard back from our client. Kershaw didn't recognize the woman who had allegedly scammed Boter, but I didn't expect him to. "Who did Greene say contacted him about his winnings?"

Justin pushed the police folder closer to me. "It doesn't say."

I reread the report and Taylor's notes. "I'll have to ask."

Justin hit a button. "I sent you Greene's work schedule for the rest of this week. He should be getting home around six a.m. He's working tonight, delivering to area businesses from a centralized warehouse."

"Including a grocery store," I said.

"Is that important?"

"That's the same grocery store Boter manages."

"Huh?" Justin tore off a piece of naan and used it to scoop up the butter chicken before popping it into his mouth. "Do you think it's a coincidence?"

"I think it's a clue."

"Then you should say ah-ha."

FIFTEEN

I was waiting beside Eric Greene's car at 5:45 in the morning with a drink carrier resting on his hood. I hadn't slept yet and was starting to feel it. Yawning, I reached for my cup and bounced a little to get the blood circulating.

Enough of that, I thought, resting my hips beside the drink carrier and scanning the area for the umpteenth time. The parking lot was well lit. The delivery trucks were parked around the side. These weren't those big eighteen-wheelers. These were the smaller refrigerated trucks that made local deliveries from the larger shipping companies. Last leg delivery or last mile, whatever they were called.

That's how this investigation felt to me, but again, I was tired. The police and FBI had kicked things off, but they didn't deliver. Instead, Cross Security was going to take the investigation that final stretch, or so I hoped.

"Hey," a guy said, coming out of the building that boasted the delivery service's name in bright red lettering.

"Good morning," I replied.

"More like good night. You look like you could use some sleep too." He glanced at the cups beside me. "Word of advice, don't drink all four of them. I ended up in the hospital after one too many energy drinks."

"I'll take that under advisement."

He gave me a strange look before continuing to his car. On the bright side, he didn't take me for a knee-breaker, even though I had spilled curry on my shirt and hadn't changed since I wanted to keep my spare outfit clean for my meeting with Miller Industries. More importantly, the man didn't see me as a threat to his coworker. I didn't think Eric Greene had loan sharks to worry about, which went along with my theory that he, unlike Boter, wasn't on his way to becoming a degenerate gambler.

"Can I help you with something?" Greene asked, approaching from the building. He had a black windbreaker open over a neon yellow safety vest.

I held out the drink carrier. "Coffee?"

"Um...no."

"Your buddy," I indicated the now empty parking space, "said I shouldn't drink all of these myself, but if you don't want one, I think I'll risk it."

"Good for you." Greene veered a little to the right to avoid getting too close to me as he approached the driver's side door. "Do you mind? I'd like to get home."

"I was hoping we could chat before that happens. I'm a private investigator." I indicated my business card which I'd tucked into the drink carrier. "Lucien Cross, Cross Security and Investigations."

"I never heard of it."

"That may be why I haven't had any new clients lately." I sipped my drink, my hips remaining firmly planted against the hood of his car. "Detective Taylor told me what happened at the mahjong parlor. I was hoping you wouldn't mind answering a few questions." I slid off his car and turned to face him. "You're not the only one who's been scammed. Someone's zeroed out the accounts of at least two other people. I think it's connected to what happened to you."

"Can you get my money back?" Greene asked.

"Probably not, but I'll buy you breakfast in exchange for your time."

Greene eyed the coffee carrier. "Are you expecting company?"

"Nope."

"You have four coffees. Who are they for?"

"Two coffees. One is tea. The other is hot chocolate. I didn't know what you liked to drink. I wanted to cover all my bases."

"If we go to breakfast, are you going to order every item on the menu?"

"Is that what it'll take to convince you to talk to me?"

Greene grinned. "I could go for some steak and eggs."

"Sure."

I left the cup carrier with Greene, who seemed intrigued by the prospect of having three different beverages to sample, and followed him in my car to the diner of his choosing. It was the typical greasy spoon, but we beat the morning rush by about an hour.

"What'll it be?" the server asked.

"Espresso," I said, "with the veggie omelet and a side of hash browns."

Greene ordered the remaining items on the menu, including the tofu scramble. "I always wanted to try it," he said. "Figured I wouldn't like it and it'd be a waste of money. But seeing as how I have no money now, it can't hurt."

"You really don't have anything left?"

"I asked my boss for an advance, but he can't do it. I don't have family I can borrow from. A couple of guys at work invited me over for dinner or out for beers. Hopefully, I'll be able to scrape together enough by the time the bills come due."

"What about your credit cards?"

"I can use them to float for a while, but they'll have to be paid back and the interest rates are insane. I'm using them as little as possible."

The server returned with four plates, put two of them down in front of me, and put the other two in front of Greene. Another server followed behind carrying another four plates. "I'm not sure where to put these."

We rearranged the table to accommodate Greene's selections. Finally, our cups were placed on the window sill, the only remaining space near our table.

"Enjoy," the server said, bewildered.

"If you wouldn't mind, grab us a few containers to wrap this up when you get the chance," Greene said.

Greene didn't order everything to be a jerk. He ordered so he'd have food to last him the week.

"Wrap up a dozen muffins and a pie too," I said.

Greene looked at me. "You have a hell of a sweet tooth."

"It's for you."

"You don't have to."

I turned back to the server. "Do it anyway."

Greene picked up his fork and took a bite. "Thanks."

"Run through everything for me," I said.

"Where do you want me to start?"

"The beginning. *Memento* was brilliant, but I find it easier to follow the story when events happen in sequential order."

"You're weird."

"I know."

Greene laughed. "I work strange hours. Lots of nights. Lots of late shifts. There's not a lot to do on my nights off. I'm always looking for different things. There are only so many sports bars to visit. I'm too old for the clubs."

"The age limits work the other way."

"Well, I feel too old. I kind of stumbled upon the mahjong scene by accident. I deliver to some restaurants and got friendly with the owners who invited me along to their normal game, and it became routine."

"How long have you been going there?"

"A couple of months. I'm not very good. We don't play for much. The night of the raid, I must have stepped in something because I was on a streak. It's like the game suddenly clicked."

"How much did you win?"

"About two hundred bucks. It wasn't anything major. Like I said, we never played for much. That's why when someone reached out, offering to pay up, I figured it was legit."

"Because it was a small sum?"

Greene nodded. "I thought it was their way of encouraging me to go back once things were up and running again."

"Were you planning on going back?"

"No. I knew gambling wasn't legal, but it didn't seem like a crime or anything that came with a risk. We were a group of people playing games. Sure, it cost money, but it wasn't substantial, life-changing amounts. But after the police busted in and arrested everyone, I was done. I have too much to lose. The point wasn't to play. The point was to find something to do, somewhere to socialize while the rest of the world slept."

"I get that," I said.

"Yeah, so I figured, if the people running the game wanted to pay me for my trouble, I'd take it so as not to be disrespectful and quietly bow out."

"Do you know the person who contacted you?"

Greene looked uncomfortable and focused on dividing a stack of pancakes in half. "I never asked who was calling. The person on the other end did most of the talking. The details she provided were enough for me to make some assumptions. It was stupid. I should have asked more questions. I should have said no."

I asked a few questions, but the number had been blocked and he had no idea how the person subverted his bank's security. "Check your contact information," I said. "In one instance, the notification alerts had been rerouted. In another, the caller impersonated an authorized user."

"I don't have anyone else on my account." Greene pulled out his phone and opened his banking app. "Son of a bitch. The multi-factor authentication's some weird ass shit."

"Let me see." I took the phone from him and wrote down the number and e-mail address. "Neither of these is yours?"

"No."

"What about the PIN?"

"That's mine."

"The same asshole has got to be behind this." I wrote down the name of his bank. None of the victims banked at the same place, but banking practices were uniform throughout. If the scammer was targeting different victims with different banks, there would be less chance bank staff or security protocols would flag anything since they didn't know about the existing threat. "Let me ask you another question. Do you play cards?"

"No."

"Not even online?"

"No."

"Do you owe anyone money?"

Greene shook his head.

"What about enemies?"

"Well, I did piss off some schmuck on the turnpike earlier tonight."

"Other than that?"

"I know it may not seem like it and you probably won't believe me, but my world's pretty small. There aren't a lot of people in it, and the ones who are aren't out to get me."

"I believe it. It just doesn't help." I showed him the photo taken at Chelsea's, another place he'd never been. "Do you recognize this woman?"

"What do you think?"

"I'd be remiss if I didn't ask."

The server returned with a dozen containers. I helped Greene relocate the leftovers, which he marked and labeled with a sharpie he pulled from his shirt pocket. After I paid for our meal, I followed Greene to his car.

"Thanks for breakfast, Lucien." He held out his hand. "I'm sorry I couldn't be of more use."

"Hang on a sec." I reached into my pocket and pulled out my wallet. Before I even opened it, Greene put his hand on my wrist. "I'm not looking for a handout. This will keep me squared away for the week. I'll figure something out. But I appreciate the offer." He chuckled. "You should be careful. The scammer may show up at your door with her hand out."

"Wouldn't that be interesting?"

SIXTEEN

"I don't like that look on your face," Justin said when I stepped off the elevator. "Whatever you're thinking, stop it right now."

"Is Miller here yet?" I asked.

"No."

"Good, that should give me enough time to change." I went into my office and opened the closet. My spare suit was safely zipped inside a garment bag. I undid the zipper, pulled the jacket off the hanger, and reached for a clean shirt.

Justin followed me into my office, studying the tattoo on my back. "When you flex your shoulder blades, it looks like the wings are moving."

I eyed him through the mirror. "You mean my rhomboids?"

"Sure." Justin continued to stare at me.

"You need to get some sleep. You're starting to scare me."

"That's not the problem."

I turned, buttoning my shirt. "There's a problem?"

"Darrow."

"What did he do?"

"He called right before you got here to say he had a possible lead and was going to speak to her."

"Who?"

"Eloise Boter."

My head swam on account of the sudden spike in my blood pressure. I blinked a few times. That guy was right. I shouldn't have had that many espressos in such a short amount of time. But the caffeine wouldn't put me in the ground. Darrow would. "How did he find out about her?"

"I don't know."

"You don't know? I need you to know."

"Amir's going over everything again to make sure Darrow didn't go near our servers or access our system. I have building security checking to make sure he didn't find some way to splice the wires or hack in from some other part of the building outside of our offices, and I have our security footage dialed up on my computer, ready to review."

"Okay." I checked the time, aware of the ding of the elevator. Miller was always early. It was one thing I usually liked about him. But today wasn't most days. "I will be in a client meeting. Once I'm finished, I'd like answers."

"I'll have them." The way Justin said that gave me confidence he would find out how Darrow knew what he knew.

"Make sure that machete and shovel are handy too."

"Maybe we won't need them."

"I've never been that lucky."

My meeting with Mr. Miller didn't take long. He liked it when I got to the point, and since he wasn't a client, at least not yet, I didn't bother dancing around things. The last time I did, he had no interest in signing on the dotted line.

"We've been over this. You know what Cross Security has to offer." I indicated the revised proposal. "Obviously, you're interested since you asked for a second meeting. It's no secret your last firm screwed you without so much as buying you dinner first."

"Oh, they bought dinner," Miller said. "Then I took it up the ass."

"Happens." I sat back in the chair. "That's our fee

schedule. Equipment costs are always extra, but you'll get a quote before we start work. There are a few suppliers I trust, but you can always purchase your own equipment and have someone else perform the installation. Hardware isn't my priority."

"We have equipment. I'm just wondering how shitty it is."

"You want an assessment, so how about we get something on the books? I'll take a look at the work your previous firm did and tell you what to keep and what to improve. If you like what you hear, you sign. If you don't, I won't waste my time with a third meeting."

Miller chuckled uncertainly, unsure if he should be insulted. "I thought you'd be more of an ass-kisser."

"You caught me on a bad day. But you have a boardroom full of yes men who'd be happy to pucker up. That's not what you want from a security firm. You want someone who'll tell you the truth and won't worry about hurting your feelings in the process."

"True." Miller looked over the proposal again. "I'll have my assistant call to set up that assessment, and we'll take it from there."

"Excellent." I extended my hand. "I'm looking forward to working with you, Mr. Miller."

As soon as the elevator whisked him away, I sat on the edge of Justin's desk. "All right. What's the damage?"

"Darrow didn't cheat. He found Eloise Boter by chance." Justin showed me some posts she'd made on an online forum.

"I had everything flagged. Why wasn't I notified when she made that post?"

"You flagged casinos and gambling scams. She didn't use any of those keywords. She wanted to know what to do if someone's bank account is emptied."

"How the hell did Darrow find that?"

"He's better with keywords," Justin suggested.

"Fuck."

"I don't know, boss. I'm guessing that's what happened, but you should ask Darrow."

"You said he was on his way to speak to Eloise."

"When he called to say he'd be getting to the office late this morning, that was the reason why. However, I don't know if he's made contact yet. According to her schedule, she isn't expected at work until ten."

I checked the time. It was just after 8:30. I might be able to catch her before Darrow did, but that would depend on where he planned to make his approach. "Did he call her to set up a meeting?"

"I don't know."

"You didn't think to ask him that?"

"I did, but he rambled on about how he'd tell us everything if his lead panned out and then hung up."

"Pull his phone records. Hell, pull our phone records, and find out if he made contact."

"I already asked Amir to look into it. We haven't found anything on our line or Darrow's, but—"

"He could have a second number we don't know about." I wouldn't put anything past the other private eye. I almost wondered if he made things overly complicated to annoy me, but that would be a very self-centered view of things. He must have picked up these paranoid habits from working oppo and needing to cover his tracks. "Are the company cars outfitted and ready to go?"

"Yeah, but Darrow didn't take a company car. He took his own."

"Does he know what the company cars look like?"

Justin shrugged.

"Let's hope not. I don't want him to see me coming." Even as I grabbed the keys, I knew how insane that sounded. We were on the same side, allegedly. We should be working together. But I wanted to know what was what first. That was the only way I could ensure he wasn't withholding information or planning a takedown that I didn't see coming.

Damn, I really was paranoid.

SEVENTEEN

When I arrived at Eloise Boter's address, I immediately spotted the blue SUV with the dented rear. The D.C. plates had been exchanged for local plates, but I'd know that vehicle anywhere.

Parking the silver sedan in a space a block away, I wondered if Darrow was waiting for her to come out or if he'd already gone inside. Instead of stepping out of my car, I dialed Eloise's number. When it went to voicemail, I told her who I was and why I wanted to speak to her. Then I hung up.

The clock on the dash counted the minutes as they ticked by. All I knew for certain was Darrow was in the area. He could be speaking to Eloise inside her apartment, or he could be staking out the lobby, hoping to intercept her the moment she headed for the front door. Or he could be waiting inside his damaged SUV, like a crazed stalker.

I glanced around the car. "Glass houses," I mumbled.

I'd decided to knock on her door, like a normal human, when my phone rang. It was Eloise.

"Hi," I said, "this is Lucien Cross of Cross Security and Investigations."

"I got your message," she said. "I'm not sure how you

found me."

"Has anyone else reached out to you?"

"Like who?"

At least I'd beaten Darrow to the punch. "Another investigator is working the case. I thought he may have spoken to you. I have a few questions regarding your father and his bank account."

"I didn't take his money," she said. "The bank insisted I emptied the account, but I didn't do it. I've only ever put money in. I wouldn't take it out. I know he needs it. Sure, I have had conversations with his landlord about paying his rent directly, but I'm afraid if I do that he'll really get into hot water with someone. This way, I know he can cover his debts. That he won't get hurt."

"How bad is his gambling?" I asked, letting her take the conversation in a direction I hadn't anticipated.

"He's the equivalent of a functioning alcoholic. He has an addiction. It controls him, but he can still be productive when necessary. He scrapes by."

"With your help."

"Yeah, I know. I'm making it worse, but I don't know what else to do."

"Unfortunately, I don't have a solution."

"That's not your job. You called to find the scammer. I don't know who approached him or how she gained access to his account."

"Are you sure he didn't lose the money and make up the story?"

"I spoke to the bank manager directly. A woman emptied his account."

"What did your father tell you?"

She repeated a version of the story I had already heard. However, the Nathan Boter in her tale had a less defeatist attitude about the final hand he played and had only left the table because nature had come calling and wouldn't leave a message. "When he found out he won, he was floored by the other player's honesty. They exchanged information, and when she reached out to make the transfer, he thanked her again."

"Did he get her name?"

"Claudia Bellman," Eloise said, "but the police said that was a phony name. They couldn't track her down. That sounds suspicious to me. There are cameras everywhere. How could they not know who she is?"

"Did she go to the bank?"

"No, but she was at the damn restaurant where he plays cards in the back."

I already pulled that footage, but facial rec hadn't IDed her yet. "I'm going to send you a photo. Tell me if you recognize this woman."

"I don't. Is she the one who emptied my father's bank account?"

"That's a strong possibility. I'm still working on figuring a few things out." I glanced at the time. "Your father manages a grocery store."

"Uh-huh."

"Tell me about that. Has he ever mentioned problems with anyone at work? Maybe he fired someone? Or there's an employee who's always looking to pick up extra shifts, who's desperate to make more money?"

"I don't know."

"Has he ever mentioned anyone to you for any reason?"

"Not that I recall."

"What about customers?"

Eloise sighed. "I don't think so. We don't really talk about his job."

"I'll have to follow up with him on that." Eric Greene delivered to that store. Since he and Nathan Boter were both scammed, I had trouble believing that was a coincidence, but it could have been. "Do you know if your father works nights?"

"Sometimes."

"Does he supervise deliveries?"

"Not usually, unless there's a problem."

"What sort of problem?"

"Beats me." She made a sound. "I hate to cut this short, but I have to get ready for work. You can call me back tonight if you have more questions. I don't mind answering them. I want to know who did this to my dad."

"I appreciate your time. I'll be in touch if anything

surfaces." I had a feeling Eloise would call me if I didn't call her. With any luck, I'd have something to tell her the next time we spoke.

I opened the glove box and checked beneath the seats. Justin was right. The car had been outfitted. Basic tools of the trade had been placed inside the vehicle. I didn't check the trunk, but I didn't think it was empty. However, I wasn't driving this for the new car smell or access to zip ties and lock picks. I took it so Darrow wouldn't notice me.

Now I had a decision to make. Should I let him approach Eloise, even though we'd just spoken? Or should I stop him before he made Cross Security look incompetent?

Given that Nathan Boter wasn't a paying customer and Eloise hadn't said anything particularly helpful or damning concerning the investigation and had made no mention of hiring me to handle this, I would let it play out. From here, I had a front row seat to whatever Darrow was about to do, even if I had no idea where he was.

I could call and ask, I reasoned. That would be the easiest solution, but that felt like admitting defeat. I wasn't ready to do that. Instead, I waited.

Seventeen minutes later, Eloise exited her apartment. Ace Darrow wasn't beside her. He didn't chase her out of the building.

I turned my attention to his parked car. He didn't step out, even as Eloise opened the driver's side door to her red compact and slid behind the wheel. Maybe he planned on following her to the office. He'd followed me plenty of times, or so he said.

Even after she pulled away, his SUV remained parked. I gave the apartment building another look. Darrow wasn't near the doors or sitting on any of the benches outside.

Getting out of my car, I walked down the sidewalk. If he was dead inside the SUV, I'd feel like an idiot. But since I doubted he had made a break in the case that resulted in his death, I wasn't surprised when I peered through the window to find the front seat empty. The bastard wasn't here.

"You son of a bitch." I knew where he was. I just wasn't

sure what I should do about it.

Curiosity won out over self-preservation. Eloise Boter's apartment building didn't have a doorman or even the most basic of security measures. Anyone could walk right in. That made getting deliveries easier. The same held true for home invasions.

I kept my hands in my pockets as I made my way up the stairs. When I arrived at Eloise's door, I noticed the scratches on the lock. For a man with plenty of experience, Darrow was sloppy. I wondered if he'd been caught on the security cameras, if they even worked. I'd spotted two since entering the building.

Knocking on the door, I waited. The last time Darrow and I scouted the same apartment, he jumped out the window. However, this building didn't have a fire escape, so maybe he'd be a little smarter about things this time.

I knocked again. "Is anyone home?"

The door opened. "Lucien," Darrow hissed, "what are you doing here?" He grabbed my arm and yanked me inside. Peering through the peephole to make sure I hadn't been followed, he said, "Are you trying to get me caught?"

"What are you doing here?"

"What are you doing here?" he countered. "This is my investigation. I told Justin where I was going. Why did you show up? Were you afraid I couldn't handle this on my own?"

"Handle what?" I looked around, hoping Eloise didn't have a security system or surveillance set up inside her apartment to make up for the lack of security inside the building. "I was under the impression you were following a lead, that you planned to question a," I held up my palms and shrugged, "lead, suspect, witness? Who is this woman, and what does she have to do with Alan Kershaw getting ripped off?"

"I don't know."

"You don't know? What does that mean? You picked her name out of a hat?"

"Her father was allegedly scammed too. Someone emptied his bank account. I looked into him. He works at a grocery store. I looked through Kershaw's financials. He's been to that store twice in the last month."

"That's your connection?"

"Isn't that enough?" Darrow went back to searching a decorative box filled with receipts and old bills. "Alan Kershaw and Nathan Boter were scammed in a similar fashion. Their checking accounts were zeroed out. I checked with the bank regarding Boter's issues. The bank manager was under the impression Boter's daughter emptied his account, so I'm searching her place."

"Connect the dots for me," I said. "What's your theory?"

"Eloise Boter used to work at that same grocery store when she was in college during her summer breaks. She crossed paths with Kershaw several times. They could have struck up a conversation. She realized he was loaded, found out he liked to gamble online, and targeted him."

"Eloise Boter graduated college two years ago," I said.

"Right, which means she has student loans and rent and plenty of other expenses. That information on Kershaw may have come in handy."

"She has a good job. She covers her father's rent half the time."

Darrow turned to look at me. "How do you know that?"

"I spoke to Nathan Boter."

"And you didn't tell me?"

"I don't have to tell you. You work for me."

Darrow gave me a dirty look. "You don't play fair."

"I'm not playing at all."

"What else haven't you told me?"

"You first," I said, but Darrow didn't budge. "Let's get back to Nathan Boter. I'm sure you looked into him. He likes to gamble."

"Yeah, just like Kershaw."

I resisted the urge to point out that Kershaw's gambling habits were nothing like Boter's. Instead, I said, "Who do you think emptied Nathan Boter's bank account?"

"His daughter."

"Why would she? She's the one who gave him the money."

"They had a fight."

I wasn't sure if he was making that up or if he had proof

to back it. "About what?"

"Money. Eloise wants to move to a nicer place, but her father said she should save up for a while before making a decision. They fought about that, about how she wastes her money, and she said the biggest waste of money was supporting him. She could have scammed Kershaw and taken back the money she gave her father. This could be about revenge."

That didn't sound like the woman I'd spoken to only minutes earlier. "Why would she want revenge on Kershaw? How do they connect?"

"The grocery store."

"Did anything happen there?"

"I don't know. Possibly, or she discovered Kershaw's also a gambler and figured she'd make him suffer too."

"Do you have proof?"

"Not yet."

"How do you know she fought with her father? Or did you make that story up in your head too?"

"No, smartass. Eloise's neighbor heard them arguing."

"You spoke to her neighbors?"

"That's how you find dirt. Neighbors, friends, colleagues. It's best to talk to everyone, Lucien. I know you're not much of a people person, but that's not doing you any favors."

"What neighbor?"

Darrow pointed to the right. "She walks her dog every morning at seven. I ran into her, and we had a pleasant chat while she took poochie for a stroll."

I had too many questions to ask, most of which weren't relevant, but the sheer amount threatened to make my head explode. "Do you have any other basis for thinking Eloise is behind this? Have you found the funds she allegedly stole?"

"No. That's why I wanted to search her place before I speak to her. If I find something, I can confront her about it."

"What if you don't find anything?" I used a pen to pick my way through the items on her coffee table. There was nothing of interest. I moved into the kitchen, reading the notes on her fridge. She was out of butter and coconut water.

"Then I keep looking." Darrow poked his head into the kitchen. "I already checked in there. If you want to help, search the bedroom."

EIGHTEEN

"I told you Eloise Boter has nothing to do with our client's bank account being emptied."

Ace Darrow rolled his eyes. "Just because we didn't find anything doesn't mean there isn't anything to find."

"No. That's exactly what that means. We looked, physically and electronically. She isn't involved. The bank got it wrong. They are blaming her instead of the actual thief. That's how they cover their asses and avoid an investigation and review by the treasury department."

"How long have you known about Boter?" Darrow asked.

"Not long. He approached me when I was leaving the federal building. He overheard my conversation with Agent Olsen and thought we could help each other out."

"It sounds like he made you his mark."

"He didn't make me his mark." Talking to Darrow reminded me of conversations with my father, the instructors at the academy, and Jablonsky. Was I the only person on this planet capable of rational thought? Lots of people thought I was paranoid, but this was some next level craziness. "Boter's another victim. I'm guessing he and Kershaw were scammed by the same person, but I can't say for certain."

"So you've been looking into this too."

"I had some time."

"You don't trust me," Darrow said.

"Why should I?"

"Then why did you hire me?"

"We are not having this conversation again."

"Fine." Darrow peered at the filing cabinet behind my desk, practically salivating. "Let me update you on the progress I've made."

"By all means."

Darrow had run down every person Alan Kershaw had ever met and sorted them into friends and enemies. The supposed enemies were then classified by threat level. I couldn't help but wonder if Darrow was serious or if this was some drawn-out joke. But by the time he got to the end, I was still waiting for the punchline.

"I'd say Alan Kershaw was scammed by a random third party. That's why Eloise Boter fits as a suspect," Darrow said.

"And if it's not her?"

"I checked Kershaw's internet history and did a deep dive to see what I could uncover about him from old posts and online dating profiles."

"Kershaw has a dating profile?" I asked. "He said he isn't looking to date."

"Missed that, did you?" Darrow pulled a page out of the folder, showing me a printed screenshot.

I scanned the page and entered the information into my computer. However, it didn't lead to Alan Kershaw's dating profile. It led to an error message that such a profile didn't exist.

"He took it down a few months ago," Darrow said, "but nothing posted online is ever truly lost to the ether." He indicated a section he highlighted. "That would answer one of his account security questions. The rest could be determined from more in-depth searches into public records and looking into his college pals' social media pages. A few of his friends are rather nostalgic about their misspent youth and posted lots of things about the places they went and things they did."

"You think whoever scammed Kershaw stalked him first?"

"It's a chicken and egg situation. It'd be impossible to determine which happened first, but the scammer must have accessed his dating profile before choosing to target him."

"Couldn't the scammer have pulled up the information the same way you did?" I asked.

"Not a lot of people know how to do this."

"Someone who sends fake e-mails and hacks into bank accounts should be savvy enough to do that."

"Good point," Darrow admitted.

"That means we're no closer than we were before."

"Well, we do have the Nathan Boter angle to explore, assuming the same party is responsible for both crimes. I still say Eloise is behind this. She had means and motive."

"No, she doesn't."

"Yes, she does. She's mad at her father. She has hardly any savings because she's always covering his ass. That would put a chip on her shoulder when it comes to gamblers, and she knew Alan Kershaw was one too."

"Walk me through that thought process."

Darrow beamed. "Like I said before, Kershaw's been to that grocery store. Eloise worked as a cashier. Maybe her father introduced her to Kershaw since they gambled together."

"Eee, wrong." I imitated a game show buzzer. "Kershaw and Boter don't gamble at the same places."

"That we know of," Darrow insisted.

"They don't. You've done the research. Does anything indicate they know one another?"

"No, but—"

"But nothing."

"Okay, fine. Maybe that's not how Eloise learned Kershaw was a gambler. Maybe he said something to her. Maybe she saw the app on his phone when he put it down on the register. Maybe it came up in conversation."

"Alan Kershaw doesn't know Eloise Boter either."

"He shops at that store."

"Everyone in that neighborhood shops at that store."

"See," Darrow looked smug, "they crossed paths. They knew one another."

"I don't know any of the people who work at my supermarket."

"That's because you're not a people person."

"No, that's because I'm too busy to strike up conversations with everyone on the planet, just like Alan Kershaw."

"Are you sure?"

I was until Darrow asked. This felt like a gotcha moment, but I stuck to my guns. "Kershaw and Nathan Boter aren't friends. They don't travel in the same circles. Their lives are very different. They don't gamble the same way. Eloise had no reason to know Kershaw plays poker online. She couldn't have targeted him like that."

"Are you sure?"

"She's a secondary victim, the innocent bystander who got caught in the crossfire."

After Darrow and I left her apartment, I returned to the office and dug up everything I could on Boter's daughter. She was clean. No priors. No criminal ties. No reason to want to rip off her old man, the grocery delivery driver, and a random shopper at her old man's store. If anything, Nathan Boter would have had a greater motive than his daughter. He needed the money to fund his habit.

"Well, you know the statistics. Crimes of opportunity, where the offender has no ties to the victim, are the least likely to be solved. You told Alan Kershaw that when you spoke to him. The FBI must have said the same thing. Tell him we did our best, collect our fee, and let's move on," Darrow said.

"That's how you operate?"

"This is business. We do what we say and try to deliver. Either way, we still get paid."

"Uh-huh."

"That's your problem right there, Lucien." Darrow pointed at my face. "You get bogged down in these things. That's how you get in trouble. That's how you get blamed. And that's how you almost got yourself killed the last time we worked on a case together."

"We weren't working together."

"Well, now that we are, I suggest you take my advice. Get paid and find a new client. This case is unsolvable."

That word zapped my brain like a bolt of lightning. "Unsolvable? Are you kidding me?"

Darrow made himself comfortable, sinking down in the chair and crossing his right ankle over his left knee. "Do you know something I don't? You already told me the grocery store angle is a bust, even though that connects our victims. But hey, what do I know?"

I pointed a finger at him. "I'm not that easily played."

"Seriously, Lucien, what are you doing? You wanted me to look into this matter, but you've been hamstringing me every step of the way. And now that we have something solid, you don't want to explore it further. It's like the cat got your tongue. Are you afraid I'm going to steal your thunder? I get it. You don't like me. To be honest, I'm not particularly fond of you either. But I'm here now, and I'm doing my damnedest to help. No one, and I mean no one, will ever want to work for you if you pull this shit on them." Darrow glanced at my open office door. "That would explain the lack of investigators in this place. You really should have that ego of yours checked. It's killing your business."

"There's a third connection to the grocery store, but I'm telling you, Eloise Boter isn't the scammer. In fact, I'm pretty sure the grocery store is a misdirect, nothing more than an unfortunate coincidence." Against my better judgment, I told Darrow about Eric Greene. "You've been trying to connect the victims. What we should focus on is figuring out who connects to each of the crime scenes."

"The banks?"

"No, the casinos."

Darrow plucked the printed photo of the woman who'd spoken to Nathan Boter at Chelsea's off my desk. "If it's not Eloise, this has to be our scammer."

"Agreed, but we don't know who she is. Facial rec hasn't come back with anything yet. I showed her photo to Kershaw and Greene, but neither of them recognized her."

Darrow studied the photo more carefully. "She's wearing a wig. Maybe even a fake nose or chin. It's hard to tell from this low-quality image."

"How do you know that's a wig?" I'd been convinced the dye job looked weird, but I never would have guessed wig. Her hair looked real. It just didn't look right on her.

"I know disguises. This is high-end. Let me run with this."

"By all means."

"You know, you could have saved us both a lot of time if you'd shown me this the moment you got it."

"I've been busy."

"Busy not resolving your client's problem."

I grumbled as Darrow left my office. The worst part was he was right. I'd be damned if I let that happen again. I would be more transparent with him from here on out, but I'd have to keep a closer eye on him too. He'd already bugged our client's apartment and broke in to search another victim's place. I didn't want him to rack up any more unnecessary offenses. Sure, taking a creative license to situations often put private eyes on the wrong side of the law, but Darrow took too many liberties. That would get him caught, and I didn't need to have to bail him out or explain his practices to Kershaw or anyone else.

"You're justifying it in your head," Justin said from my doorway.

"Stop doing that," I hissed.

"Then stop thinking dumb things. You know he's right. You made the wrong choice, but we all know why you did. What none of us understands is why you hired him in the first place." Justin held up his hand. "But we're not going around on that again. I came in here to tell you Miller Industries set up that assessment. It's on your calendar. Tuesday at 1 p.m."

"Fine."

"Also, I've taken the liberty of handing out keys to our employees. I gave Darrow his. Amir knows to keep tabs on his movements."

"Thanks."

"One last thing, boss. I got copies of the footage taken at

the mahjong parlor the night it was raided. I had Amir run a side-by-side comparison. The woman who spoke to Nathan Boter at Chelsea's appears to have been playing mahjong the night Eric Greene hit his winning streak. She wasn't at his table. She was playing with the high-rollers, but I'm pretty sure it's her. I e-mailed you a copy of the footage."

I brought it up and watched, confused how Justin had gotten access to the arresting officer's body cam footage. The woman at the table had jet black hair halfway down her back. She'd lost the glasses, and her features looked a lot more delicate, her nose and chin less pronounced, and the wrinkles had vanished. If anything, she looked a decade younger.

"There's no way that's the same woman," I said.

"Amir said there's a good chance it is. You heard what Darrow said. He knows disguises. Maybe you should ask him."

"You were eavesdropping again?"

"It's not my fault the intercom's always on."

"You're the one who turns it on. In fact, why aren't you using it to tell me this?"

"I prefer having these conversations face to face. That way, I can watch the vein at your temple jump."

"Is there any chance she was playing poker with Alan Kershaw online?"

"I'll have Amir pull up the list of players who were in the same online game as Kershaw for the last..."

"Let's go back six months. Kershaw doesn't play a lot. Hopefully, that won't give us too many possibilities."

"You got it, boss." Justin paused in the doorway. "Do you want me to forward that list to Darrow?"

"You might as well. We're in this together now."

NINETEEN

Ace Darrow had reached out to his contacts in the costume design and makeup industries to see what he could dig up. No sales had been made to any Claudia Bellmans, but that wasn't her real name. Unfortunately, we didn't have it. Darrow thought we'd identify her from the wig, but no one recognized the frosted one from Chelsea's or the jet black one she wore at the mahjong parlor.

"I'll keep looking," Darrow said, "but I doubt she got this locally."

"Explain to me how you have local connections when you came from D.C."

"I've done plenty of work here. I couldn't always pack for the occasion since I wasn't sure what my research and surveillance endeavors would require, so I made friends with people who could help me out. The theater district offers plenty of resources, if you know where to look."

"I guess you don't know where to look."

"I know where to look. She doesn't." Darrow studied the images again. "I'm telling you, Lucien, these are high-end pieces. Whoever made them knew what they were doing. Maybe our scammer isn't local. She could be from Hollywood."

"People who live in Hollywood don't call it Hollywood."

"How would you know?"

"I know," I said. "Plus, Eloise is local. By your logic, it can't be her."

"It's her," he insisted.

"No, it isn't." I didn't have time to waste on this argument again. "Whatever. Let me know if you find anything else."

Despite my insistence, Darrow remained adamant that the grocery store was the key to identifying the person responsible for ripping off our client. Since that was the only thing that connected the three victims, he assumed the scammer would choose her next target from that same grocery store.

Since nothing I said mattered, Darrow was analyzing the grocery store's records. It, like most markets, had a loyalty program. Darrow had gained access to the list of customers, employees, and vendors and was combing through it for something that would lead us to the scammer.

However, I had better things to do with my time. Anything would be more productive than that. So I told him I'd look into the gambling establishments. The only downside was I needed help from the police department.

Detective Taylor tucked the stem of her sunglasses into her collar, scanning the coffee shop until she spotted me at a two-seater near the bathrooms. An untouched cup sat in front of the empty chair. She popped the lid off and gave it a sniff before taking a sip.

"You bought me coffee," she said.

"It was the least I could do. Justin said you sent over the body cam footage. I wasn't expecting that. I'm pretty sure that violates—"

"What you mean to say is thank you."

"Right. Thank you. Anyway, I noticed something on the footage."

"Oh yeah?"

I held out my phone with the video frozen and zoomed in on the woman at the other table. "She made contact with Nathan Boter. She introduced herself to him as Claudia

Bellman, but she's no Claudia Bellman."

"Boter's the other victim?"

"Yeah."

Taylor narrowed her eyes at the screen before taking a photo of the photo. The way she did things reminded me a little of Darrow, but I didn't want to think too hard about that or I'd start to think I was crazy and the rest of the world was sane. Surely, that wasn't the case, not under these circumstances.

"She was wearing a disguise when she was at Chelsea's. This may also be a disguise," I said.

"Disguise?" Taylor leaned back and sipped her drink. "You mean the hair and makeup?"

"Yeah."

"Since you're sure she isn't Claudia Bellman, who do you think she is?"

"I dunno. That's why I asked you out for coffee."

"I thought it was because you liked me."

I was almost certain she was messing with me, but she delivered the line so seriously, I couldn't help but wonder if that was her way of baiting me into flirting with her. "Eric Greene was arrested during the raid. I'm guessing everyone at the mahjong parlor was brought in."

"That is the nature of a raid," Taylor said.

"That means you know who she is. I was hoping you wouldn't mind telling me."

Taylor studied the photo before sending a text, presumably to someone in the department, maybe her partner or a tech. "I take it you believe this woman is responsible for ripping off Eric Greene, Nathan Boter, and Alan Kershaw."

"She was in the vicinity of two of the victims prior to their bank accounts being emptied. That's worth exploring."

"But she wasn't playing at the same table as Eric Greene, so how did she learn enough about him to rip him off?"

"You tell me. You brought everyone in. You must have put them in holding cells."

"Men and women are detained separately."

"They could have been next to each other during booking. Hell, they could have shared a squad car."

Taylor's phone beeped. "Jasmine O'Neal."

"That's it?" I'd never gotten information out of a cop that easily. Even Sara made me work for it.

"What do you want? I can put her name in an envelope and open it dramatically before reading it to you, but that seems like a waste. You wanted the name. I gave you her name."

"Okay, great." I stood to leave.

She grabbed my wrist. "Not so fast, Lucien." She held firm. Her eyes told me to sit back down. "I told you how this was going to work. I give you something. You give me something."

"I don't have anything to give."

"Finish the conversation. You believe Jasmine O'Neal is responsible. What evidence do you have?"

"None yet. It's a hunch."

"A hunch, huh?"

"Based on what Boter told me. He said this woman scammed him. I'd say that's worth exploring."

Taylor let go of my wrist. "Except it wasn't this woman, was it?" She tapped on her phone before holding it out to me. On it was surveillance footage from Chelsea's. "This lady doesn't look anything like Jasmine O'Neal."

"I already explained she's in disguise."

"And you're certain of that?"

"Amir wasn't a hundred percent, but he's never a hundred percent on anything. Scientists, go figure."

"Amir?"

"Amir Karam. Look him up if you want. His credentials speak for themselves."

"I know who your resident tech expert is."

"Then why did you say his name like you had no idea who I was talking about?"

Taylor glared at me.

I liked that look even less than the possibility she'd been keeping tabs on my operation or that she thought lying about keeping tabs on my employees was a sound play. "What's the problem? His word should be golden."

"I need evidence. A conversation is circumstantial. The woman who approached Boter at Chelsea's didn't scam him that night and gave him a fake name. That's not proof. That's circumstantial. Sure, he allegedly gave her his information, but we don't know it's the same woman. We don't even know if that's what happened. We can't even be certain Claudia Bellman is Jasmine O'Neal. You said Amir wasn't a hundred percent."

"He was sure enough," I argued. "Bring Boter in and ask him if that's who he spoke to. It'd be a good idea if you brought O'Neal in too. Boter may recognize her voice from the phone call. That should be enough to get you a warrant."

"Fine." Taylor didn't look convinced. "But when this doesn't pan, you better have something else for me."

"I don't work for you. Don't expect me to do your job for you."

"Then don't expect me to do yours for you." She left after that.

"Honey not vinegar," I mumbled, but it was too late. The damage had been done.

Once I returned to work, I stopped by Darrow's office. "The police arrested Jasmine O'Neal during the raid. We believe she's the same woman who approached Nathan Boter at Chelsea's using the alias Claudia Bellman," I said.

"Wow, someone's in a sharing mood." Darrow entered her name into the computer. "I'll see what I can pull up and cross-reference this to the list I have from the wig shops and costume places. If she made any purchases or inquiries, someone may remember."

"Great."

Darrow glanced at me. "Want to try that again without the sarcasm?"

"Not particularly." I jerked my chin toward his computer. "Have you found anything on the grocery store?"

"I'm still digging. You're welcome to help. I have tons of potentials to analyze."

"Start with O'Neal. See if she was a customer or employee. That might save you some time."

"Lucien, you have a lot to learn."

Shaking my head, I left his office and headed upstairs.

"How'd your coffee date go?" Justin asked.

"I'm pretty sure it wasn't a date."

Justin cocked his head to the side. "Did the detective put the moves on you?"

"I don't even know."

"Has it really been that long, boss?"

"She gave me a name. Jasmine O'Neal. That's who they arrested during the raid. I sent the details to Amir. He says it's possible O'Neal was in disguise when she approached Nathan Boter. We need to find everything we can on her. More importantly, I'm wondering what the police charged her with or if they have anything on her."

"Did you ask Detective Taylor those questions?"

"I didn't get the chance."

Justin gave me a look. "You need to think before you say or do anything stupid."

"I can get access to the records on my own. I have my ways."

"Stubborn," Justin muttered as I went past his desk and into my office.

Thankfully, the backdoor I'd created into the police department's database allowed me access to the files I needed.

Jasmine O'Neal, thirty-two, no known priors. I copied her phone number and address. The police had released her with a warning, which was the same thing they'd done to Eric Greene. They had little interest in building cases against the gamblers, especially ones without records and no known criminal ties.

On the surface, O'Neal looked clean. I opened the file Amir had sent of the poker players Alan Kershaw interacted with online. Jasmine O'Neal was one of them.

"I knew it."

"Knew what?" Justin asked.

"O'Neal has to be responsible. At the very least, she's involved or knows who is."

"Do you want me to let Kershaw know? Or do you want to handle that yourself?"

I rocked back in my chair, staring at the name on my screen. Telling him now would be premature, but if he recognized her name or had some sort of connection to her, it'd be best to find out. "I'll do it." Usually, I'd wait until I had solid, irrefutable proof, but his case didn't require anything of the sort. I couldn't get his money back. All I could do was share leads and let him use that information however he wished.

Reaching for the phone, I dialed Kershaw while I brought up everything I could find on Jasmine O'Neal. The woman wasn't who I expected. She had a good job at a marketing firm, lived in a nice apartment, and had no known criminal ties.

"I may have identified the party who scammed you," I said. "Have you ever heard of Jasmine O'Neal?"

"The name doesn't ring a bell," Kershaw said.

"She plays poker at the same online casino. Her handle is JazzGirl." Even as I read that to him, I entered it to see if she used that name on any other accounts.

"I don't recognize the name, but I don't pay a lot of attention unless I see the same player over and over again."

"You don't think she played against you more than once?" I asked.

"It's possible, but it must not have been that often, not that I play often."

Amir could pull the exact time and date they were at the same virtual table. He could also see if they shared any communications or interactions online.

"Do you know what possessed her to steal from me?" Kershaw asked. "I don't believe I've ever met or spoken to this woman. Why would she do this?"

"She may have been looking for a payday." But that didn't fit with the facts I had. When this was a nameless, faceless scammer, that theory made sense. When the scammer was an innocent who had been forced to act by a powerful criminal element, that still made sense. But Jasmine O'Neal wasn't locked away in a dark dungeon with armed men forcing her to work behind a computer. So what motivated her to pick her targets?

"Well, she got one." The bitterness reminded me how

annoyed Kershaw was with the situation. "Do you think the FBI has discovered this yet?"

"Probably not. The local police may be looking into it. It's hard to say for certain."

"Did you tip them off?"

"That's also hard to say." I wasn't sure what Taylor planned to do with the intel. She insisted this was a quid pro quo, but I hadn't handed her evidence on a silver platter. Maybe she'd follow up. Maybe she wouldn't. I could usually read people better, but she was an odd one.

"I'll inform Agent Olsen and see what he has to say. Thanks for doing this. Tell Darrow the same."

"Sure," I said, wondering how Darrow planned on retrieving the bugs he planted.

TWENTY

"Mr. Cross," Agent Olsen was waiting in the lobby when I arrived at work the next day, "we need to talk."

"Did you lose your phone?"

Olsen wasn't amused. "I heard you like to get an early start. Since your office was on my way, I thought it might be easier to have this conversation in person."

"Who told you I like to get an early start?"

"I hear things."

Jablonsky. Maybe Darrow. I wasn't sure. "Why don't you get to the point before you waste more daylight?"

"Alan Kershaw called me last night."

"So you didn't lose your phone."

"Mr. Cross, these are serious matters." Olsen rubbed a hand down his face and stared out the front door of my building. "Kershaw told me you identified the woman who stole his money."

"I told him I wasn't sure, but there's a strong possibility I found her."

"Who is she?"

"A local with ties to two other victims. It looks like you got it wrong. This isn't some overseas syndicate ripping off

Americans to fund terrorist plots."

"Do you have a name?"

"Kershaw didn't tell you?"

"I'd like you to tell me."

I wasn't sure what game the FBI agent was playing. Why would he think Kershaw would lie to him, unless he thought I was lying to Kershaw. "Jasmine O'Neal, but she also calls herself Claudia Bellman. I'm not sure what other aliases she might be using, but those are the two I happened across."

"How do you know it's her?" Olsen asked. "Did you trace the funds to her bank account?"

"I'm a private investigator. How would I have the resources to do that?"

Olsen squinted at me. "Amir Karam used to teach at Quantico. He works for you now."

"Mr. Karam isn't a hacker."

"No, but he has several specialties. Forensics being one. Cybercrimes being another."

"He never mentioned that to me." This was why I didn't want to deal with the FBI. Too many questions always led to trouble. "Are you planning on making a point soon or should I have my breakfast delivered to the lobby?"

"Did you trace the stolen funds back to Jasmine O'Neal?"

"No."

"Yet, you told Alan Kershaw she was responsible."

"She was in the right place at the right time. She lied to Nathan Boter and concealed her identity with a disguise. Upstanding citizens don't do that. Criminals do." That would explain Darrow's wardrobe.

"That's a simplistic view of things. I didn't expect a guy like you to only see in black and white."

I didn't. I just wanted the Feds off my back. "I'll admit it was premature to provide Kershaw with the name. However, it is your job to investigate. After all, you told me to stay away from this. By telling my client, I knew you'd hear about it. It's your turn to look into this. Find out what's what, and file charges. Or don't. That's up to you. You're the FBI agent. I'm a nobody with a nicer suit."

"I want your files."

"Files?"

"Whatever evidence you've collected that led to this conclusion."

"Talk to the PD. They arrested Jasmine O'Neal for playing mahjong. While you're at it, get surveillance footage from Chelsea's Bar and Grill from the night Nathan Boter told you he was scammed. If you look closely, you may recognize a familiar face buried beneath prosthetics and a wig."

"That's not how cases are built."

"I wouldn't know. I'm not part of the law enforcement community. I work private security. Protecting clients and their assets is what we do here. But I'd think following up on a tip would be in your purview. Maybe I'm wrong. My bad."

Olsen put his sunglasses back on. He could have doubled as an extra in *Men in Black*. "In that case, stay away from this investigation. I won't tell you again."

Again, the familiar itch nagged at me. "Sure. No problem."

*   *   *

Even though I had shared my suspicions about the scammer's identity with my client days ago, questions remained that I couldn't quite shake. It must have been a slow week. There was no other explanation for why I was still looking into this when the FBI told me to back off. There was nothing I could do to fix things for Kershaw. I'd gotten him a name. That was it. That was all he wanted. As far as he was concerned, our business was concluded. Yet, I couldn't help myself.

I didn't want to admit it, but something wasn't sitting right. I should have dug deeper before I shared the name with Kershaw. That would have held Olsen at bay and given me more time to compile evidence to give to Taylor. But I screwed up, again. By now, I should have been used to it.

Detective Taylor had brought Nathan Boter in, went

over his statement, the surveillance footage, and showed him what she had from the raid. Boter didn't believe O'Neal was the same woman who he'd spoken to at Chelsea's. Without his corroboration, Taylor couldn't get approval to bring O'Neal in for another round of questioning, not without evidence, which meant the ball was in my court again.

Darrow was still digging through whatever records and intel he thought would prove useful. I was pretty sure the grocery store was a waste of time. I'd already connected the scammer to our three victims. We no longer needed to find out how they were connected. We needed to find out how O'Neal connected to them. Had she targeted them specifically, or had they been easy marks? I needed to find out more about this woman.

Jasmine O'Neal worked at Good Day Marketers. It was a marketing firm that specialized in online advertising and so-called organic reach campaigns. The premise of those campaigns was to create social media accounts dedicated to a product category, run advertising campaigns to gain followers and boost traffic, and provide enough content to keep people coming back for more. Those accounts would then be used to market products and services to the existing audience base without the use of overt advertising and sponsored ads. Instead, the promoted products and services would seem like recommendations from a trusted source, making the audience more likely to engage and buy.

I wasn't sure what role O'Neal played at Good Day Marketers. Her title was marketing manager. That could mean pretty much anything, from taking a hands-off approach to working behind the scenes, optimizing SEO, and tickling the algorithms to gain more exposure at a lower cost. Her degree was in programming with a minor in graphic design. She'd have the knowhow to make the e-mail Kershaw received, and she'd been physically present prior to Boter and Greene being scammed at those two underground casinos. But I didn't know her motivation. Maybe that's why I couldn't let this go.

Good Day Marketers was a small operation. They hadn't

worked for any major brands. The campaigns they ran were mostly for independently owned companies, everything from niche beauty products to self-promoting artists. The company hadn't been flagged by any watchdog agencies. An online search didn't reveal any negative reports regarding Good Day Marketers' services. They delivered what they promised.

Expanding my search, I tried to figure out if any of the people who followed these social media accounts had been scammed. Perhaps that was how the marketing firm really made its money. But I didn't have much luck navigating through the mess. There were too many campaigns, too many linked accounts, and too many possibilities.

When my phone rang, I picked it up. "Cross Security," I said.

"That's my line," Justin mumbled from outside my door.

It was Amir. "I sent you a list of Jasmine O'Neal's online gambling activity. The highlighted portions are the dates and times that coincide with Alan Kershaw's presence at the same virtual poker tables."

"How much overlap is there?" I asked, clicking on the waiting file.

"Not a lot. O'Neal spent a great deal of time online gambling, but she and Kershaw barely crossed paths. They never spoke or messaged. I don't know why she'd pick him, assuming she's responsible."

"You don't think she is?"

"I don't know, Lucien. She's the common denominator, but it could be circumstantial."

The extensive list of dates and times made me wonder when this woman slept or ate. "It looks like online gambling could be her full-time job." She'd only played against Kershaw on three separate occasions, one of which corresponded with him winning. The other two times, he'd busted and left the table early. "She logged a lot of hours."

"That's not the only place she gambles," Amir said. "She doesn't use that handle anywhere else, but I traced her IP. She frequents several other online casinos too."

"How many hours a week are we talking?"

"Dozens. She plays a couple hours a day, every day."

"All right, thanks."

I put the phone down and stared at the screen. Between the online casinos, Chelsea's, and the mahjong parlor, the woman wouldn't have time to do much else. If anyone had a gambling addiction, it should be her, but given what I knew about Good Day Marketers, I wondered if this was research for their next big advertising campaign.

Pressing the button on the intercom, I said, "Hey, Justin, can you get me a meeting with Good Day Marketers? I want to see if they can help with our advertising dilemma. See if you can get me a meeting with Jasmine O'Neal specifically."

Justin rolled his chair in front of my open door. "Sure thing, boss."

"You could have used the intercom," I said. "It's always on."

"Then I couldn't see your face when I tell you Darrow wants to speak to you."

"Why?"

"I don't know. Was I supposed to ask?"

"I wouldn't want you to put yourself out."

He grinned. "That's what I figured."

I gave the information Amir had sent one last look before getting up from behind my desk. Since I'd been sitting all day, I took the stairs, needing to move before my back locked up or my legs went permanently numb.

Darrow was waiting at the elevator when I came through the stairwell door. He didn't see me, so I snuck up behind him and cleared my throat. He jumped, which gave me the tiniest bit of joy. I'd have to talk to someone about that sadistic streak before it became an issue.

"You wanted to see me," I said.

"Lucien," he looked around the reception area, confused how I'd materialized without him noticing, "I wanted to talk to you about something."

"I'm aware of that. What's up?"

Darrow glanced at Janet, who busied herself with changing out the toner cartridges in the copier. "I'm still looking into Kershaw's case."

"I know."

"Why?"

"What do you mean why?" Had Olsen spoken to him too?

"We identified the scammer. You informed Kershaw of our progress. He sent payment for our services. Aren't we done?"

"Oh," I stepped to the side and gestured to the elevator, "I get it. You're free to go. I appreciate your assistance. Don't call us. We'll call you."

"Lucien, come on," Darrow made an exaggerated eye roll, "you know that's not what I'm saying. What I want to know is why we're still digging."

"Have you found anything?"

Darrow glanced at Janet again, as if she were an enemy spy. I wasn't sure why he distrusted the receptionist. Sure, she'd been keeping an eye on him, but that was because he couldn't be trusted. "I'm only halfway through my research into the grocery store. But I found something interesting."

"What is it?"

Darrow led me to his office and leaned over the computer while he enlarged the document he'd been reading. "There. Do you see that?" He slid the cursor back and forth over one line in an employee's job application. "This person interned at Good Day Marketers. I told you someone at that grocery store was responsible for targeting the victims."

I read the name on the application. Charlie Steed. "Does he have a record?"

"No."

Darrow clicked another document. "He's the same age as Eloise Boter."

I wasn't going to waste my breath reminding Darrow she wasn't involved. "Is that significant?"

"They could have dated."

"Let's stick with the facts. Steed interned at Good Day Marketers. Do we know any details about that?"

"Yeah," Darrow looked smug, "Steed reported directly to Jasmine O'Neal."

TWENTY-ONE

I wasn't sure which was worse. Darrow may have been right or I could be wrong. Like everyone else involved in this case, Charlie Steed didn't have a criminal record or known criminal ties. He had been a business major who interned with Good Day Marketers during his senior year. There was nothing remarkable or questionable about that. A lot of college students pursued internships.

However, upon graduating, Steed didn't get hired by that marketing firm or any marketing firm. And unlike the majority of his classmates who went on to pursue advanced degrees, mostly MBAs or JDs, Steed took a step back and applied to every job he could find.

Nathan Boter hired him as assistant manager. Steed had access to everything he'd need to pinpoint potential targets, or so Darrow insisted. However, I couldn't quite wrap my mind around that. Knowing the details of a delivery was different from knowing intimate details about the driver. The same was true of customers who participated in the loyalty program. How would Steed know Kershaw gambled online occasionally or Greene played mahjong on his days off?

For shits and giggles, I stopped by the grocery store to

pick up an application for a loyalty card. Unlike its larger competitors, the store didn't have any way of signing up online. It had to be done in person.

The clerk working the customer service desk handed me a clipboard. I scanned the questions. Name. Address. Phone Number. Those were basic. Some questions near the bottom got far more personal. The asterisk told me they were optional and for statistical purposes only, but I didn't know why a grocery store needed to know my household income.

A few other questions gave me pause. Answering these questions would make it easier to gain access to bank records or steal my identity. Had Kershaw filled out the form? Maybe Darrow wasn't as far off the mark as I thought.

I handed the clipboard back without writing anything down. "The pen doesn't work," I said.

The clerk searched for another one.

"That's okay. I'm in a rush. I'll fill one out next time." On my way back to the car, I called Darrow. "Is Eric Greene a loyalty club member?"

"Hang on." Darrow dropped something and cursed. A moment later, he returned. "How did you know that?"

"Lucky guess."

"I'm telling you—"

"I know." But that didn't mean he was right. "I'm heading to a meeting at Good Day Marketers. I'll update you on everything when I get back to the office."

"I'll be waiting. I would say with bells, but you don't like bells." The glee in Darrow's voice made my stomach turn. He was getting a perverse pleasure out of this. That was another thing I didn't like.

During the drive, I tried to prepare myself by rehearsing the questions I wanted to ask. However, when I arrived, I was thrown off my game. The place was poorly lit and tiny, not at all what I expected from an advertising agency.

The guy working the front desk didn't look up as I approached. He wore a hooded sweatshirt with the hood up and the sleeves ripped off. A mop of purple hair poked out from beneath the brown hood. Even after clearing my throat, he still didn't acknowledge my presence. I was on time. He should have been expecting me.

I knocked on the desk in front of him. "Hey," I said.

He jerked backward as if I'd struck him. With his head up, I could see the earbuds in his ears. He took them out, leaving his hood on as he peered at me. "You scared me."

"I'm Lucien Cross," I said. "I have an appointment."

"That doesn't mean you can scare me."

"I'm sorry."

"Good." He held up his finger before swiveling in his chair. "Rita, tell Vinnie Lucien's here."

I couldn't see Rita or Vinnie, but the guy in front of me gave someone down the hallway a thumbs up before turning back to face me. I wondered if this was Justin's role model.

"Nice operation you have here," I said.

"It's a sweet gig." He pointed to the Keurig machine on a side table. "Help yourself."

"I'm good, thanks." I rested my forearms on the counter and leaned forward, wishing I'd remained in my sweats from the gym so I'd fit in better. "Do you happen to know Charlie? He used to work here."

"Charlie?"

"Steed," I said. "He was an intern."

"Um...no. Sorry."

"Lucien," a man called from the rear hallway, "we're ready for you."

The guy I'd been speaking to gestured behind him. "Right back there."

I observed the cracked plaster and uneven flooring as I went down the hallway, passing two small offices which looked basic, except for the oversized bean bag chairs. Neither was labeled. The man who'd called my name stood beside an open doorway.

He held out his hand. "I'm Vincent Lyman. I hear you're in the market for some marketing." He looked proud of himself, as if that had been extremely clever. "Why don't you tell me about your company and I'll show you our packages?"

With any luck, he was speaking about their advertising

options, but given the vibes I was getting from this place, I remained leery. "I thought I was meeting with Jasmine O'Neal."

"Jazz has a full plate. I assure you, I'm perfectly capable of meeting your needs. Why don't you tell me what you're hoping to accomplish?"

Walking out now wouldn't help matters. "I recently started my own business."

"Congrats, man." He clapped me on the shoulder as I entered the room.

I took a seat in a metal folding chair that had been set up in front of a table that looked exactly like the kind they had at the academy, which could seat four students, their notebooks, laptops, and textbooks. "We've been in operation for a little while. At first, it was crickets. Then business started to pick up, but now, crickets again."

"It's the economy." Vincent sat in a chair which had been duct-taped together. "What business are you in?"

"Security."

He scrutinized me more closely. "Are you a bouncer or bodyguard?"

"Something like that."

"Do you work clubs?"

"More like private events."

"Weddings and such?"

"Sure," I said.

Vincent smiled. "I can work with that." He rolled his chair to my side of the table and put the laptop between us. "What we do here is make magic happen. We operate tons of pages which provide helpful resources to interested parties. Our initial investment is what helped us build our audience. Now we've gotten so big, we get lots of search engine traffic without lifting a finger. All our profiles and pages have the right people going to them. Let me show you an example we used for a local line of baby food."

He opened several profiles and pages which appeared to be run by mommy bloggers and recipe creators. Every post was related to the topic of childcare. Dispersed within were mentions of this new baby food line and recommendations to try it.

"As you know, word of mouth is the best form of advertising. Having a trusted friend suggest something because they love it makes you more likely to consider that the next time you're shopping. Good Day Marketers can do the same for you."

"Who runs all these pages?" I asked. "Do you have consultants or actual mothers on staff?"

"God no. A lot of it is automated. We have a few content creators who feed everything in, and it gets posted at regular intervals."

I didn't ask where the content came from. "How big is your team?"

"You met Jeff. Rita's our office assistant. She's around here somewhere. Then there are the marketing managers. That's me and a few other people."

"Jasmine O'Neal?"

Vincent cocked his head to the side. "Yes. Do you know her?"

"My assistant made this appointment. He mentioned the name, but we've never met."

"She's on vacation this week."

"I thought she was busy."

"Yes, busy on vacation. She's working to set up some travel pages for a client." That was a convenient excuse for her absence. "We share responsibilities. I'm sure she'll work on your campaign at some point. We'll all work on it. We believe in collaborating and sharing here at Good Day Marketers."

"What about interns? A friend of a friend was supposed to have worked here at one point maybe a year or so ago. Charlie Steed?"

"Ah, yes. He's a bright guy, helped us out of more jams than you'd imagine."

"He doesn't work here now?" I asked.

"He moved on to bigger and better things, but we wish him the best."

Pushing too hard would send up red flags. Asking about O'Neal made Vincent uneasy, but I wondered if this could be a domestic click farm of sorts. From the looks of things, I wouldn't be surprised to learn they were running their own online scams from inside the building, using their pages and audiences to target and retarget individuals. Everything they were doing involved manipulation, but that was the point of marketing and advertising—to influence consumer behavior.

"I'm curious what kind of computing power an operation like this uses. You must have server rooms and an entire tech department," I said.

"Nope. It's just us and our laptops." Vincent spun the device around so I could see the logo on the lid. "They're nice laptops, but you could easily order one from the manufacturer. The computers aren't what make our advertising campaigns special. Our approach does." He picked up the computer and centered it in front of him. "Let's get into specifics. How wide-reaching a campaign were you thinking?"

"Local."

"Okay." He tapped on the trackpad. "What types of events do you cover? You said weddings, right?"

"Sure."

Vincent gave me a confused look. "What else?"

"Private parties. Anything that involves a guest list."

"That could be anything from bar mitzvahs to corporate retreats."

I smiled. "Now you're getting it. I want to expand my business. The sky's the limit."

Vincent returned my smile, feeling more at ease now that I was playing along. "I like your style, Lucien. You've got gumption. I'm sure we can help make your dreams come true."

"Before we get too far into this, what will this run me?"

"That depends on if we can reuse existing pages or if we have to start from scratch. Since you're a unique business with a unique offering, we may have to experiment. We can start with casting a small net, suggesting you to our wedding and party planning audience and take it from there. Start-up cost will be ten thousand for the first three months."

I whistled. "Before we get too far into this, I'm going to have to think about it."

"Sure. If you have any questions, check out the FAQ on our website."

I peered out the door. "How many marketing managers did you say worked here?"

"There are four of us. We'd all be involved at some point."

"Would I meet with everyone?"

"We don't normally do that. We have our own in-house meetings where we exchange insights, but I guess we could make an exception if you had something important you wanted to discuss with the team. We can always set up a video chat to save you the trouble of coming back here. Most clients don't show up at our door. As you can see, we don't look like the big ad agencies."

"I was picturing a modern-day *Mad Men*."

"That's why we handle most things online. I know our offices can be a little off-putting."

Vincent was smooth. Whether that was the salesman in him or he'd been practicing the lie for a while, I wasn't sure, but I chose to go along with it.

The world was a different place. Employees worked remotely. The tech industry was famous for its casual attire and trendy workspaces, thanks to intrepid individuals who'd taken Silicon Valley by storm. But this didn't feel like a fad. This felt like the kind of place where opening the wrong door would lead to a dungeon filled with human remains.

"Given the nature of my business, I'm usually forced to conduct meetings in person. Sometimes, I forget the rest of the world doesn't function like that," I said.

"I can appreciate that." Vincent assessed me again. "When would you want us to start, assuming you decide this is worth your time?"

Before I could respond, my phone buzzed. "Excuse me for a sec."

"Hey, boss, I thought you should know Alan Kershaw was attacked last night," Justin said.

"Where is he?"

"Mercy General."

"I'll call you back in a minute." I put the phone in my

pocket. "I'm sorry to cut this short, but I have a personal emergency."

"Sure, no problem. Get in touch and let me know if you'd like to proceed or if you have any other questions I can answer." Vincent stood and offered me his hand. "It was nice meeting you."

"Even face to face?" I asked.

"Surprisingly, yes."

TWENTY-TWO

I hated hospitals. I'd gotten used to them, but that didn't mean I enjoyed spending time inside of them. However, Alan Kershaw was a client, technically a former client, but since I was still looking into the matter, I had an obligation to see if the assault connected to the case.

A police officer was seated near the doorway to his room. I kept my distance, not wanting to answer any more questions. My last two run-ins with law enforcement hadn't ended well.

"Lucien," Almeada stepped out of Kershaw's room and joined me at the end of the hallway, "I wasn't expecting you to show up so quickly. It's the middle of the workday. Is business really that bad?"

"Don't worry. You'll still get your retainer checks." I jerked my chin toward Kershaw's room. "How is he?"

"Pretty banged up. Broken arm, two broken ribs, and a concussion."

"Did he see who did it?"

Almeada shook his head. "Someone jumped him when he was heading back to his car."

"Where was he?"

"At work. He'd just left the office."

"Where was he parked?"

"On the street."

"Did anyone see it happen?"

"It was late. Not a lot of people hang around the business district at that time of night."

"What was he doing at the office that late?" I asked.

"Why don't you ask him these questions?"

"The nurse told me he wasn't in any condition for visitors. Since you're his lawyer, I figured you were the exception to the rule. And given the uniform stationed near his door, I can only assume the police had questions, which would explain why you're here."

Almeada patted me on the shoulder. "Business will pick up. You make a good detective when you aren't being self-destructive or moronic."

"Most detectives are self-destructive. Have you seen the old movies?"

"Those are movies, Lucien, not real life."

"Maybe I should pick up smoking and develop a drinking problem."

"Stop being ridiculous."

That was easier than dealing with the current situation, especially since the pit in my stomach told me I was the reason Kershaw was in the hospital, either directly or indirectly. "Did Kershaw recognize the person who attacked him?"

"I told you he didn't get a good look. The attacker came up from behind him."

"What about a description?"

"I thought you didn't want to bump up against the police on any more investigations."

I waited.

"Whoever hit him was bigger than he was. Taller, stronger, just overall bigger," Almeada said.

"How much bigger? Incredible Hulk or Bruce Banner?"

"Banner isn't that big."

"No, but he could knock the shit out of Kershaw."

Almeada considered the two options. "I'd say somewhere in the middle."

"Anything else? Hair color? Eye color? Skin color?"

The headshake said it all. "He came at Kershaw with a baseball bat. It was a Louisville Slugger if that helps."

"Anything else?"

"He smashed the windows on Kershaw's car."

That may have been telling. "The attacker has anger issues but refrained from bashing in Kershaw's skull or turning him into a bloody pulp."

"He's pretty bloody," Almeada said. "I have photos which I took in case we need them for trial." He handed me his phone. Kershaw would be feeling this for a while.

"The police should take their own photos for evidence." I gave him back his phone.

"These aren't for criminal proceedings. They're for a civil trial. Kershaw can sue for damages."

"We have to catch the person first."

"We?" Almeada's lips curled in the corner.

"The police," I clarified, but we both knew I hadn't been able to give this up, even before it got to this point. The assault wouldn't scare me off. It'd only make me slightly more cautious but a lot more interested. "Despite how bloody Kershaw may be, that bat could have opened his head like a melon. It didn't, which means the attacker held back."

"He had the foresight not to turn into a killer," Almeada said. "That's smart. Homicide charges are a lot harder to beat."

"It depends on how you want to look at it. Either the attack was a warning, or the car windows were smashed because the guy needed an outlet for his rage." I considered the possibilities, but I couldn't figure out what Alan Kershaw would have done that angered someone that much.

"Do you think his attacker is the same person who emptied his bank account?" Almeada asked.

"I was under the impression Jasmine O'Neal emptied his account. She's smaller than Kershaw. The bat would even the playing field, but she wouldn't match the description, no matter how big her wig is."

"Maybe you got it wrong."

I sighed. "I hate it when that happens."

"I'd think you'd be used to it by now."

"Hey."

Almeada shrugged. "I'm just calling it like I see it."

"Well, don't." I ran a hand through my hair. "What do the police think? Do they have a theory?"

"Not yet. The investigation is just getting underway, but Officer Smoltz is under the impression this was a failed mugging."

I didn't believe that. "Was anything stolen?"

"Everything. Kershaw's wallet, his phone, watch, whatever else he had of value."

"They left the car."

"Well, yeah. The windows were broken."

I called Amir. "Ping Kershaw's number. We need to get a location for his phone."

Amir worked some magic, but the phone was turned off.

"Don't you think the police did that?" Almeada said when I relayed the news to him.

"Not yet. Investigations take a lot longer when the cops wait for approval and follow the rules. I should get going. Are you hanging around here?"

"I'll be heading out soon. The only reason I came was because Kershaw requested an attorney. Since I had an opening, they sent me."

"You're a named partner. No one sends you to do shit."

"Tell that to the managing partner." Almeada gave me a look. "Do you need me to stay here?"

"It'd be nice to have some idea what's going on." I glanced at the cop again. "Get me what you can on the police investigation."

"What are you going to do with that information?"

"Hell if I know." But I had the beginnings of a plan. Today had shaken a few things loose, hopefully more than Kershaw's teeth.

There were two more stops I had planned to make before returning to the office. One was to see Charlie Steed. The other was to perform recon on Jasmine O'Neal. But those things could wait. Darrow had Kershaw under surveillance. With any luck, he'd gotten footage of the attack. If not, the bugs in Kershaw's apartment may have been telling in terms of who would be angry enough to bash in his car windows.

I called Justin on my way back to the office to update him on the situation.

"How's Kershaw?" Justin asked. "Did you see him?"

"The nurse wouldn't let him have any visitors."

"That's not good."

"Almeada took a few photos. They don't look good either. But Kershaw should make a full recovery. I'll have to go back later to check on him."

"Do you know if he's blaming us for this?"

"I don't know why he would. Did you go after him with a Louisville Slugger last night?"

"No, boss, I prefer aluminum bats." Justin chuckled, a nervous reaction to the situation. "If he's not blaming us, why are you blaming yourself?"

"I'm not."

"The quiet suggests otherwise. You only get introspective when you're bogged down in an investigation or throwing a pity party. I can get some streamers for the occasion. Maybe some noisemakers. Pointy hats. Confetti poppers."

"If you want to get me something, find out precisely where the attack happened and let's start collecting surveillance footage. I should be arriving in five minutes. Make sure Darrow is waiting for me."

"On it, boss."

I went back over everything from my meeting at Good Day Marketers. They were hiding something. Vincent had been unnecessarily cagey. For someone who wanted to sell his services, he should have been more accommodating. Instead, he acted like allowing me to meet him in person was going above and beyond normal expectations. Sure, it may not have been how he usually conducted business, but why have an office space and not use it?

The meeting room had been prepared for me. The two offices I passed on the way didn't look like much of anything. But the place was larger on the outside than the inside, which meant there were other hallways and rooms that I hadn't seen. Again, I revisited the thought they could be running online scams, using servers and massive computing power to do whatever it was they were doing. But if they were operating the way he suggested, they wouldn't need any of that.

Someone could generate or curate everything by themselves. What appeared to be a large operation could be much smaller. So what were they doing with the rest of the space? Or were there a lot more than four people running the place?

By the time I took the elevator up to Cross Security, the vertigo had set in. Part of my brain was turning over Good Day Marketers, another part was going over the details of the three scammed men, and another part was dissecting the limited facts I had concerning the assault.

"Lucien," Darrow looked up when I barged into his office, "Justin said you were on your way."

"Did you know Kershaw was attacked last night?"

"How could I possibly know that?"

"You have him under surveillance," I said. "I want to see the footage."

"I don't have footage. I have trackers and listening devices."

"Show it to me."

Darrow held up his palms, less comfortable with my presence given my volatile mood. "Give me a second." I moved closer to his desk while he tapped on his phone screen. A second later, he pointed to the large monitor on the wall. "I put it up there so it'd be easier to see." He didn't want me getting too close, which was smart.

The red blip on the screen was in the center of the city's impound lot. The police had taken the car in, presumably for evidence collection. I sent a text to Justin, telling him I wanted that report too.

"Why didn't you notice this?" I asked.

"We already had this conversation about how Kershaw isn't a client anymore. I had no reason to continue monitoring his activity."

"What are you going to do when the police find your tracker?" I asked.

"Shit."

"That better not link back to me or Cross Security." I didn't supply Darrow with the gear. He bought that on his own. I hadn't touched it. I hadn't so much as seen it. However, I didn't put it past him to throw me under the bus when the cops came knocking, especially since he was working from my office.

"It won't. It's clean. It won't link to anyone." He stared at the blip on the screen. "I'll need to deactivate it, so they can't trace the signal back to me."

"Not yet." Since it was still showing the impound lot, no one had found it yet. More than likely, processing the vehicle for evidence wasn't a priority given the backlog of cases and the crime being an aggravated assault rather than a homicide. "I need to know everywhere Kershaw's been since you started tracking him."

"I already told you."

"I want everything," I said. "If he stopped to get a cup of coffee on his way to work, I want to know about it. Every minute the tracker was activated, I want to know where it was."

Darrow pulled up the details. I watched as the blip moved quickly on the map, going backward, then forward, then backward as the side of the screen filled with coordinates and times. Every stop, including traffic lights, resulted in another entry. Since Darrow had been watching our client for weeks, the list was long.

"Save the file," I said, handing Darrow the flash drive I kept on me.

He took it from my hand and plugged it into the side of his computer. "We could have been doing this the entire time. It would have saved on all that printing."

I didn't trust him not to slip me some hidden malware so he could spy or sabotage my servers, but since I was watching him every second while he saved the file, I wasn't too concerned.

"Print a copy to be on the safe side." I pulled out the drive once the file was saved. "Then you can deactivate it."

"Isn't that nice of you?" he muttered sarcastically.

I gave him a look. "I told you not to plant it."

"But it came in handy, didn't it?"

"If it came in handy, you would have realized something was wrong sooner. We could have been ahead of the police instead of behind. Maybe we could have done something to stop it."

"You can't save the world, Lucien."

"I know that," I snapped. Fighting with Darrow was wasting too much time. That was the one thing we didn't have. "What about the other bugs you planted?"

"The listening devices?"

"And whatever else you may have done."

"I didn't do anything else."

I wasn't sure I believed him, but again, I was reminded of the potential time crunch. "You said Kershaw didn't deviate a lot. You didn't get anything useful from his conversation, but I still want those audio tracks."

"I already told you—"

"I want the originals."

He held out his hand. "I can't print them. I'll have to save them on something."

"Where are they?"

"They get exported to the cloud, but I've downloaded them onto this computer."

"I'll pull them from cloud storage later. Right now, play them for me."

Darrow had the surveillance devices set to only record when they picked up sound. Anything that wasn't white noise would get recorded. That would save us a lot of time. Of course, things like a neighbor leaving or people talking in the hallway would trigger the recording to start, but that was easy enough to filter out.

"Here." Darrow hit play. "Given the time this was recorded, I'd say it was made yesterday morning."

"Kershaw never returned home last night." The tracker on his car verified that. He'd gone to the office and was attacked outside his building, never making it back.

"This is the last conversation he had at home before someone tried to knock his block off."

I listened to his side of the conversation. Kershaw didn't sound stressed or anxious. He sounded normal.

"He's talking to his oldest daughter," Darrow said.

I nodded, unsure how he'd figured that out. Kershaw hadn't used her name, but the honey and sweetie tipped me off that he was speaking to someone he was close to.

"The police and FBI have a suspect. They'll do their best. I'm just glad to have this behind me." Kershaw paused. *"No, I didn't do much. Cross Security handled it for me. Mr. Cross found a few other victims. That's how he got a name. It's up to the police now."* He paused again. *"You don't have to worry, honey. I'm fine. It wasn't that much. My lawyer suggested I take a few additional precautions to ensure this doesn't happen again. We just have to keep an eye on things to make sure the thief doesn't come back for more. That's why I need you to keep an eye on your accounts and credit cards."* Kershaw paused again. *"Okay, I'll let you go. Have a good day. I love you."*

"Did Kershaw hire you to do any of that work?" Darrow asked.

"No."

"I figured he would have since he gave you such a glowing review."

"It's basic. He could use the service from his credit card company if he wanted to monitor his finances. He doesn't need a security firm to do that for him."

"Still, that has to be a slap in the face."

I glared at Darrow. "What about the sounds you recorded the night before?"

Darrow clicked on the previous entry. We listened to muffled, staticky talking. "I'd say that's the TV."

I opened a visual representation of the audio files, searching for peaks. Gunshots, yelling, anything like that would stand out against the muffled TV. But there was nothing.

"Lucien, there are hundreds of hours here. I've listened to almost all the recordings, well, everything up until you supposedly solved the case, so I don't know what you expect to find. If someone threatened Kershaw, he would have said something. I bet he would have gone to the police. I don't think he had any idea someone was coming for him."

"Probably not." I stared at the long list of files. "Give me your cloud storage log-in."

"That's an invasion of privacy. I'll give you the files, but that's it."

I had enough to think about without wondering what Darrow was hiding. "Fine." I handed him the flash drive again. "Once the transfer completes, I'm dropping that off with Amir. Then you and I are going to Kershaw's apartment."

"Are you out of your fucking mind?"

"Do you want the police to find the surveillance devices you planted, on the off chance they want to search Kershaw's apartment and he gives them permission?"

"No."

"In that case, let's go."

TWENTY-THREE

"This is how you get caught," Darrow said. "You should never move the body."

"We aren't moving bodies."

"Not this time." The look on Darrow's face bothered me. "You never want to involve yourself in police investigations either. You don't want them poking around in your business or arresting you, but yet, you think it's a good idea to give them a reason to turn their attention to you and our involvement with Kershaw. Showing up here is a bad idea. It was an assault. It happened elsewhere. The victim is alive. There is no reason in the world the police would come here, but now, if they hear two people were snooping around in Kershaw's apartment, they'll come looking. And you know what they're going to find? They're going to find us."

"You should have thought about that before you bugged his apartment."

I wasn't too concerned. Almeada would cover for me if necessary. Since he was Kershaw's attorney or temporary attorney, he could say Kershaw asked that we retrieve some personal effects for him and Almeada sent me. The lie was basic enough that it would fly, especially since the defense attorney had teeth, and the police department had learned the hard way his bite was worse than his bark.

I didn't expect to find much of anything. What I wanted to know was what other kinds of surveillance equipment Darrow had installed. I didn't buy that this was audio-only, particularly since he didn't want me accessing his cloud, which is what Amir was doing while we were out of the office.

I followed Darrow through the apartment. He had planted the surveillance devices in the usual places on his way to the bathroom. However, Darrow hadn't gone to the bathroom. Instead, he bugged Kershaw's bedroom.

"The guy doesn't have much in the way of a sex life. Whatever self-pleasure he may have enjoyed didn't happen in here." Darrow retrieved the bug from the bedside lamp. "That should be it." But the way Darrow peered around the room told me he had something else to retrieve. "You said his property was taken."

"Wallet, phone, whatever he had on him," I said.

Darrow bit his lip while he looked around the room. "Huh. Okay. Do you know if he had his laptop with him?"

"Almeada didn't say." I narrowed my eyes. "What are you thinking?"

Darrow left the bedroom and went into Kershaw's home office. "I guess he didn't take it to work." Opening the lid, Darrow bypassed the log-in screen with practiced ease and a familiarity that made me uncomfortable. Once he was in, he entered a few commands.

"You son of a bitch. What did I tell you?" I asked.

Darrow deactivated the keystroke monitor and deleted the program. "No harm. No foul."

"You hacked his computer. Do you realize how bad that would look if the FBI confiscated his device? They'd think we emptied his bank account." I shook my head. "No. They'd think you emptied his bank account, and you know what, I'd help them build a case against you."

Darrow sighed. "You are such a drama queen. The crime already happened. If they wanted to check his computer, they would have already done so. This way, we had a bird's eye view of what he was doing, what kinds of illegal activity and other gambling endeavors in which he partook."

I couldn't believe I was asking since I knew the answer, but I asked anyway. "What did you find?"

Darrow mumbled, "He's clean."

I wanted to punch him, but that would have to wait until we were back at the office. "What else did you do?"

"That's it. I swear."

"Let's go." I waited for him to leave the room, gave it one last look, and followed him out the door. We didn't speak again until we were inside the car. "Are there any other surprises you forgot to mention?"

"Asked and answered," Darrow said.

"Fine. New question. Do you have any idea why someone would attack Alan Kershaw?"

"The attack happened at the office. That would indicate—"

"I know. A work-related incident or a random act of violence, but you've gone off the deep end, looking into our client. Tell me what you know."

"You meant to say I've been performing a deep dive."

"I said what I meant."

Darrow glared at me. "Y'know, you should be nicer if you want me to cooperate."

I didn't waste my breath making threats. Darrow didn't respond to them. Instead, he'd find some way to infuriate me. "Since you're such an excellent investigator," I said through gritted teeth, "what have you found?"

"I'll ignore the patronizing tone." His shoulders hitched. "I don't know. You kept saying our client was clean. I've been digging and digging, but I have yet to find anything. His children may have questionable ties, his son in particular, but nothing solid has come from those searches either."

"All right." I focused my attention on the road ahead of us, wondering what Amir found and if Darrow was on the level. I wished I could trust him, but I didn't. And I didn't think I ever would, not when he concealed things from me and his motives remained murky.

"I'm telling you, whoever's responsible connects to the grocery store. You went there to ask questions. Maybe that's why Kershaw got clubbed."

"That was after Kershaw was assaulted. I asked about their loyalty program. That was it."

Darrow pointed to the approaching sign. "We could check it out now. The damage is already done. What's the harm?"

I glanced at Darrow. He was wearing a football jersey with a matching cap. It was toned down compared to his normal disguises. "Do not introduce yourself to anyone. Do not say you work for me. Is that clear?"

"What do you want me to do?"

"I don't know. Shop around. Chips and beer would go with your outfit."

Darrow plucked the jersey away from his chest. "Do you like it? I got a great deal. This guy was selling a bunch of them on the sidewalk a few blocks from your building."

After parking the car, I got out. I didn't wait for Darrow. Not wanting to be seen with him had nothing to do with his outfit. I had questions that I wanted to ask Charlie Steed. Handling that now would save time later.

I made my way to the customer service desk while Darrow disappeared down the frozen food aisle. The clerk working the desk was the same one I'd spoken to earlier.

"Are you back to fill out the application?"

"Maybe later. I was hoping to speak to the assistant manager," I said.

"He's on break. He should be back in about fifteen minutes."

"Great," I said. "I'll look around while I wait."

"You could fill out the application."

Wondering why the clerk was so pushy, I faked my phone vibrating and pulled it out. Holding up a finger to indicate I'd only be a minute, I pretended to answer while I walked away. The grocery store had seemed innocent enough, but now I was having doubts. It was that kind of day.

I spotted Darrow filling a basket with frozen appetizers while he spoke to the employee restocking the shelves. Darrow blended in with his surroundings, and unlike the questions I'd just asked, his didn't seem to be drawing any undue attention to himself.

Making my way to the back of the store, I spotted an employees only sign on the swinging doors. I pushed my way through, getting assaulted by the smell of soggy cardboard and fish. A few men with boxcutters were unloading a pallet. They wore insulated gloves and heavy coats to keep warm in the freezer. They paid me no heed as I moved past them and through another door which led to a brightly lit hallway.

On the left was the break room. Charlie Steed sat alone at a table. He had a paper cup in front of him and a half-eaten sandwich from the deli. The sticker on the side said it was half price with an expiration date of today. He was watching something on his phone, his earbuds making him even less approachable. Given the places I'd worked as a kid, I could understand why the assistant manager wanted to hide for a few minutes. Jobs like this were brutal.

"Is that any good?" I asked, taking a seat across from him.

He looked up as if he was about to berate me only to realize he didn't know who I was. "No one's allowed back here."

"I know," I said. "I saw the sign."

"All right, so what are you doing here?"

This was why wearing a suit was beneficial. If Darrow showed up in his jersey and jeans, Steed would think he was about to get mugged. "I wanted to speak to you in private. I thought this would be a good place to do it. It's come to my attention you interned at Good Day Marketers."

Steed flipped his phone face down on the table and took out his earbuds. "That was a while ago."

"You reported to Jasmine O'Neal," I said.

"Yeah, so?"

"I work for a law firm." I flashed him Almeada's business card. It may have been a stretch, but it wasn't a complete lie. I had done work for them a time or two.

"Shit." Steed shook his head while he closed the plastic container around his sandwich. "I knew what they were doing was wrong. They said it wasn't. That's how business is now. It's how the future will look, but it always felt underhanded to me. Like fraud."

"Funny you should say that." I leaned back in my chair, non-threatening, just a pal with whom he could talk trash. "Anything you'd be willing to share would be greatly appreciated. Of course, you'll be compensated for your time."

"I don't want this linking back to me. If you promise you can leave my name out of it, that I won't have to testify, I'll tell you what I can."

"You have my word."

He studied me a moment longer, assessing my suit as if everyone at law firms dressed like this. "Okay. What do you want to know?"

TWENTY-FOUR

"Why don't we start with the basics?" I suggested. "I'm aware of Good Day Marketers' mission statement. In fact, you could say I was walked through their supposed advertising strategies. However, we all know that's not really what's going on there. That's not how they're making their money."

"You're right." Steed glanced at the door. Uncomfortable, he got up, peered down the hallway, and closed the door to the break room. "They turn a profit on the sites and profiles they create. Everything is monetized. The entire goal is monetization. They make even more off online ads than the paid endorsements and advertisements they provide."

This wasn't what I had in mind, but I didn't want to interrupt. I wanted Steed to lead the conversation. My only hope was we'd end up somewhere pertinent.

"The content is total bull crap. It's generated garbage. They do a half-assed copy and paste job, feed it into the automation software, and have fresh shit posted regularly, except none of it is fresh. Half of it isn't even accurate, I don't think. I don't know." He shrugged. "It's all stolen. That's how these large language models provide output.

They regurgitate whatever was input into them. And let's not even get into the potential FTC violations by their failure to disclose."

"Did you voice your issues to anyone in charge?" I asked. "Did you talk to your boss about it?"

"You mean Jasmine?" Steed rolled his eyes. "She didn't see anything wrong with it. She claimed everything was carefully checked and curated, but it wasn't. They don't have enough people on staff for that. Out of spite, she assigned me to fact-check every generated article they posted." He folded his arms over his chest, unsure what to do with himself or possibly to contain the rage. "I'm not a research assistant, and even if I was, I would have done my own searches and written my own articles. What they're doing is wrong. It's stupid. It's nothing but shoveling more horse manure at the masses."

"Agreed," I said.

Steed let out a relieved sigh, as if he'd been vindicated. "Finally. Someone gets it. Everyone at Good Day Marketers thought I was insane. They treated me like a squeaky wheel. Everything they made me do felt punitive."

"What did they make you do?"

"Besides the fact-checking, it was coffee runs and monitoring community feedback."

"What exactly did that entail?"

"Deleting any negative comments that weren't completely off the wall. They needed some to make things look legit, but if someone posted the truth about this slop or the money-grabbing that was going on behind the scenes, I had to make it disappear. In between, they expected me to leave a handful of other comments as different users. They had several computers set up to make that easier. Everything they did was about manipulating the system, at least on the social media sites. Whatever went on with the sites they created themselves, that they had domain over, was even worse."

"Domain," I chuckled, hoping to ease the tension radiating off him.

"The wordplay isn't lost on me." Steed puffed out his cheeks and blew out a breath. "I didn't care for any of that."

"Did you notice anything else going on at Good Day Marketers?"

"Like what?"

"Tell me about Jasmine O'Neal."

"She's a bitch."

"Besides that. Did you notice any personal quirks? Maybe she had a few vices she kept secret."

"Everyone at that place was super secretive. They kept the doors locked. I'd have to knock and wait to be let in."

"Any chance they have a dungeon full of bodies?"

Steed's left eyebrow twitched. "Are you serious?"

"Sure, why not?"

"I never noticed a dungeon. But there were several areas that I wasn't allowed to go. What are you thinking? They're filming porn in there?"

"You'd know better than I would." Though that had never come to mind.

"I've never seen anyone go in or out. In fact, besides Jasmine and Vincent, it was rare I'd even glimpse another human being. They never even had food delivered. They'd make me go pick it up. They didn't want anyone in that office who wasn't supposed to be there."

"I was there," I said, "earlier today. I met Vincent. He mentioned Rita, and there was another man at the front desk. Jeff, I think his name was." I described him, but Steed didn't know him, which I didn't think he would.

"Rita, huh? He really said Rita?"

"He said she was an assistant."

"I assisted Jasmine. Vincent had Rita. For all those months that I interned there, I never once met Rita. She often got mentioned, but she must have been invisible. She didn't leave when we did. She never went past me. I wouldn't even be able to describe her."

"What about the other marketing managers?"

"What other marketing managers?"

"I was under the impression there were four."

"Whoever told you that was lying. There are two, Jasmine and Vincent, unless things have drastically changed since I left, which is totally possible."

Steed gave me a few things to look into and think about,

but nothing he said was helpful to Kershaw's predicament.

"What about gambling?" I asked.

"Gambling?"

"Does Jasmine O'Neal like to gamble?"

"I don't know." Steed closed his eyes, searching his memory. "I'm sorry."

"Let's get back to how Good Day Marketers makes money." I held up my hand before he repeated himself. "Besides what you've already mentioned about their posts and comment manipulation, are they doing anything else underhanded that's unrelated to that?"

"Ask me directly whatever it is you think they've done."

"Are they running scams? Phishing? Identity theft? Anything like that?"

"I don't have proof, but that wouldn't surprise me. They were always monitoring their audience to the point of invading people's privacy. The tracking cookies they used would collect a lot of data that they shouldn't have been able to access."

"Are we talking malware? Hacking?"

"They were doing something like that."

"Did you ever come across any posts that someone's bank account had been wiped out?"

"No." Steed studied me closely. "Did that happen?"

"I don't know."

The PA system kicked on, requesting assistance in the bread aisle. "I should get back to work." But he didn't budge from his seat. "I'm sorry I couldn't be more help, but you mentioned something about compensation."

I slipped a few twenties out of my pocket. "Make sure you keep this between us. If I have any follow-up questions, I know where to find you."

"I'll be here." Steed pocketed the cash and left the break room.

Before following him, I sent Amir a text. We'd need to monitor Charlie Steed's phone and internet activity. His anger at Good Day Marketers seemed genuine, but it never hurt to make sure. The last thing I needed was for him to tip off his former employers that someone was on to their operation.

However, if he did, it'd turn into a fire sale. If I could get there quickly enough, I'd have all the evidence needed to bury them. Damn, when did I become so optimistic?

* * *

"How did your talk with Charlie Steed go?" Darrow asked.

"It could have gone better. He told me all about their marketing operation, how they make their legitimate money, but he didn't have much to offer in terms of illegal activities."

"Do you believe him?"

"I don't know."

Darrow punched my shoulder. "Look at you, finally learning not to take someone at face value."

"How did your conversation go?"

"I learned a lot."

"Oh?"

"Did you know they stock thirty-seven different brands of frozen pizza? Did you even know there were thirty-seven brands of pizza?"

"Ace," I hissed.

He grinned. "I'm just messing with you, Lucien. It's what we do. Plus, it's fun to watch your face get red and your knuckles turn white."

"What did you ask about?"

"I asked specifically about the assistant manager, how closely he monitors the employees and the customers. Y'know, things like that."

"You still think Steed is providing Good Day Marketers with marks?" I asked.

"Wow, that's one giant leap. So now you're sure Good Day Marketers is behind the zero bank balances, and yet, you just got through telling me you weren't taking Steed at his word. Tsk, tsk. You can't have it both ways."

"We've already established Jasmine O'Neal is involved, even if the advertising firm isn't. I'm using the names interchangeably at this point. So did you find any proof Steed is involved?"

"No."

"What do his subordinates think of him?"

"They like him. They think he's fair. He doesn't do a lot of micromanaging, but he's always keeping an eye on everything."

"Everything?" I asked.

Darrow poked me in the arm. "See, I knew you'd be interested. Your good buddy keeps an eye on the number of active customers. He tracks the loyalty cards to see if business is on an uptick or tumbling downhill."

"He was a business major. He has experience in marketing."

"Do you think that's all it is?"

"Do you know if he and Kershaw ever crossed paths?"

"Not beyond whatever limited interactions they would have had in the store," Darrow said. "But I can tell you Steed oversaw a few of the deliveries that Eric Greene made."

"Did they talk?"

"The guys I spoke to said Steed talks to everyone. He's always friendly. Always interested. I took that to mean he asks lots of questions."

"You're projecting."

"How would you describe friendly? For me, it always starts with a greeting, followed by how are you. From there, it can get a lot more specific, personally and professionally, depending on if the other party is willing to go along."

"You must do great on the dating scene," I said.

"I hold my own." Darrow hadn't caught on to the sarcasm.

"All right, let's head back, see what Amir has for us, and take it from there."

"I like this side of you, Lucien. I'm glad you finally came around to working together. You know what they say. Two heads are better than one."

TWENTY-FIVE

While we were gone, Amir had taken a peek at Darrow's cloud storage account. I didn't get the full report, but the looks Amir was giving Darrow told me it'd be best to remain cautious around the seasoned private eye. He struck me as a bumbling fool, but I'd seen enough to know some of that was an act.

"Charlie Steed hasn't reached out to anyone from Good Day Marketers," Amir said. "From what I can tell, he hasn't spoken to anyone in the company since his internship ended. His phone records and e-mails support that. I looked into his offline activities, but there's no overlap."

"Does he gamble?" I asked.

"I didn't find so much as a discarded lotto scratcher."

"Did you go through his trash?" Darrow asked.

"Electronically speaking," Amir said.

"Yeah, well, unless you actually check, you can't know for sure."

"I thought you didn't do a lot of legwork, Ace," I said. "You're the computer guy. Not the sift through the trash guy."

"Research is research. I've been in plenty of dumpsters."

"I'll bet."

Amir met my eyes. "Darrow's right, but I have no reason to think otherwise."

"That's good enough for me," I said. "What about the rest of the gang at Good Day Marketers?"

"I pulled up the employee profiles and ran background checks. Vincent wasn't lying to you. Four people are listed as marketing managers. Two of them aren't local. They work remotely. One is based in Texas, the other in British Columbia."

"And Rita?"

"I haven't found anything on Rita. I'll have to go through their tax filings to see how many W-2s and 1099s they issued. But that'll take calling in some favors and pulling some strings."

"Hold off for now," I said. "Let Agent Olsen deal with that." I glanced at the phone. "Maybe you should tip him off. You used to be one of them. I bet you still have the windbreaker in your closet."

"Are you sure you want to do that?" Darrow asked.

"This isn't my case. I told that to Kershaw when we met, but since he's in no condition to have a conversation or share our intel with his FBI contact, we'll help him out," I said.

Amir nodded. "Is there anything else I can do?"

"I guess that's it," I said. We couldn't talk in front of Darrow. "If you need to update me on something, I'll be upstairs in my office."

"Very good, sir," Amir said.

I herded Darrow back to the elevator. "See what you can find on this mysterious Rita," I said. "You excel at compiling background information. This should be firmly in your wheelhouse."

"All right, I'm on it."

If Darrow found any of this suspicious, he didn't let on. I rode with him to his floor and made sure he was settled into his office before I pushed the button on the elevator for my floor. When I got there, Justin was waiting with the information Almeada had sent over regarding the police investigation.

He joined me in my office, shutting the door behind

him. I didn't ask before pouring two drinks and putting one down in front of him.

"Isn't it a little early to start drinking?" Justin eyed the glass.

"Not on a day like today." I checked my messages and e-mails, but Amir wouldn't send anything damning to me, not when I was worried Darrow would find a way to hack our system. "What are the police doing?"

"The usual. They're canvassing the area in search of witnesses. They've collected security cam footage from the cameras in the area. Those include the building where Kershaw works, a nearby parking garage, an ATM across the street, and the security camera from the adjacent deli."

"Do we have access to that footage?"

"The ATM is the only thing we haven't gotten. Everything else wasn't too hard to collect."

"Did you pull the funds from our emergency account?"

"You mean the cash you keep in the locked drawer?"

"Yep."

Justin smiled. "Yeah."

I unlocked the drawer and did a quick count. It didn't cost that much. "Have you had time to watch it?"

"Yes, but there's not much. It happened the way Almeada told you. The techs have the footage now. They'll see if there's anything they can enhance or pull that will help us identify the attacker."

"Could it be Jasmine O'Neal?" I asked.

Justin shook his head. "I've seen photos of her, even the footage of her in disguise. Whoever attacked Kershaw looked like a big guy." Before I could ask the next question, Justin pointed to my keyboard. "You can dial up the footage yourself. I sent copies to your dropbox."

I opened the files, finding everything Justin said to be accurate. "Do you know if Kershaw's permitted visitors yet?"

"His children are with him now. Well, his oldest daughter and son. His youngest promised to be there after class. She has one late afternoon class and didn't want to miss it with midterms coming up."

I was starting to wonder how everyone else knew things

I didn't. "How did you find that out?"

"Almeada told me. He was there when Kershaw spoke to her on the phone."

"Is he still at the hospital?"

"No, he left once he got the intel you wanted."

"What about Kershaw's car? Did the police find any evidence on it?"

"They've only done preliminaries at this point. It's not a priority."

"Figured," I muttered.

"They found several sets of prints on the exterior, but you saw the footage. The assailant wore gloves. The prints on Kershaw's car could be from anyone walking by. Sara doesn't think it'll mean much of anything."

"Was there anything else?"

"Nope."

I sipped my drink and thought about things. When I couldn't make heads or tails out of what was going on, I filled Justin in on everything that had happened today. Unfortunately, my executive assistant didn't have any helpful insights to share. I couldn't blame him. I wasn't even sure if the assault and the scam were connected.

"Did Amir tell you what he found in the cloud?" I asked.

Justin picked up the glass, swirled the liquor around, and took a sip. "Lucien, it'd be best not to react right away."

My skin prickled. "What did he find?"

Justin took another sip, urging me to do the same. "Darrow has an entire file of blackmail saved."

"To use against me?" I'd kill him.

"Not you. Alan Kershaw."

"What does he have on Kershaw? I thought he was clean."

"He is, but Darrow's saving whatever questionable or embarrassing details he found."

"Like what?"

"For starters, Kershaw's adult browsing habits."

"Adult browsing habits?" I gave Justin a look. It had been a long day. "You mean he knows the type of porn Kershaw enjoys. Is it anything illegal?"

"No."

"So who cares?"

"Beats me, but Darrow's background is in doing opposition research. Details like that could bury otherwise viable candidates."

"Only the morons running on family values." I tried to shake away my annoyance with our political system. "Alan Kershaw has zero interest in any of that. He would never run for office. What else does Darrow have on him?"

"The rest has to do with Kershaw's children. They're young adults with active dating lives."

"He has photos."

"And videos."

"The kinds I told him not to save?" I asked.

"They're all adults. Nothing Amir found falls into exploitation of minors."

"At least there's that." I was seeing red. "Is it possible any of that connects to whoever emptied Kershaw's bank account?"

"No. Amir believes the information Darrow saved is purely meant to be used as leverage against our client."

"Do we know why? Or is this just another way for Darrow to screw with me and my business?"

Justin didn't say anything.

"That fucking bastard. I'm going to kill him."

Justin grabbed my arm before I made it around the desk. "Lucien, sit down."

"He can't blackmail our client, our client who less than twenty-four hours ago was brutally assaulted. Shit. Do you think Darrow had something to do with that? Where the hell was he when Kershaw was getting knocked around?"

"He'd already gone home for the night."

"Supposedly." I reached for the phone. "Darrow planted trackers on Kershaw's car. He knew where our client was. He easily could have orchestrated the attack. And I helped him cover his tracks. He made me a fucking accomplice."

"Lucien, stop." Justin's harsh tone temporarily halted the spiral. "You're jumping to a lot of conclusions. You need proof."

I punched in the digits for Amir's extension. "Find out

where Darrow was when Kershaw was attacked last night. He had the company car. Where the hell was it parked?"

"It was outside his place," Amir said.

"What about his phone?"

"Hold, please."

I focused on Justin who was perched on the edge of his seat, as if preparing to tackle me to the ground if I made a break for the exit. "Where are we on that shovel and machete?"

"They're close if we need them," Justin said, "but I hope we don't need them, boss."

"Me too."

A moment later, Amir came back on the line. "His phone pinged somewhere in his neighborhood. I'd say he was probably at home."

"Does Darrow fit the description of the man who attacked Kershaw?"

"It's possible," Amir said.

I fought the flinch off my face. "All right. Thanks."

"I take it Justin filled you in," Amir said.

"He did. What have you done with the files?"

"They remain. I wasn't sure you wanted him to know we'd accessed them."

"Monitor his activity. Let me know if he adds anything else to his cloud account or if he downloads any of that shit. Do we know if he has other copies?"

"I don't know. The only thing I can say for certain is he didn't pull those things using a company computer or our network. He did that on his own time, using his own equipment."

"That means whatever copies of the files he has must be off-site, probably at his place, on his personal computer or mobile device."

"It's not on his phone. I already checked," Amir said.

"That leaves his computer, tablet, and any public computer he could have accessed."

"Focus on the small wins," Amir suggested.

Biting off a retort which my tech expert did not deserve, I put the phone down and stared at Justin. "Do you want to dig the hole or cut the body into little pieces?"

Justin scowled. "You have to be certain."

"Who else knows about this?"

"Amir, you, and me."

"Amir's certain it's blackmail. I agree. What's your vote?"

"Technically, it's not blackmail until he uses it against Kershaw for personal gain. Right now, it could be anything. It could be his insurance policy, like the kind you have for that one troublesome former client."

"That's different. That's necessary to protect myself should certain facts come to light. Frankly, it probably won't save me, but it'd mitigate some of the damage. But this case, Kershaw's case, isn't that. Kershaw is a good guy. He got scammed. There is no reason why Darrow needs to dangle the threat of mutually assured destruction over his head." I sighed. "Is there any chance Darrow's behind the scam?"

"You mean emptying out people's bank accounts?"

"Yeah, unless there's some other scam going around that I don't know about."

Justin shook his head. "We would have figured that out. You looked into this independently. If anything overlapped with Darrow, you would have noticed immediately."

"Not if it was after I brought him on board. At that point, he could have used his position to cover his tracks, to lead me in the wrong direction."

"Stop being paranoid. You wouldn't let him lead you anywhere." Justin considered what I'd said. "For argument's sake, let's say Kershaw getting scammed is personal."

"That's how it seems, given that the other two victims are also local."

"Right, but we don't know who has a grudge against Kershaw. However, if Darrow figured it out and approached that guy, maybe he's working for him instead of us."

TWENTY-SIX

Now would have been the perfect time to have other trained investigators on the payroll. One of them could keep an eye on Darrow, track his movements, and see what other sneaky, underhanded things he was up to. However, I hadn't hired anyone. That was on me. But this shit that Darrow was pulling was entirely on him.

The tracker in the company car and Amir keeping an eye on where Darrow's cell phone pinged would have to do. Even after backtracking Darrow's movements since I hired him, I still couldn't figure out who he was working for or even if he was working for someone else.

The cop who'd been stationed outside Alan Kershaw's room was gone now. The police had decided Kershaw wasn't in any danger of the attacker returning. I wasn't sure that was true. But if it was Darrow, at least I'd get advanced notice he was on his way.

I stepped into the room, finding two sets of eyes staring at me. I cleared my throat, unsure if I should make the introduction or wait for Kershaw to do it.

He tore his gaze from the television. His face was bruised, making him nearly unrecognizable. Again, the thought that Darrow could be responsible or that I caused the attacker to strike made my stomach ache.

"Mr. Cross," Kershaw took an uneasy breath, preparing himself before lifting higher in the bed, "it's nice of you to show. Mr. Almeada said you were here earlier."

"I heard what happened and wanted to make sure you were okay."

Kershaw's son looked up from his phone. "Are you the dick my father hired?"

"Yes," I said.

Kershaw gave his son a sharp look. "Be respectful."

"Do the police have any leads?" I interjected, hoping to stop an argument.

"They're looking into it." Kershaw gave his daughter's hand a squeeze. "Why don't you take your brother and sister out for dinner? The three of you have been cooped up in here for the last few hours. I'm sure you're starving."

She smiled at her father. "Sure, Daddy. No problem."

Her siblings weren't as easily persuaded. They didn't trust me and didn't want to leave their father alone with me. But they reluctantly agreed and followed her out of the room.

I didn't blame them. I wouldn't want me anywhere near a loved one either. A brief thought of Jade across the country came to mind. It was no wonder I encouraged her to go. Being near me was dangerous for everyone.

"Do you mind if I sit?" I indicated the empty chair beside his bed.

"Help yourself." Kershaw muted the television. "Why do you think this happened?"

"I was hoping you could tell me."

"The police think it may have been a random mugging. The asshole took my wallet and phone. He even ripped the watch off my wrist."

"Smartwatch?" I asked.

"No."

I didn't have to ask. The only other kind of watch Kershaw would wear would be an expensive timepiece. "They may be able to track that. Items of value tend to show up in pawn shops or get unloaded online."

"That's what the cop said. I gave him the serial number

and everything. He said they'd keep an eye out."

"Did you notice anything specific about the person who attacked you?"

"He was a good-sized guy."

"My size?" I asked.

"Heavier. Maybe broader."

"Darrow's size?"

Kershaw considered the question. "I guess. Maybe a little taller. I'm not really sure."

I fought to keep the anger down. "I'm wondering if this connects to whoever scammed you."

"By adding injury to insult?"

"Yeah," I said.

"I was thinking the same thing. But you said a woman was responsible. Whoever came at me with that bat wasn't built like most women I know."

"Jasmine O'Neal may not have attacked you. She may not have even scammed you. But I have every reason to believe she's involved."

"You said this could be a dangerous situation, that criminal organizations are behind these kinds of operations."

"Sometimes. Most of the time."

"Is that why someone came after me? Do I have to worry about a hitter coming back to finish the job?"

"I don't think so. If whoever attacked you wanted you dead, you'd be dead. The assault appears to be a warning."

Kershaw grew increasingly uncomfortable, fidgeting with his good hand for something to grasp—the remote, the blanket, the wires hooked to the bed, whatever he could find. "Why would someone want to warn me off?"

"You wanted the person who scammed you to get caught. He or she probably didn't like that."

"How would they even know I reported any of this?"

Thoughts of Darrow double-crossing me came to mind. That was only a slightly more pleasant possibility than the thought my question asking had led to this. "Your name could have surfaced during the investigation. Or the guilty party assumed you came forward since you lost the most and weren't involved in any illegal activities at the time."

"Do you really think this connects? The police said it was a random mugging."

"It's possible, I suppose."

"You don't put much credence in their theories."

"The simplest solution is usually the right one, except when there are extenuating circumstances to consider. I don't believe they are taking any of that into consideration. But I have been known to be a paranoid, delusional alarmist."

"You didn't mention that during our consultation."

"It scares away prospective clients, but I did warn you I didn't think I'd be able to do much for you." I gestured at the bed. "For what it's worth, I am sorry I wasn't able to prevent this from happening. I have security teams on standby. With your approval, I'd like to assign one to keep an eye on you and have additional teams keep watch over your children in case any threats follow them home."

"Do you think that's necessary?"

"It's precautionary."

"Fine. I don't care, whatever the cost."

"No charge," I said.

"You're a terrible businessman. You tried to turn down my case, and now you're working for free."

"Let me worry about that." I sent a text to Justin. He could coordinate the security detail. I had enough teams on standby to cover the Kershaws. The tricky part would be making sure they didn't let Ace Darrow anywhere near the family without tipping off Darrow. "Did the attacker say anything to you?"

"Not a word."

"Would you mind walking me through the attack? I've read the statement you provided the police, but I'd like to hear it firsthand, so I can interject if anything comes to mind."

"I was almost to my car. I stayed late to finish a presentation that was due the next day."

"Was the building empty?"

"Security is always there, but most of my colleagues had gone home for the night. I had parked on the street instead of in the garage. The area's usually pretty busy. People are around during normal business hours, and it's well lit. I didn't expect to get jumped."

"Was anyone else out?"

"A few people. It was quiet but not eerily so. I was just about to unlock my car when something struck me from behind. I went flying and face-planted beside the rear wheel. By the time I rolled over, he was on me. All I saw was the wooden bat. He was nothing more than a shadow. All dark clothing. He had his face covered. I put my hands up to protect myself." Kershaw held up his good hand, as if reliving the attack. "That's when he broke my arm. He hit me once more, which broke my ribs, then he went to town on my car. The last thing I remember was glass raining down everywhere. Then I get a little fuzzy."

"That's called a concussion," I said. "You said he didn't say anything. Did you?"

"I screamed. I told him to stop. I yelled for help."

"Did you hit him back?"

"I never got the chance."

The possible rage the attacker took out on the windows wasn't because he'd gotten upset that Kershaw popped him in the nose. "The attack sounds more like a warning than a mugging. Muggers wouldn't typically hang around to take a few swings at your car," I said.

"He was like a bully on the playground."

"But he didn't say anything? He didn't warn you to back off or keep quiet? He didn't tell you to stay away from the police?"

Kershaw shook his head. That didn't fit with my warning theory. Most warnings had a vocal element.

"He didn't mention me, did he?" I asked.

Kershaw snickered, as if I'd made a joke. "He didn't say a word."

"Okay. I just wanted to make sure. Maybe the cops are right. Maybe this isn't related. If it is, he should have warned you to stay away or back off. Something like that."

"Damn. That means I've been targeted twice in the span of a few weeks. First, my bank account. Now this. Do I have 'easy target' tattooed on my forehead?"

"Not that I can see, but it could be written in invisible

ink that only shows up under UV light."

"Thanks a lot."

"If it makes you feel any better, I have a cosmic kick me sign I have yet to shake."

"Maybe you should have mentioned that during our consultation."

TWENTY-SEVEN

Once my security teams were in place, I left the hospital. Alan Kershaw and his three children would be safe. More than anything, I wanted to confront Darrow. But something told me to wait. I wanted to know the reason he had saved blackmail on our client. Going straight at him wouldn't result in answers. Instead, it would force him to tip his hand and enact whatever doomsday scheme he had.

"Darrow is not an evil genius," I reminded myself, but I wasn't convinced.

I drove around for a while, trying to figure out what to do. Jasmine O'Neal was the only lead I had. If it hadn't been for the assault, I'd say she was my prime suspect. Now, I wasn't sure. Maybe everyone at Good Day Marketers was involved. Jasmine reached out to the victims, convinced them to trust her, and gained the sensitive intel she needed to empty their bank accounts. Meanwhile, Vincent or Jeff could rough up anyone who got in the way.

I'd seen their hands though. Neither had the hands of a fighter. They had the hands of people who spent too many hours at a computer. Their knuckles weren't bruised or callused. They didn't have any scars or cuts. Maybe that's why the attacker used a baseball bat.

Unsure what else to do, I looked up Jasmine O'Neal's address and headed to her apartment. Her neighborhood was nicer than Darrow's but not as nice as mine. Building security would be tough to crack, should I have to break in. How could a woman who worked in an office that looked as questionable as Good Day Marketers afford a place like this?

Again, thoughts of organized crime and terrorist cells came to mind. "There's that paranoia." I texted Amir and asked him to run backgrounds on everyone from Good Day Marketers and see if they had ties to organized crime. Since he was still figuring out who worked there, this could take a while.

I looked up at O'Neal's apartment. Maybe I should knock.

I let that thought play out, considering the various possible scenarios. Most of them didn't end well for me. On the tamer end of the spectrum, she'd slam the door in my face. On the other end, she'd lure me inside and shoot me. Even if she didn't resort to violence, I didn't think she'd confess, unless she was certain she could get away with it, which brought me back to all the ways she could murder me.

While I was debating if I should try my luck or tip my hand, afraid of what that could mean for Kershaw or her other victims, I called Almeada and filled him in on the rest of my day. He wasn't surprised when I told him about Darrow's possible blackmail scheme. However, he refrained from saying *I told you so.*

"Are you going to turn him in?" Almeada asked.

"Should I?"

"No."

"That's what I figured."

"What are you going to do?"

"I haven't decided yet. Right now, we're monitoring the situation. My immediate plan is to intervene if Darrow tries something. However, if he plans to sit on this for a while, I don't know how to proceed."

"Couldn't you delete the files?"

"I doubt those are his only copies. If he pulled them off the internet, he could do it again."

"Couldn't anyone do that?" Almeada asked. "Maybe it's not blackmail. Maybe it's a teachable moment."

"The last thing Kershaw needs is someone else teaching him a lesson."

"Promise me one thing, Lucien. Should something happen to Darrow, make sure you don't tell me about your involvement."

"Wouldn't that be privileged?"

"Regardless, I don't want to know."

"All right. I won't tell you I have a shovel and fifty pounds of lye in my trunk."

"Lucien, that better be a fucking joke."

"I'm not supposed to tell you, remember?"

He sighed, exasperated. The tone indicated he realized I was teasing, but the slightest bit of uncertainty remained when he said, "How about we grab a drink? My treat."

I looked up at the window again. The interior lights were dim. Jasmine O'Neal could have been asleep or out. I had no way of knowing, and I had yet to come up with a foolproof plan to get her to confess. "Yeah, okay. Where do you want to go?"

"You pick."

"Spark," I said.

"I'm not sure that's the best idea."

"Then you shouldn't have said I could pick."

"Fine. I'll meet you there. On the bright side, I won't have to worry about you murdering anyone inside the club. The owner has a strict policy against anything that would give the police grounds to enter his establishment."

"That leaves plenty of other options," I said. In fact, there was a good chance there might be something exciting happening in the back room. Whatever it was was bound to be more fun than going over the details of this case again. "Give me a few minutes. I want to knock on a door first."

"Whose door?"

"Jasmine O'Neal's."

"Hold off on that."

"Why?" I asked.

"Let's give the police a chance to do it first."

"I didn't know they were planning on doing anything."

"I'll give them a nudge."

"Since when do they listen to defense attorneys?"

"Lucien, if you want me to pay for drinks, stop asking questions and get your ass to the club."

"Fine."

When I arrived at Spark, I found a smaller crowd than usual. There was no line outside. The doorman, George, nodded to me as I approached.

"Good evening, Mr. Cross."

"Is Mr. Almeada here?" I asked.

"Not yet."

"Tell him I'll be waiting for him at the bar."

George nodded again. "Very good, sir."

His manners reminded me of a butler, but the way he filled out the black suit made me wonder if he couldn't pick up my car and throw it through the nearest building. He wasn't particularly tall, but he was solid. He had the hands of a fighter and the scar tissue around his eyes and nose to back it up. If he was a little taller, I'd consider him a suspect in the assault.

I made my way across the darkened club. The strobing lights kept things interesting. As usual, scantily clad dancers filled the cages. They were always beautiful, just like everyone else who worked here. The waitstaff wore silver, which would catch the lights and shimmer. Everything about this place screamed glitz and glam, but it was all for show.

"You should have named this place Mercury," I said as I slid onto a stool.

Axel Kincaid, the club's owner, was behind the bar. He had regular bartenders on payroll, but half the time, he was behind the bar with his jacket off, his shirt half unbuttoned, and his sleeves rolled up. I never asked why he did it, but given that he had an apartment upstairs, I was pretty sure working the bar made it easier to pick up women, men, or whatever he was interested in at that particular moment.

"Mercury, huh?" Axel grabbed the gin off the top shelf

and reached for a glass from underneath the bar. "Why?"

"Look at this place." I spun on the stool, indicating the room. "It's liquid silver."

"Mercury was the Roman god of merchants and monetary gain. He was also the god of trickery and thieves."

I shrugged. "It's also a failed car company."

"Are you trying to say something, Lucien?"

"You brought up thieves." I sipped the gin and tonic he had poured. "I was simply stating a fact."

"I'm wondering if I should regret allowing you membership to my club. You're starting to sound like your father."

I held up my palms. "Point taken. No more barbs." I hadn't meant the Mercury comment to be an insult, but Kincaid would take things however he wanted. Most of the time, he wanted to see if he could scare me.

"What brings you here tonight?" He poured himself a shot of tequila and leaned against the bar. "You look like you could use a pick-me-up." He eyed my drink. "I have a reputation for being able to get anyone whatever they want at any time. What would you like?"

I thought about it. "You don't sell drugs or run a brothel. So how exactly are you fulfilling those requests?"

"I know people. I can make things happen outside these doors and away from my property, but we aren't talking about that. You already have your own connection on speed dial, not that you use his services for their intended purposes either."

"How is Freddy?" I asked.

"The last I heard, he was enjoying a sandy beach somewhere tropical. He should be back from vacation soon." Kincaid gave me a wicked smile. "Should I take that to mean there's something I could help you with in the meantime?"

"Maybe you could provide some information. Like you said, you have connections."

He looked me up and down. "Information isn't part of Spark's wish fulfillment. I deal in the tangible."

"Just not inside your club."

"I have a lot to lose. That's why I'm careful what I allow inside my club."

"You have rules about what you allow to happen here. I'm wondering what happens when someone breaks those rules."

"It depends. I have a zero tolerance policy when it comes to drug dealers and sex workers. Neither is permitted on the premises. People can show up already intoxicated. They can go outside and do whatever they want, but in here, I run a clean business." Kincaid sighed. "Based on your questions, I take it you're here to work. You know I have rules about that too. I don't want any of my members to think I let someone spy on them."

"That's not my intent. I'm waiting for Almeada."

"You need legal advice?"

"Not yet. We'll see how the night plays out."

Kincaid picked up his glass and clinked it against mine before downing the shot and pouring another. I took another sip, assessing the club owner. Axel Kincaid had a juvie record a mile long. He'd also been one of the best car thieves around. Supposedly, he was reformed. He went legit, bought a club, and ran a self-proclaimed clean business, except for the illegal casino he ran out of the back room and whatever off-property events he orchestrated for his interested members.

He'd been careful to keep me away from anything too horrific. Even though we'd bonded over our shared disdain for my father specifically and the police department in general, he knew we could easily end up on opposite sides of an issue. And since we shared an attorney and several clients, that would be bad for both of us.

"You're dialed into a lot of things," I said. "Maybe you can help me with something. It could be beneficial to us both."

Kincaid made a noncommittal gesture and waited for me to go on.

"Someone's been ripping off gamblers. I know of three people who have had their bank accounts drained by someone pretending to be interested in paying them back for a jackpot they won."

"That sounds...ridiculous."

"The scam is a little more complicated than that. It's always a variation, but it's an offshoot of the same premise." I gave him the details, leaving out names and locations. "I was curious if anyone at Spark has experienced something similar."

"If anything like that happened here, I'd take care of the scammer."

"You have fifty pounds of lye and a shovel in your trunk too?"

Kincaid didn't answer. He didn't find that funny because, unlike me, he was serious about eliminating the problem permanently. Who knew what he could be hiding in his trunk?

"So you haven't heard anything about this happening in other establishments? You're dialed in to the competition. I'd think you would have heard something," I said, hoping to goad him into answering my questions.

"You're the private detective. Shouldn't you have some idea who's responsible?" Kincaid knew something, but he didn't want to speak out of turn. He wanted me to show my hand first.

"A woman approached all three victims. She used different names and changed her appearance, but I have some idea who it could be."

"You have me waiting on tenterhooks."

"Jasmine O'Neal. In one instance, she introduced herself as Claudia Bellman."

"The online marketer?"

"You know her?"

Kincaid grinned. "I know of her."

"Of course, you do."

"She approached me a few weeks ago." Kincaid went to the cash register and popped open the drawer. Beneath the tray, he had her business card. "She was doing research on gambling, how it exists outside of the major hubs, where gamblers go, and what they enjoy."

"Did she tell you why she wanted to know those things?"

"She's working on an advertising campaign. She was in the research phase. Once she collects enough data, she plans to construct some webpages, set up advertising to boost online traffic, and see if anything takes off. Given the nature of the campaign, she wants to make sure she attracts the right crowd. That's why she came here. She thought I'd have valuable insights to share."

"What did you tell her?"

"That I had no interest in sharing proprietary information."

"How did she take that?"

"She offered to mention Spark at no cost. I declined."

"You don't like her method of organic advertising?"

"The internet is full of shit. I run a decent business. I'm not looking to expand. She wanted to use Spark for her personal gain, as fodder for her websites and social media pages. I have no interest in being exploited like that, despite whatever supposed benefits would go along with the so-called free advertising. Truth be told, I have a very specific clientele. What she's doing relies mostly on bottom-feeding scum. I have standards. Should I wish my business to expand, I'll let it happen naturally, but I find it best to keep a low profile. Word of mouth is why new members seek me out. It's what led you to showing up at my doorstep."

"That was Freddy's doing."

"You're proving my point. It keeps things at a nice steady simmer, if you will."

"How did she take the rejection?" I asked.

"I'm not concerned."

"I'm guessing your bank account would be significantly more substantial should she decide to empty it out."

"She'd never be able to touch it," Kincaid said. The unspoken threat hung in the air, as if the sentence remained unfinished. "What I don't understand is why she'd be involved in scamming her potential audience. That would be bad for business. It would deter gamblers from future gambling endeavors."

"I don't get that either."

"But you're sure she's behind it?"

"Sure is subjective."

Kincaid thought about what I said. "I have some

business to attend to. Are you planning on joining the game later tonight?" He indicated the hallway which led to the back room where he held illegal poker games.

"I haven't decided yet."

"You should."

TWENTY-EIGHT

Almeada sat beside me and ordered an Old Fashioned. "I hope you weren't waiting long."

"Kincaid kept me company."

Almeada sipped his drink. "That's why you look like that."

"What do I look like?"

"Like the wheels are turning in your head. What dumbass idea are you cooking up now?"

"Nothing." I grinned. "Is this a test? You told me not to tell you things."

"I told you not to tell me if you killed someone." Almeada glanced around, but no one had overheard us. Even if they had, discussions like this weren't that uncommon inside the hallowed halls of Spark. "What did Kincaid say?"

"He invited me to play poker tonight."

"That's the last thing you need with everything going on."

"I'm not going to lose my shirt or bet my pink slip, if that's what you're worried about."

"Do people do that?"

"I've seen it happen."

He swiveled on his stool, scoping out the VIP section for a table. Once he spotted an empty one away from everyone else, we made our way to it and sat down. I didn't consider myself a regular. I came here on occasion, mainly to play or blow off steam. But my attorney was a frequent flyer. However, since he was usually here to conduct business, no one hovered near our table or bothered to ask if we wanted bottle service or refills. They assumed this was another of Almeada's client meetings. Maybe it was.

"You aren't billing me for this, are you?" I asked.

"I wasn't planning on it, but if you're offering—"

"I'm not."

"Too bad." He watched the entertainment in the nearest cage. "Have you figured out what to do about Darrow?"

"No."

"What about the Kershaw situation?"

"Jasmine O'Neal has been researching gambling establishments. I'm not sure when that started. I just found out she approached Kincaid a few weeks ago for tips and tricks. That may explain why she was at Chelsea's, the mahjong parlor, and that online casino. She should be in the process of setting things up that will appeal to an audience of gamblers who don't necessarily care if what they're doing is illegal." I mulled it over. "I need to find out who her client is. It's stupid for her to use that research to run these scams. That would make getting caught a lot easier."

"Apparently not, since you have nothing but conjecture."

"That's not helpful."

"It's called free advice."

But now that I had the thought, I couldn't shake it. "Maybe she's not running these scams. Or her alleged research isn't research. It's just the excuse she's giving people. Well, Kincaid, since he's the only one who's mentioned this to me."

"If she is conducting research, she would have spoken to other club owners and people running afterhours games. That shouldn't be too hard for you to figure out. Make a few calls. You know people. Hell, you used to play at every underground game there was."

"That's when I was more fun."

"Fun? That's when I'd get calls at four o'clock in the morning from lockup." He eyed me. "You're less attention-seeking now, but you have yet to lose that self-destructive streak."

"Are we back on the subject of Darrow?"

"What are you going to do about him?"

"I'll figure it out when the time comes. For now, this is about containment. I don't have to put out the fire, but I have to make sure it doesn't spread." I reached for my phone and left a message for Justin. We had to find out if the photos and videos Darrow had collected could be found online or if he'd gotten them through a more thorough search. "I hate this for Kershaw. He's been scammed and attacked. Now, he's potentially the target of future blackmail."

"Do you know if anyone's out to get him?"

"That's just it," I said. "He doesn't have enemies. There's no rhyme or reason to this." I had Darrow check. He'd done that deep dive and didn't find anything, or so he said. Maybe he had. "Are the police really going to pay O'Neal a visit?"

"I suggested they should. I don't know if they will, but Kershaw believed she could be responsible for stealing his money. After making that claim to authorities, he was attacked. They have a responsibility to follow up." Almeada checked his phone for messages.

"When is that happening?"

"It should have happened earlier, after the police spoke to Kershaw at the hospital, but they've had trouble locating O'Neal. She wasn't at work. When they went by her home, she wasn't there either."

"In that case, I could have knocked."

"Knowing you, you may have found the door unlocked."

"It happens."

"Only when you shove your picks into the lock first."

"Unlocked is unlocked. I can't be expected to know exactly how it happened."

"Right now, you have more than enough on your plate.

Don't go looking for trouble."

"Speaking of, I should really get back to the office. I need to check on a few things."

"I thought you were playing cards with Kincaid."

Dammit. I wanted to go through Darrow's research and see if there was something I missed, but Kincaid's parting words suggested if I stuck around he'd get me what I wanted, and that wasn't an eight ball or a sexy companion. It was a break in this case. "I guess I'll be heading back to the office afterward." I gave Almeada a sideways look. "Are you sure you don't want to play a few hands? It'll be fun."

"I'm paying for our drinks tonight. I'm not handing over my money to you. That is not how our relationship works."

"You like it better when I pay you."

Almeada smiled. "That's always worked out best for us. Why mess with the status quo?"

"I thought it might be exciting to change things up."

"If you want to get paid, I'll let you do some investigating for one of my clients. However, I usually deduct that from your tab instead. Would you rather me hand you the cash, so you can hand it back to me with a bit more on top?"

I pointed at him. "This is why I'm not as much fun as I used to be."

"It's called growing up, Lucien. You have more responsibilities now."

We parted ways near the bar. Almeada had a car waiting to take him home. I didn't have that luxury. Instead, I'd parked my new Porsche in the side alley with the other exotic sports cars.

A few weeks ago, I'd seen a guy bet his pink slip at the poker table. I couldn't imagine ever being that drunk or desperate, but maybe if my bank account had a couple more zeroes, I wouldn't care so much.

"Are you ready to play, Lucien?" Kincaid asked, coming up beside me. He clapped me on the back. "A couple of tables are heating up." He gestured to the rear hallway. "You know the way."

"I need another drink first."

"I'll have one brought to you."

I went down the familiar path and waited for the bouncer outside the interior door to let me inside. I wasn't sure the man was a bouncer. Kincaid had referred to him as his general manager, but he looked more like security, armed security. No one was permitted to carry a weapon without Kincaid's approval. Yet, when I installed his security system, he didn't ask for metal detectors. Instead, he had plenty of eyes in the sky to keep watch on things, like the cage bosses at a casino.

I slid into an empty chair at one of the tables. "What are we playing tonight?"

"Seven card."

Nodding, I reached into my pocket, pulled out the cash, and waited for the dealer to exchange it for a corresponding stack of chips. "Best of luck," I said to my competition.

Poker was a way to decompress after a long day. The risk was monetary. At least within these walls, no one was going to get murdered. Briefly, I wondered if Kincaid would take cheaters into a back room where they'd be beaten or worse. But I didn't want to think too hard about that.

I looked around the table at the competition. I recognized most of the people, except for the woman sitting across from me. I'd seen enough photos of Jasmine O'Neal to know that wasn't her, unless she'd gotten even better at her disguises. But I didn't think Kincaid would allow O'Neal inside his club after turning her offer down. Given my suspicions concerning her and the three victims, I couldn't help but think she'd hold a grudge against Kincaid. He'd want to make sure she kept her distance.

"Hey," Dennis Powers, a client who had followed me from one career to the other, nudged me, "I had a system crash the other day. I'm wishing I'd gone with you on the cyber security front and not just the hardware installation. Any chance I could get an upgrade and you could fit me in sometime this week?"

"Call the office in the morning," I said. "I'll move some things around."

"Thanks."

"No problem."

The woman across the table kept my attention. Her chip pile was dwindling, but she wasn't playing aggressively. She'd fold after making her first bet. No one played like that. It served no purpose. Not once did she see her bet through.

I kept an eye on her for the next few hands. Her tactics didn't change. I'm sure the other players noticed, but they didn't care. She was padding the pot for them.

"Do you work for Kincaid?" I asked.

She looked up, the confusion evident on her face. She made a show of looking to her left and right before pointing to her chest. "I'm sorry. Did you ask me something?"

"I asked if you work here?"

The three other people at the table looked annoyed that I had stopped the game to ask a question.

"No," she said.

"My mistake." I tried charming. "I thought you may have been one of the dancers. Every single one of them is objectively beautiful, just like you."

She returned my smile. "Flirting will get you nowhere, Mr. Cross."

"I didn't realize I introduced myself." In fact, no one at the table had used my name, not even Dennis. "What's your name?"

"Tessa."

"I'll try to remember that."

She went with flirtatious, but I wasn't buying it. However, I held the smile, feeling very much like I'd walked into a scene from *Casino Royale*. As long as I didn't let her seduce me, I'd have nothing to worry about.

"All in." She pushed her tiny stack into the middle of the table.

I matched her bet, tossing my chips into the center. "I call."

The guy to my left with the hoodie and sunglasses wasn't going to let us duke it out alone. He decided to raise. The other players folded.

I met his raise, setting up a side bet. My cards were

trash. The odds I'd win were abysmal, but I wanted to play this out. Once we laid down, the rest of the players would play more aggressively against me, believing everything was a bluff, and I'd be able to take them to the cleaners. But that wasn't my main objective.

Right now, I wanted to see what Tessa planned to do or why she'd been determining every players' tell without giving anything away. Maybe she finally had that winning hand, but I didn't think so. She wanted an excuse to leave. She didn't like that I'd confronted her.

Once we flipped our cards, Tessa was out of chips. I hadn't bet enough to lose my shirt. I was only down by half. There'd be plenty of opportunities to recover. If she were here to play cards, she would find more cash and start playing for real. Instead, she pushed her chair out and picked up her wine glass. I wasn't surprised.

"Good game, gentlemen." She avoided eye contact as she headed for the door.

I shuffled my chips with one hand, watching until she disappeared from sight. Then I anted up and played three more hands. Revealing my bluff gave the guy in the hoodie a false sense of victory. He played more aggressively. For a winner, he shouldn't be on tilt, but he was excited.

I folded on the fourth hand, surprised when Dennis went all in.

Poker gave me insight into human behavior. Once the players around me became predictable, I'd cash out. However, I hadn't predicted that last hand. I needed to pay more attention. Tonight was a bad night to play. I wasn't focused. Tessa had derailed me.

"Shit." Hoodie stared at the cards in front of him. Dennis had a straight flush. Hoodie only had two pair. That wasn't a great hand to go all in, not with five-figures on the line.

Dennis smiled and raked in his winnings, carefully stacking his chips beside him.

Hoodie checked his pockets a few times, but he didn't have any more cash. If he had an expensive watch or pink slip in his pocket, he would have exchanged it for more chips, but he didn't have anything of value on him. He pointed a finger at Dennis. "Next time. I mean it. Next time."

"I'll be here." Dennis finished stacking his chips.

Could a poker game be what caused the scammer to target Alan Kershaw? I let that thought float around the back of my mind. The deposits in his account didn't indicate any recent or large wins. Whoever ripped off his bank account didn't appear to have done it to get back the money they lost. Still, I couldn't entirely dismiss the possibility, regardless if O'Neal was behind the scam or not. After all, she'd played against Kershaw. Had she lost big to him?

The dealer kept an eye on Hoodie while she shuffled the cards. Hoodie was mad, but he wasn't going to try anything. His body language didn't indicate he was ready for a fight. In fact, he looked defeated and tired.

"Watch my chips," I said. "I'll be back in a few minutes." I picked up my empty glass, indicating that was the reason I was leaving the table.

I returned to the bar before Hoodie made it out of the back room. Spark's regular crowd kept the bartenders busy, and with Kincaid otherwise occupied in the VIP section, I didn't have to worry about anyone rushing to get me a refill.

Hoodie trudged toward me, his face buried in his phone. He took a seat five stools away, not even noticing I was there. However, Tessa noticed and made sure to avoid looking at me. Despite her earlier flirtation, she didn't want to talk to me. As soon as Hoodie tucked the phone away, she appeared behind him.

From this distance, I couldn't hear what they were saying, so I picked up my glass and moved closer, pushing my way between two of the occupied stools while I attempted to flag down the bartender.

"Tough table," she said. "Who knocked you out?"

"Powers," Hoodie said. "That guy has the best luck. He won the other night too. He's really been cleaning house lately."

"So I heard." She ran her hand along his forearm. "Better luck next time."

"You too." Hoodie waited for the shot to be delivered, downed it in one gulp, and headed for the exit.

Tessa went back to her table. She didn't acknowledge me, but I knew she'd seen me. I didn't think she and Hoodie had been working together to cheat at poker. If they had, they were the two worst cheaters on the planet.

We weren't playing blackjack, so counting cards was out. But this woman was up to something.

Once I got my refill, I returned to the poker game. Kincaid joined me at the table, taking the seat left by Hoodie. He pushed his rolled-up sleeves higher on his forearms and slouched in the chair.

"Is everyone having fun?" Kincaid asked.

Powers grinned. "I'm hot again tonight."

"It looks like it." Kincaid glanced at the dealer. She gave him a half shrug. For the briefest moment, I wondered if she was feeding Powers winning hands, but I didn't think so. The only reason that would happen would be if Kincaid wanted it to happen, and he wouldn't risk angering everyone else by doing that. The look was meant as a way for him to ask if she thought Powers was cheating. "What about you, Lucien? Is this what you wanted?"

"Not exactly."

"I'll have to work on that." Kincaid gestured to a server to bring me another drink, even though I'd just gotten one.

I left it untouched beside me. As soon as I broke even, I excused myself. I wasn't in the mood to play. I wasn't sure what I wanted to do, but it wasn't this. I thought Kincaid had intel for me, but it no longer seemed like it.

Once I was back inside the main room of the club, I spotted Tessa lingering near the bar. Her actions had made me suspicious, or maybe that was a result of Kincaid's earlier suggestion. Either way, I couldn't help myself. Instead of making an approach, I decided to keep an eye on her. I had to know who she was and what she was doing.

TWENTY-NINE

I waited outside in my car, figuring I'd follow her when she left. That would be the fastest way to gain intel. And if she left with someone, then I'd know that too.

Tessa, last name unknown, wasn't a regular member of Spark. At least she hadn't been when Kincaid had me run background checks on his members. Assuming she hadn't recently joined, she was here with someone. Hoodie left, so I didn't think they were together.

She knew my name. I didn't like that. I wanted to know if she planned to target me or if she'd researched every one of Spark's poker players. It may have been the paranoia rearing its ugly head, but I suspected she had something to do with Jasmine O'Neal.

George, Kincaid's doorman and head of security, knocked on my window and gestured that I roll it down. "Is there a problem?" he asked.

"No problem. I'm waiting to sober up a little. For some reason, the police love to pull me over."

"It's the car," he said.

"Really? I thought it was my name."

"That could be too, but I'd think they'd be afraid to mess with their boss's son."

"They're not that smart."

George looked like he wasn't buying it. "Mr. Kincaid would be happy to let you sober up inside."

"I don't want to be an inconvenience."

George wasn't buying that either. "Mr. Kincaid isn't comfortable with you conducting business on the property."

"Powers asked if I could take a look at things for him. I didn't instigate."

"That's not what Mr. Kincaid was referring to."

"I'm not on the property. I'm outside."

"You're parked in the alley. Kincaid considers this part of the property."

"Axel knows what I'm doing out here. We had a conversation earlier."

George tried to open my door, but like anyone who grew up with a cop for a father, I locked my doors the second I got inside the car. "Come inside. Mr. Kincaid would like to have a word." George didn't threaten or bully. Instead, he turned and headed for the side door. Once he reached the door, he pulled it open and waited for me, his arms crossed over his chest. That left no room for argument.

I ran a hand through my hair and went through the side door. It opened at the rear of the hallway, allowing me a glimpse of the locker room and other offices on my way to Kincaid's.

George waited for me to enter and closed the door behind me. He didn't join us.

Kincaid was behind his desk, watching the hidden camera feeds on his monitor.

"I thought you'd still be playing," I said.

"I lost interest after you left. Your friend, Mr. Powers, has been on one hell of a winning streak lately."

"Do you think he's cheating?"

Kincaid shook his head. "Marcy would have noticed."

"Are you sure she isn't behind it?"

He chuckled at the screen in front of him. "I would have noticed."

I cleared my throat. Being in Kincaid's office always made me nervous. I wasn't sure why, but I didn't like the feeling. I liked it even less that he knew that. "What can you tell me about Tessa?"

"The woman who left the table before I arrived?" Kincaid knew everything, but he liked to pretend he didn't until it served his purposes to be the smartest man in the room. That was something else I didn't like. "How would I know anything about her?"

"Is she the reason you wanted me to join the poker game tonight?" I sunk into the oversized chair across from his desk. "I've run background checks on your members since that's what you hired me to do. She isn't familiar. That tells me she isn't a regular, or she's new. Which is it?"

"She's been showing up on the nights Spark offers poker in the back room. She always gets in as someone's guest. George has pointed out that she'll hang around outside. As soon as someone shows up alone, she'll make her way to the door, chat them up, and get in under the guise of guest. We've been letting her do this for the last few weeks to see what she does."

"What does she do?"

"She loses a lot of money at the tables."

"Always?"

"Always."

"Why?" I asked.

"I was hoping you could tell me that."

"She knows my name," I said.

"A lot of people know your name, Lucien. Half of them are your clients. People talk."

"Maybe, but we've never been here on the same nights, at least not that I recall."

"No, you haven't."

"Are you sure she doesn't know any of the members?"

"She might. I can't be sure. I thought that might be something you could look into."

"And I thought business was slow." Getting up, I indicated his monitor. "Do you mind?"

Kincaid scooted over, making room behind his desk.

I rewound the footage, finding a good shot of her before snapping a photo with my phone. "Let's see what facial rec turns up." I sent the image to Amir, knowing he'd already left for the night, but I had hired staff to man the lab 24/7. Someone else would get the message and get started on that.

Returning to the live feed, I zeroed in on Tessa. She remained at a table near the bar. She had a wine glass in front of her, but she didn't have any interest in finishing it.

"Do you think this woman has something to do with Jasmine O'Neal or her marketing firm?" Kincaid asked.

"You tell me."

"She might."

"Might?"

Kincaid smiled again. He knew something, but he was waiting for the perfect moment to execute the big reveal.

"Has anyone approached her?" I asked.

"Tonight?"

"Any night."

"On occasion. It always looks like harmless flirtation or brief conversations. Nothing overtly suspicious."

I gave him a sideways look. "How closely do you monitor your guests?"

"I'm an astute proprietor."

"Uh-huh."

Kincaid left the current feed from the bar playing on one monitor before cycling through the other camera feeds on the other monitor. "Since I have you here, I was wondering if you know this guy." He pointed to a person on the screen dressed in Spark's server uniform. "Fox performed the background check, but he thinks we're missing something."

"Are you screwing with me? That's Malloy. He and I went through the academy together before I got kicked out."

"He's a cop?"

"He was the last I heard, but now he looks like a waiter. Times are tough, I guess."

"They're about to get a lot tougher."

I didn't like that, but I didn't voice it. Kincaid wasn't stupid enough to hurt a cop. He valued his freedom far too much.

"Do you think Tessa could be a cop too?" he asked.

"That would explain how she knows my name." I

thought back to Detective Taylor. "Give me a sec." I sent the photo of Tessa to Sara and then I dialed her number. When she answered, I asked, "Is she one of yours?"

"Lucien—"

"A cop, Sara. Is she a cop?"

"No."

"Are you sure?"

"I can't be certain, but she doesn't work out of this precinct."

"All right. Thanks." I hung up before she could ask me any questions. My phone buzzed a moment later. Sara was calling back. Instead of answering, I sent her a text, told her I was in the middle of conducting surveillance, and would call her back as soon as I was finished.

"All right. Since you answered my question, I'll answer yours." Kincaid handed me a business card. *Tessa Gold – Gold Bar Gaming.* "She claims to represent a gaming company from Atlantic City that was looking to expand. Spark may be new, but it's gained quite the reputation. Tessa wanted to check out the operation."

"When did she approach you?"

"A few weeks ago."

"After you turned down Jasmine O'Neal?"

Kincaid nodded. "I'm having trouble believing that's a coincidence."

"Did you check her out?" I asked.

"Not in the way you mean."

"You don't know if she's legit?"

"Fox is looking into it. He has contacts in AC who work with the gaming commission."

"I assume she must have ties to Jasmine O'Neal."

"One would think Jasmine would have started her research there. The place is lousy with casinos and all sorts of gambling, legal and illegal. With all those opportunities, I don't see why she'd bother with anything local."

Given the song and dance Vincent had performed for me, I had to assume if any of this was legit, the client was local, which meant O'Neal wanted to hit the local market and target the proper demographics, the people who didn't want to make the drive but still wanted to divest themselves of their money as quickly and easily as possible.

"I guess I'll have to ask O'Neal when I talk to her." I nodded to the live feed. "Do you want me to ask Tessa a few questions in the meantime?"

"You know I don't appreciate you conducting business inside Spark. Interrogations at the bar could scare away my members."

"Since you know who she is, is that why you've been letting her get away with sneaking into Spark?"

"I'm not sure who she is," Kincaid said, his voice becoming harsh. "I know who she claims to be, but it hasn't been verified."

"Why would she lie about that?"

"She could be working for Jasmine. After all, you said Jasmine's been using disguises to sneak into other establishments. Hiring someone to do the dirty work wouldn't be beneath her. It'd be the next step to gaining the intel she wants."

I let everything sink in. The knowledge overload threatened to trigger one of my headaches. This was a lead. It had to be. Though, my stance on coincidences existing was again shaken. "Did you happen to mention me to Tessa in conversation?"

"No."

"That makes this more interesting, doesn't it?"

"I wouldn't call that interesting."

"That's why you're not a private detective." I glanced at the other monitor, spotting Fox speaking to Malloy. "Do you want to clue me in as to why an undercover cop is working at your club?"

Kincaid pretended he didn't hear the question.

"Why are you under investigation?"

"Ask your father."

"Do you think Malloy's the only one?" I asked.

Kincaid glanced from one monitor to another. "He's the only new hire. His background check came out a little too perfect. That's why Fox was suspicious. We've been keeping an eye on him ever since."

"When did he start working here?"

"A few days after Tessa showed up."

It could have been unfortunate timing, but it was all very strange. "Where did you meet Tessa?"

"She showed up one morning after we closed, knocked on the door, and introduced herself. Everyone had gone home. I gave her a quick tour. She gave me her business card, and we talked business." Kincaid's eyebrows inched upward suggestively.

"Do you sleep with everyone who knocks on your door?" I asked.

"Feeling left out, Lucien?"

"You're a good-looking guy, but no. I'm just not sure how one thing led to another. If she was here on business, how did she end up in your bed?"

"She's a closer. She wanted to close the deal."

"What deal?"

Kincaid considered my point, as if the thought had never struck him before. Had this man never been rejected? I assessed his suit, silk shirt, and the tousled way he wore his hair. Maybe I should give that a try. Or maybe it was the fleet of Maseratis and Bugattis outside that made him irresistible. "I'm not sure," he admitted.

"Did you sleep with Jasmine O'Neal too?"

"No."

"Did Tessa come on to you?"

"She's beautiful. It wasn't one-sided."

Sleeping with the club owner would make him a little less suspicious and a little more open to allowing her to hang out at his club. "Is there anything else you can tell me?"

"Interrogations bore me, Lucien. At least the way you do them."

"This isn't an interrogation."

"It feels like one."

"You want to be interrogated, ask Malloy to do the honors."

Kincaid held up a finger. "Wait here."

THIRTY

Before I could object, Axel Kincaid left the office.

Edging around his desk, I reached for the keyboard. Since I'd installed the security cameras, I knew where most of them were. I also knew Kincaid had several on a private system that only he monitored. All I had to do was figure out how to log into that system.

Before I could get in, the office door opened. Kincaid ushered Malloy into the room. *Dammit, what was his first name? James? Jerry? Julius?*

"Mr. Kincaid, I don't—" Malloy stopped midsentence. "Lucien fucking Cross."

"Hey, you even remembered my middle name." I gave him a big smile and sunk into Kincaid's chair. "How are you...Jebediah?"

Malloy glared at me. "Still with the wisecracks, I see."

"It seems you weren't very truthful on your application." Kincaid made a tsk noise and stood in front of the door, blocking Malloy from leaving. "You can correct that by telling us why you're here."

"The city pays shit." Malloy looked back at me. "You know that."

"So you're moonlighting." Kincaid nodded, as if he

believed him, which he didn't. "Why didn't you disclose that on your application? In fact, Mr. Malloy, you didn't even list your real name or social security number. Should I contact someone about fraud and identity theft?"

"A lot of that going around right now," I said.

"We're not interested in you, Mr. Kincaid. Not this time." Malloy sighed. "We needed access to your club."

"And you knew I'd never agree. Do you have a warrant?" Kincaid asked.

"No."

Kincaid remained still. Dangerous energy radiated off him, electrifying the air. Even across the room, I felt it. Surely, an undercover cop like Malloy picked up on it too.

"Hey," I said, hoping to keep the cop from getting ripped to pieces, "how about you tell us who's on your radar?"

"I can't do that."

"You're going to." Kincaid hadn't moved. His voice sounded like a growl.

"Cross," Malloy didn't look at Kincaid for fear he'd be incinerated by the death glare, "you know how ops work. I can't say."

"Your cover is blown. Give us the name and we won't file a complaint or sue the department for abuse of power, among other things," I promised. Kincaid's glare shifted to me, but I didn't cower. Instead, I looked him straight in the eye. "Isn't that right, Axel?"

After a silent battle of wills, Kincaid tilted his head to the side. "Accept before I take the offer off the table."

"Vice is looking into reports of a grifter preying on gamblers. Since Spark is rumored to have cards and betting on the premises, I was sent to gather intel," Malloy said.

"This is a nightclub. There is no such activity on the premises," Kincaid said. "I dare you to find evidence to the contrary."

To his credit, Malloy held his ground. "If you say so."

Kincaid was careful about who he allowed entry to the back room, that included staff. Since Malloy was new. He'd been kept away from that room and the hallway.

"Who's the grifter?" I asked.

Malloy shook his head. "I don't know."

"What about the victims? Who's already been targeted?"

"You're a real piece of work, Cross. Are you doing this to spit in daddy's face? I always knew you were no better than a criminal. You never saw things black and white. You always wanted to operate in the grey. That's how you got kicked out."

"Tonight, the tables have turned." Kincaid opened the door, revealing the bouncer from earlier. "Fox, take him to collect his belongings and escort him from the premises. If he shows up again, he better have a warrant with him." Kincaid leaned in close. "Mr. Cross may have threatened legal actions, but I'm not nearly as civilized. Make sure I don't see you again or no one will ever see you again."

Malloy gave him that hardened, dead-eye stare most cops mastered by the time they graduated from patrol. "Oh, I'll see you again, Mr. Kincaid. I imagine sooner rather than later."

Fox pulled Malloy from the room before Kincaid could do anything stupid and gave his boss a warning look. I'd seen that look thousands of times on Justin's face. Apparently, I wasn't the only one who needed his employees to keep him in line.

"That could have gone better," I said.

Kincaid glared at me. "Get out of my seat."

I held up my palms and stepped away from his computer. "Do you believe him?"

"The cop?" Kincaid asked, as if the notion threatened the very fabric of his reality. "I find it hard to believe that any undercover operation being conducted inside my club without my consent doesn't have anything to do with me."

"Usually, I'd agree. Right now, I'm not sure."

Kincaid hated the police more than I did. Everything he did was to minimize the chances of police interference. He didn't want anyone to OD or get shot inside his club, which is why he kept out drugs and weapons. He also kept sex workers out so vice would have less reason to come knocking and fewer opportunities to turn a low-level criminal into a snitch.

Champagne Problems

I pointed to the monitor. "You said they showed up around the same time. Assuming what Malloy said is true, the police must have gotten a tip or some piece of intel that led them here." Taylor told me Kershaw wasn't the first. Maybe that's why Malloy was investigating.

"You think he's interested in Tessa?" Kincaid settled behind his desk and checked the previously recorded footage. "I never saw the two of them make contact."

"Either that or she tipped him."

"Are you sure she's not a cop?"

"I'm pretty sure," I said.

"I need you to be certain."

"I'll find out."

Kincaid sighed. "How long will that take?"

"It depends."

"On what?"

I jerked my thumb toward the door. "How badly is your guy going to rough up Malloy?"

"Fox won't touch him."

I stood, buttoning my jacket and heading for the door. "That should make this a little easier."

"What about Tessa?"

"Keep an eye on her for me."

I went out the side door which opened into the alley. My car remained where it was. George had returned to his post out front. I peered around, looking for a dark sedan with the telltale bars, but Malloy was smarter than that. He didn't drive an unmarked to the club. But there was no way an undercover cop would be given a six-figure car to drive while pretending to be a server. The car would have to match his cover identity.

Stepping out of the alleyway, I looked around until I found the most nondescript vehicle on the street. It was white. A basic model. Nothing fancy or special about it. The kind of car that would get the driver from point A to point B without a problem, but the ride wouldn't necessarily be smooth or quiet and there was a good chance the air conditioner or radio didn't work.

I moved down the street, keeping my hands at my sides. Once I was close enough to see Malloy inside, appearing to

- 198 -

be in conversation with himself, I picked up the pace. More than likely, he was calling to report his cover had been blown. If I hurried, I could offer to corroborate his side of things to his superior.

Knocking on the window, I gave him a big, friendly wave and tugged on the door handle. Unlike me, he hadn't learned to lock his doors. That was stupid. I would have mentioned it, but he was already having a bad enough night. *Honey not vinegar*, I reminded myself.

"Lucien, the fuck are you doing now?" he asked, stabbing the disconnect on his phone. "Are you here to gloat? Because I have half a mind to bring you in for interfering in a police investigation."

"I didn't know you were undercover. Kincaid asked if I recognized you. I answered truthfully. Whatever happened wasn't my fault." God, what was his name? It was a J. Jonas? No. It wasn't that. I already tried Jebediah. What about Jeremiah? No, that would be too bullfroggy. "Jeremy," I said.

His eyes flicked to mine. "What?"

I grinned. *Got it right.* "I'm sorry."

"Yeah, fine. Whatever. What are you even doing here?"

"Working."

"I should have known you worked for Kincaid."

"I don't work for Kincaid. Okay, technically, I installed his security system, but I'm not here because of that."

Malloy's eyes lit up. "You installed his security system?"

"Focus," I said. "I was hoping we could help each other out. I feel bad about busting your cover. Let me make it up to you. You said you were looking for a grifter. I take it we're after the same person." Malloy didn't say anything, leaving me to volunteer more information. "My client, Alan Kershaw, was scammed. It didn't happen at Spark. It happened online. My investigation led to two other men who also had their bank accounts drained. Again, not at Spark. I'm pretty sure it's the same scammer, possibly Jasmine O'Neal or someone who connects to her."

"Good Day Marketers." Malloy affirmed what I already suspected. "We don't have any proof. Do you?"

"Nothing concrete."

"That doesn't help me."

"What does Tessa Gold have to do with any of this?"

Malloy eyed the club, giving away the reason he was parked outside. He was waiting for her. "I don't know."

"She told Kincaid she represents a gaming company in Atlantic City. The funny thing about that gaming company, it's named after her."

"Gold Bar Gaming. Yeah, I know. But that could be a coincidence."

"They're teaching that now?" I asked.

"What?"

I shook the pointless musing away. "Have you run a check on it yet?"

"Have you?"

"I just found out about this an hour ago," I said.

"That's how it always works for you. You show up, and bam, you get the information just like that. The rest of us work our asses off and what do we have to show for it? I'll tell you what I got for all my hard work and trouble. Absolutely nothing."

"At least you're not bitter."

"Bite me."

"You sound bitter. I may need some syrup and whipped cream first."

He rolled his eyes. "You're an ass."

"I've been called worse." I peered out the window, but no one had left Spark since our departure. "Let's start over. What do you know about Jasmine O'Neal?"

"She got picked up in a raid not long ago. She told the arresting officers she was conducting research for a marketing campaign, that she didn't realize what she was doing was illegal, and apologized for her ignorance. They gave her a warning and let her go."

"Ignorance isn't an excuse for breaking the law," I said.

"Wow, you remembered something you were taught."

"What else?"

"Good Day Marketers has been on cybercrimes' radar for a while. We've received a few complaints that their practices are questionable. Most of those complaints sounded like they should have been filed with the Better

Business Bureau instead of the police department, but enough claims about using fake identities and misrepresenting themselves gave cybercrimes pause."

"They thought it might be fraud."

Malloy shrugged. "Fraud, identity theft, who knows? Nothing much came from it. But since they've been flagged on the servers, whenever anyone or anything links to them, we take notice."

"O'Neal's arrest did that."

Malloy shrugged again. "The thing is, vice was already interested in identifying a grifter, someone who was preying on gamblers and wiping out their savings. This isn't new. It's an old con. We normally see it with drug dealers or addicts. You commit a crime against someone committing a crime, and they have no recourse without incriminating themselves. The victims don't go to the police, and the thieves get away with it."

"That's what you think is going on here?"

"Someone's doing it. You said you found three guys who had their accounts drained. I can point to half a dozen more that got taken to the cleaners. Our hope is to find out who's responsible."

"Are you working with Detective Taylor on this?" I asked.

"Taylor wants a piece of the action. She always does. Did she tell you about this?"

"We're sort of working together. Well, until I pissed her off." I looked back at the club. If I told Kincaid the PD was looking into Tessa Gold, he could find out why faster, but I wasn't sure what he had in his trunk, so I didn't want to risk it, not until she was safely out of his club. "I don't usually do this," I said, "but maybe we should trade notes."

"Isn't that what we're doing right now?"

"Do you have any other leads we haven't discussed?" I asked.

"Do you?"

I pointed at him. "See, that's the problem. I shared my lead. You need to share yours."

"I don't have any. My cover was compromised, remember?"

"Something led you to Spark. How did that happen?"

Malloy stared out the windshield, debating if he should answer the question. "How did you end up here?"

"Luck."

"That's bullshit."

It wasn't, but I'd prefer if he thought I knew more than I did. It'd make him more likely to share. "I followed you," I said.

He glared at me.

"Taylor," I finally said.

He rolled his eyes. "Figures. She wants this any way she can get it, even if that means going to a private dick."

"I went to her."

"That's even worse."

"Next time, I can come to you."

"Don't. After this, I'd like it if you kept your distance. My career doesn't need to go down in a blaze of glory the way yours did."

"You mean you don't want to run your own security firm and rake in the dough?"

He muttered to himself before saying, "You really think you're something because your pops lets you get away with murder."

I stopped myself before I said something that would reopen that can of worms. Malloy may not have known about the homicide investigation or the other homicide investigation, both of which had painted me as the prime suspect for a while. That didn't go away because of my father. If anything, our relationship only made it worse.

"Sure, I make it a point to avoid law enforcement. In fact, working with anyone in uniform violates the bylaws of my company charter, but I like you. And I feel bad about what happened tonight. I'm willing to make an exception this one time, Jeremy. I'll lay the rest of my cards on the table if you do the same. After that, we go our separate ways."

"No strings?"

"God, I hope not."

THIRTY-ONE

After Malloy got a surveillance unit to sit on Spark and keep tabs on the mysterious Tessa Gold, I took him back to Cross Security. By the time we arrived, the rest of the building was closed for the night. I led him to my office, not bothering with the tour. Even though I'd invited him here, I didn't want him to think this would become a regular thing.

We set up in my office with every whiteboard I could find. Unfortunately, Malloy wasn't keen on sharing most of the details of his investigation with me. He didn't name any of the victims. But I didn't need to know who had been robbed. I could potentially figure those details out on my own, except I hadn't. Sara hadn't said anything to me. Was Malloy on the level about any of this?

"Walk me through your thought process," I said.

"What thought process?"

"How you ended up waiting tables at Spark."

"After Jasmine O'Neal was arrested, we had a unit keep tabs on where she was going. She went there."

"Kincaid told her to leave," I said.

"Right. Cut to O'Neal taking a day trip to Atlantic City."

"You followed her there?" To conduct surveillance

across state lines required jumping through a lot of hoops.

"Unofficially."

"Have you spoken to the Feds?"

"The Feebs wanted us to back off. They said now that we were dealing with an issue involving multiple states, it fell under their jurisdiction. But since we don't know that's the case, my lieutenant told me to stay the course."

"How did he feel about you following a suspect all the way to Jersey?"

"It was my day off. I went for the day to unwind. It's not my fault if I happened to see someone I recognized."

Yet another reminder of why I didn't like the police. They had rules, which they often broke when it suited their purposes. I almost wondered if I was a hypocrite until I remembered I didn't have to follow the same rules, and I wasn't looking to pin a particular offense on a specific party. Whatever happened, happened.

"Don't you want to know where Jasmine O'Neal went?" he asked.

I reached for my coffee cup. "Only if you want to tell me."

Malloy looked confused. "I thought we were sharing intel."

"We are."

"Then why don't you want to know?"

"I want to know," I said. "I was just being—"

"A pain in the ass?"

"Pretty much."

"She went to one of the big name casinos, walks in, and heads over to the coffee shop they have there. Tessa Gold was waiting for her. I took a seat at the table behind them, but I couldn't really hear what they were saying. The acoustics aren't great as it is, and all those damn slot machines kept going off the entire time."

"You didn't bring a directional mic with you?"

"Who the hell do you think I am?"

"I would have brought one."

"How would I have gotten approval? Even if I had, I didn't have a warrant. Plus, how the hell do you think I could have gotten surveillance equipment like that inside a casino? You know they have a million eyes in the sky. I would have been grabbed up and taken into a back room."

"You watch too many movies," I said.

"You don't think that happens?"

"Not if you flash a badge."

"I was cutting corners. As a P.I., I thought you'd understand that." He drained his coffee cup and pushed it closer to me, as if expecting me to get up and get him a refill. "Anyway, they sat at that table for over an hour, chatting. At the end, O'Neal slid an envelope across the table and left."

"What kind of envelope?"

"White #10."

"Was it thick? Thin?"

"It had some bulk."

"Do you think it held cash?"

"I'm not sure. Gold immediately stuck it in her bag. She didn't leave when O'Neal did."

"And you followed O'Neal."

"It was the sound choice. She was my suspect."

"What did she do after she left the coffee shop?"

"She checked out the gaming floor. She didn't linger at any particular table for too long."

"What was she playing?"

"Everything."

"Everything?" I'd been to my fair share of casinos. Most players gravitated toward their favorites. Gambling addicts may bet on anything, but even they had a preference or system in place. "How much did she lose?"

"She only had a hundred dollars in chips to start. When that ran out, she toured the hotel and spoke to a pit boss. After that, she left."

"Did she go anywhere else afterward?"

"No. She seemed skittish, like she was nervous to walk around. Not that I blame her. Some places are sketchy. The hotel was on the main drag, but even that can be questionable at times. You know how the boardwalk gets."

"Was it questionable that day?"

"I didn't notice any shady characters, at least none that appeared threatening or dangerous. But I'm not a woman."

"And you're a cop," I said.

"That too."

"Did she look like she wanted to go elsewhere? Like she had unfinished business?"

"Not really. She just got back in her car and came back to the city."

"She's been infiltrating illegal games around here without batting an eye. I'd think she'd be used to shady characters," I said.

"The local places are less sketchy, not as many drug dealers working the corners outside the places here."

"Have you been following her around here too?"

"I was for a while."

I slid the pad of paper toward him. "I'd like a list of places she's been and anyone she's made contact with." This would save me the trouble of making all those calls.

Malloy jerked his chin up. "Nuh-uh. It's your turn."

"I already told you—"

"Tell me again. This time, don't leave anything out."

Maybe it was the late hour, my frustration with this case and everything going on inside my company, or that Kershaw had been attacked, but I kept my word and told Malloy about my part in the investigation, leaving out Darrow's questionable involvement. "I haven't so much as glimpsed O'Neal, but based on what her associate said, I have to assume everything she's doing is research for a client."

"Do you know who the client is?" Malloy asked.

"No."

"It'd be best if you find that out."

"That's what I was thinking." I finished my coffee and grabbed Malloy's empty mug, refilling them both with what was left in the pot. I pushed it toward him, a reward for his cooperation. Maybe this was how peace treaties were negotiated. Who knows, one day I could be the spunky private eye who got handed clients and tough cases by my buddies with the badges.

The thought rolled around in my brain for a while, at first delighting me, then sickening me. It'd be nice not to worry about getting accused of murder at the drop of a hat, but I'd never fully trust anyone in uniform not to turn on me again. I wasn't stupid or naïve enough to believe anything had really changed inside the department. Sara being the only exception which proved the rule.

"Who has Jasmine O'Neal visited locally?" I asked.

"I was hoping you'd forget."

I pointed to my temple. "Steel trap."

"You already know most of the places." He pointed to the whiteboard I'd filled with details. "Chelsea's, the mahjong parlor, Spark."

"You said you had half a dozen victims that I didn't know about."

"Some of those came from private games."

"All of these games are private."

"I mean invitation only, small group settings."

"Playing poker at a friend's house isn't illegal."

"It isn't."

I stared at Malloy. "Are you going to give me names?"

"No."

"You realize I used to play a lot of cards with a lot of people. I'm going to find out anyway. Save me from having to go through my contacts."

Malloy went to the whiteboard with the marker in hand. He didn't say anything, but he wrote down what I needed to know. I knew every name on the list. I also knew none of the parties hosting the games would talk to me. If I needed details, I'd have to go to the players or victims.

"Why am I not surprised?" I said when he put the marker down. "What about the victims?"

"They didn't want to report it. Everything we have is unofficial or confidential."

"Do you have an informant?"

A strange look came over his face. "Remember what I said earlier about how the victims were being chosen. Think about it." He took another swig from his cup. "It's late. I'm gonna jet. This was fun, Lucien. I'd say we should do it again, but I don't think that's something either of us wants. However," he put his card on the coffee table, "when you get a name for O'Neal's client, the one who wants this gambling stuff researched, gimme a call."

"What's in it for me?"

"You'd be doing your civic duty. Isn't that enough?"

"No."

"What do you want?"

I wasn't sure. "I'll think about it and let you know."

"How about I forget you interfered with a police investigation?"

"That works."

He headed for the elevator. Before he even made it three steps, he'd taken out his phone to check his messages. By now, Spark would have shut down for the night. Tessa must have left, unless she and Axel were closing the same deal again. This time, it would involve handcuffs and whips and it wouldn't end the way she'd want.

Once Malloy was safely in the elevator on his way to the lobby, I called Axel. If he didn't answer, I'd assume Tessa was there. But he answered on the second ring.

"Where is she?" I asked.

"She's staying at a hotel, not as fancy as what I'd expect from someone running her own company. Fox is keeping tabs on her. Do you want the address?"

"And her room number."

"She's staying at the Park Vista. Room 708."

"Is anyone with her?"

"Not that I'm aware. She left Spark alone and entered her room alone."

"Does she know Fox is watching her?"

"No."

"Is he that good?"

"He works for me."

I let that one go. "How long is he planning on sticking around?"

"As long as he wants. He said the police are also keeping tabs."

"Malloy may be joining them."

"I'll let Fox know to keep an eye out."

With all that surveillance, I didn't need to join the party. For all I knew, Tessa Gold could be a misdirect. While we were busy seeing what she was up to, Jasmine O'Neal could be doing anything she wanted. "Would Fox mind letting me know if anything develops? I'd like to be kept in the loop and don't trust the police to do it."

"I'll make sure you get an update." Kincaid hesitated. "From now on, I'll run my new hires through you. I don't need more undercover cops snooping around in my business. Thanks for tonight."

"Sure, Axel. No problem," I said.

THIRTY-TWO

"Lucien," Justin stood in the doorway to my office, "what happened in here?"

"What do you mean?" I'd been pacing the space between the different whiteboards, studying the facts on each one and hoping to come up with something brilliant.

"Did the filing cabinet explode?"

"Why would you ask that?"

Justin pointed.

I turned to see the couch, coffee table, and floor covered in printed copies of Darrow's research. To his credit, Darrow hadn't lied or altered any facts. He'd just kept things from me, which was why I'd pulled all of that out. However, I still hadn't found anything that made the victims overlap. Jasmine O'Neal visited every underground game and online casino she could find. Anyone could be a target, unless the grocery store wasn't as meaningless as it appeared.

"What time did you get in?" Justin asked.

"I came back last night to get some work done. I meant to go home, but I got caught up in trying to make sense of this."

Justin went to the table, spotting the two cups of coffee

sitting there. "Don't tell me you're double-fisting the caffeine now."

"The second one isn't mine."

Justin looked around the room. "Y'know, you don't have to pour a real cup for your imaginary friend. He'd be just as happy with an imaginary cup." He picked it up, inspecting the rim for lipstick smears.

"He's not my friend."

"You poured a cup of coffee for your imaginary enemy?"

"Jeremy Malloy isn't imaginary." I rubbed my eyes. "It's too early in the morning for this."

My assistant moved closer to the boards, studying my notes and updated intel while he waited for me to fill him in on my night.

"Detective Malloy infiltrated Spark, which is where I went last night. While there, I met a woman. One thing led to another, and Malloy and I ended up going over the details of the case together. The three vics we know about aren't the only ones. Right now, Malloy's main lead is Jasmine O'Neal. I need to find out who she's working for and if that has anything to do with what's going on here. We believe she hired Tessa Gold to do some research for her, but that's only a theory at this point."

Justin didn't need a more thorough elaboration. He read my notes off the boards. "Question. If O'Neal is his prime suspect, why is he keeping tabs on the other woman instead?"

"O'Neal's been hard to track down. He was keeping tabs on her, but she's gone quiet. He doesn't have enough for a warrant to bring her in or search her place, but following her led him to Gold, which is why he's now seeing where that leads."

"It could be a misdirect."

"I thought the same thing." I yawned. "I'm not sure. I'm trying to determine which direction to move. Gold is under surveillance, so I'd prefer to keep my distance. But she knows my name, which I find disconcerting."

"Do you think Darrow had anything to do with that?"

I hadn't even thought about that since Darrow hadn't mentioned her. But since he'd been withholding his research, I had no way of knowing. "Do you think we have it backwards? Could Tessa Gold be Jasmine O'Neal's client?"

"That would fit, wouldn't it?" Justin asked. "Gold is hoping to do something with gaming. Based on this," he flicked the business profile I'd put together, "Gold Bar Gaming is nothing but a name. No casinos. No clubs. No nothing. Tessa Gold could be planning on opening something or starting her own underground game, but she would need customers."

"All right, let's say Gold is looking to start her own version of Spark or something along those lines. That would be reason enough for her to hire Good Day Marketers to help generate buzz. But if Gold's the client, why would O'Neal pay her?"

"Maybe that was a refund."

"An envelope of cash? That's a strange way to do business."

"It's one way to avoid taxes."

I reached for my tablet and brought up the business profile the techs had put together on Good Day Marketers. "The marketing firm doesn't rake in that much. Maybe they are taking payments under the table. But does any of this explain why several people have had their savings stolen?"

"Several? How many are we talking?"

"I don't know exactly. Nine, maybe?"

Justin thought about it. "Do you think Gold is stealing the money?"

"It's possible, but I would assume the people with the computers and knowhow would be behind it."

"Good Day Marketers?"

"Yeah."

Justin considered it. "Don't you find it suspicious that the police haven't made an arrest or brought in a suspect?"

"They don't have evidence."

"They have nine reports of people being ripped off. That should give them grounds."

"It should, except things haven't been reported through the usual channels. It's all very convoluted. Malloy said the other six victims don't want to go on the record. The way he said it made it sound like they were confidential informants."

"They could be. He works vice, right? He must have people on the inside who monitor illegal gambling and feed him tips. They may have not wanted to implicate themselves in any illegal activities."

"Yeah, that's what Taylor had said."

"Well, there you go." Justin picked up the two mugs. "Do you want me to get you a fresh cup?"

"Hang on." I took my mug from him and drank the remainder of cold coffee. It went down as smoothly as battery acid. "We still don't know why they're emptying out bank accounts or how they are choosing their victims."

"We don't even know if Good Day Marketers is responsible. That's just your best guess."

"Based on what we know." My gaze flicked to Darrow's notes. What was I missing? What had he found that he hadn't shared? "Do you think Darrow's working for someone else?"

"Lucien," Justin sighed, "I don't know."

"But he could be."

"I wouldn't put anything past that man."

"Me neither."

I scrubbed a hand over my face before going behind my desk and checking to see where Darrow was. According to the GPS in the company car, he was at home. His cell phone pinged in the same area. Unfortunately, I feared he may be smart enough to ditch the car and the phone.

"Do you think we could put a tracker on him?"

"Lucien—"

I held up my hand. "Yeah, I heard it. That's insane. I need to get some sleep. I'll be back after lunch. We'll figure this out then."

"You're joking, right?"

The panic in Justin's voice forced my mind to focus. "Do I look like I'm joking?"

"You have back-to-back meetings all day. And I got your message last night. That's why I came in early, to rearrange the afternoon so hopefully I could figure out where to fit Powers in."

"But we've been having a lull. Business took a hit. No new clients."

"Are you hoping to lose all your current ones too?"

I sighed. "I'm going to need an espresso, unless the medic on staff can give me a straight shot of adrenaline. Actually, see if he can make it a double."

"That would kill you less quickly than your coffee addiction." Justin put the tablet down. "I'll make you an espresso and bring you something to eat. Something healthy. Lots of lean protein and antioxidants."

"So the espresso doesn't kill me as quickly?"

Justin hid his chuckle. "No, so you'll have energy to keep going without crashing."

"When's the first meeting?"

"Eight."

"Wake me at 7:45. I'm going to try to nap until then."

Justin pulled my office door closed behind him. I didn't bother taking off my shoes or unbuttoning my shirt. Instead, I sprawled on the couch and pretended my office wasn't covered in notes.

Unfortunately, sleep didn't come. My thoughts remained on the case. Jasmine O'Neal and Tessa Gold were worlds away from Nathan Boter and the grocery store connection. Why would they choose to scam him? He was a nobody. The risk wasn't worth the minuscule payday. Surely, O'Neal would have known that if she'd been researching these establishments. The same was true for Eric Greene. His bank account had been tiny.

Kershaw was the only target that made sense, except he was the one who didn't fit. He hadn't been engaged in anything illegal when he was scammed. He had no reason not to report it, which was why he did. Was that why he'd been attacked?

The next thing I knew, my door opened. "Lucien?"

"Go away."

Justin entered with a tray containing my breakfast. "Stanhope usually runs late, but you shouldn't count on that." He opened the closet and unzipped a garment bag. "While you eat, I'll call his assistant and see if he's on time today." He picked up my tablet and stabbed at the screen a few times. "There's his client file, in case you want to review it."

"Who do we have after Stanhope?"

"Lindsay."

The first two meetings of the day were softballs. I hoped I could handle them in my sleep since I was far from awake. "All right. See if anything later in the day can be rescheduled. I have some things to do."

"Sleep would be good."

"Yeah. But that will require moving more than one meeting."

"I'll see what I can do." He paused in the doorway. "You know, this is why you aren't supposed to stay up all night when you have work in the morning."

I gave him a look. "This is when I'd normally call Freddy."

Justin didn't like it when I said things like that. "Why haven't you?"

"He's on vacation."

"Is that the only reason?"

On a day like today, it might have been.

THIRTY-THREE

Somehow, I made it through the day without incident. Justin had managed to cancel my lunch meeting and the one after that, so I had a three hour gap in my schedule. Instead of wasting half of that fighting traffic, I left him my phone and slept in my office. Three hours wasn't much, but it was enough for me to function.

The rest of my afternoon moved at a snail's pace. At one point, I almost put my head down on the conference room table. Luckily, Gloria came in with a tray, and I had my third espresso since waking up. The constant tapping against my sternum told me I might have overdone it, but I was awake and still alive at the present.

"Is that the last one?" I asked once the elevator doors closed.

"Yes."

"Good."

"I called you a car to take you home," Justin said. "He should be here soon."

"What about Darrow?"

"He's still here."

"Any updates on Kershaw?"

Justin rocked in his chair. "It can wait until tomorrow."

"Tell me now."

Justin looked like he wanted to protest, but arguing with me would take longer than doing as I asked. "The police didn't find any evidence on the car. They still haven't gotten an ID on the assailant. The canvass didn't turn up much of anything. A few people who'd been working late heard Kershaw's cries for help, but by the time they went to look, the attacker was gone."

"What about security?"

"Kershaw's office is a block away. They didn't hear or see anything."

I wasn't surprised. "Have you spoken to Kershaw?"

"I sent over photos of the other victims and everyone we suspect could be involved. He thought Boter and Steed looked familiar but not from the attack."

"He remembers seeing them at the grocery store."

"That'd be my guess."

"Did you ask if he remembered speaking or interacting with them?"

"He didn't think they ever had a single meaningful conversation."

"Did you tell him who they are?"

Justin nodded. "He figures maybe he's seen them at the register or the customer service desk. But that was the extent of it."

"He didn't recognize anyone else? Not Jasmine O'Neal or Tessa Gold?"

"No."

I didn't think he would. "What about Vincent and Jeff?"

"He thought Vincent looked like he might be the same size as the attacker."

"Did you fill Darrow in on this?" I asked.

"You told me to."

"Yeah." I glanced at Justin's screen. In the corner, he had the tracking software open so he could keep tabs on Darrow.

"He never left the building, boss. The only calls he made were to more costumers. Darrow's hoping to track down information on the disguise O'Neal wore as Claudia Bellman."

I didn't know why he was still on that, but I was too tired to care. "All right. When's my meeting with Powers?"

"At noon tomorrow. He's buying lunch."

That broke one of the basic tenets of schmoozing clients, but Powers wanted to show his appreciation. Since he was on a hot streak and had beaten me at poker, the least I could do was let the guy buy me lunch. "Where are we going?"

"That Japanese steakhouse on Fifth."

I fought to keep from yawning. "Anything else?"

"I pushed your first meeting of the day until ten, so you can sleep in a little. Call the service. A driver will be ready to pick you up and take you to work whenever you're ready to go."

"You set that up and signed the contract for regular service?"

"I did."

"Thanks."

"You got it, boss."

On my way to the lobby, I stopped by Darrow's office. He was sitting on the couch. A family size bag of barbecue potato chips was resting beside him. Crumbs covered his shirt, the couch, and the table. From what I could tell, he was watching football on the large monitor mounted to the wall.

"Who's winning?" I asked.

Darrow peered up at me. "No one's scored yet. I'm just taking a break."

"I don't really care. Stay. Enjoy yourself. It's fine." I tucked my hands into my pockets to keep from touching my hair. "Have you made any progress on the case?"

"Not yet. Have you?"

"Nope."

Darrow went back to watching the game.

"Have you found anything else you may have forgotten to mention?" I asked.

"I don't think so."

"Are you sure?"

He turned to look at me again. "Pretty sure. Why? What's up? Did you find anything?"

"The police didn't come up with any leads on who attacked Kershaw. They believe whoever's responsible isn't connected to the scam. Since you've done so much research, I thought you may have some idea who could be responsible."

"Assuming this was a mugging, I'm guessing it's random."

"Right." I edged toward the door. "Did you happen to run across the name Tessa Gold?"

Darrow's brow furrowed, and he bit his lip. He was trying to appear thoughtful. Instead, he looked constipated. "I don't recall."

"She may be one of Good Day Marketers' clients."

"I thought you were working that angle. I told you I'm sticking with the grocery store."

"Is she a customer or former employee?"

"Hang on." Darrow moved the bag of chips to the table, brushed the crumbs onto the floor, and wiped his hands on the front of his shirt while he made his way to the computer. Opening a spreadsheet, he typed her name into the search box. "No."

I watched the screen, figuring he may have more blackmail or secrets hiding on his computer, but he was too careful to let me see such things. "Thanks for checking."

"Do you want me to build a profile on her?"

"Not yet. Let me get more on the marketing firm first."

"Sounds good." He lumbered back to the couch and grabbed the bag of chips, like it was a security blanket. "Do you want to watch the game with me?"

Again, I found myself wondering if this was an act. For someone who'd been so keen to sign on the dotted line when I asked for his assistance, he no longer had any of that enthusiasm. Instead, he treated the entire situation with utter indifference. Maybe he was really into the game, or maybe he just wanted to be friends.

"I'm heading home. I had a late night."

"Oh really?"

"Good night, Ace."

I pushed the button for the elevator, keeping an eye on his office door. Gloria remained behind the desk. She gave me a sideways look. But she knew better than to say anything when there was a possibility Darrow could overhear us.

She waved to me when I got in the elevator. Depending on how long Darrow hung around the office would determine how long Gloria had to stay. Justin would relieve her if this turned into an all night thing, but maybe this was another of Darrow's tests.

When I made it outside, a town car was waiting for me. The driver stood beside the rear door. "Mr. Cross," he pulled open the door, "would you like to make any stops on the way home?"

"Not tonight." I slid into the back seat.

When we arrived at my apartment building, the driver turned in the seat. "Mr. Cross?"

"Hmm?" I opened my eyes, which I hadn't realized were closed.

"We're here."

"Thanks." I tugged on the door handle before he could offer to get the door for me. "Stay safe."

"Text me when you'd like to be picked up in the morning."

Nodding, I closed the door and headed for my building. My doorman had seen me coming.

"Mr. Cross, there's a cop here to see you."

"Sara?"

"She said her name was Taylor."

I turned, but my driver had already sped away. So much for making a clean break. "In the event she arrests me, call Mr. Almeada."

The doorman gave me a cockeyed look. "Does she have any reason to arrest you?"

"In my experience, that never matters." Not bothering to conceal my yawn, I entered my apartment building. The lush lobby furnishings were more inviting than ever. The decorative rugs looked thick enough that I could curl up on them and sleep for the next ten hours. Instead, I said, "Detective Taylor, what brings you by?"

She glanced at the doorman. "This is a courtesy call."

"Oh really? Are you hoping I'll invite you up to my

place? Because I'm not that kind of guy."

She snorted. "Dream on, buddy."

"That's the plan." I inhaled deeply, hoping the intake of oxygen would wake me up. "Would you mind making this quick?"

"There was another assault last night."

Again, the uncomfortable hammering in my chest started. "Kershaw?"

"No." She studied me closely. "Guess again. I'll even give you a hint. The vic had your card."

"I'm not in the mood for games."

"You're no fun." She moved closer and lowered her voice. "Charlie Steed was attacked outside the grocery store where he works."

"Is he okay?"

"He's a little banged up and shaken, but he'll be fine."

"Any idea who's behind it?"

"I was hoping you could tell me."

"How would I know?" I paused. "Shit. You can't honestly believe I had something to do with this."

She smiled, the glint in her eye bordering on sadistic. "I already ran your alibi. It was a damn good one too. Though, I am wondering what the hell you were doing with Detective Malloy. Aren't I enough of a cop for you? Did you really have to go somewhere else? I don't appreciate the two-timing, Lucien."

"He came on to me."

She waited, but I didn't volunteer any details. "Be careful. Steed had your card on him. Kershaw was your client. Things aren't looking so good for the people around you." She held out her hand. "Take care of yourself, and remember what I said. You find something, I want to know about it."

Confused, I shook her hand, smirking when she pressed an SD card into my palm. "Thanks for dropping by. I figured you'd want a statement or something."

"You're cleared," she said. "For now."

THIRTY-FOUR

Exhausted, I didn't execute all the protocols I usually followed before inserting foreign objects into my hardware. Instead, I grabbed the spare laptop I kept for non-work purposes and dug out an ancient card reader. The video files came from the surveillance camera posted on the side of the grocery store. It had a nice view of the dumpster and the loading doors. No one was around.

Charlie Steed emerged, locked the door, and set the alarm code. After giving the handle a tug to make sure everything was set, he made his way past the dumpster. He was half off the screen when he stumbled backward and crashed into the wall.

The camera didn't catch what caused Steed to stumble. He shook his head and used the side of the dumpster to steady himself. Whoever hit him didn't step into view.

Steed raised both hands to shoulder height. The surveillance footage didn't have sound, but Steed's lips moved. He was saying something. The expression on his face made me think he was trying to negotiate or deescalate the situation. Slowly, he removed the phone and wallet from his pocket and held them out.

"Stupid," I muttered, watching Steed move forward, the

items held in front of him. The smart thing to do would be toss the mugger whatever he wanted and take off running in the opposite direction. But Steed wasn't that smart.

He made it entirely off camera before something flashed across the edge of the screen. Backing it up, I slowed the speed and watched it play again. It looked like the swing of a bat. A few frames later, Steed's shoulder came into view, recognizable only by the shirt he had on.

He dropped to the ground, half of his body visible and jerking, as if someone was kicking or hitting him. Watching the beating made the pit return to my stomach. Finally, the onslaught stopped, or I had to assume it did since I couldn't see what was happening off screen. All I could see was Steed had stopped jerking from side to side.

Then he rolled completely into frame. His face was bloody, the left side already swelling. Blood trickled from his nose, lip, and chin.

I waited, but the assailant was gone. Whoever did this was smart enough to avoid the camera. I wasn't sure how many other cameras there were on the property, but for Taylor to have brought me this, I could only assume this was the best the police had found. Perhaps I could do better.

Too tired to deal with this tonight, I uploaded the video and attached a note. I hoped the techs would pick up my slack. At this rate, they might quit by the end of the week.

Before going to bed, I watched the footage one more time, freezing it when the weapon swing was caught on screen. Even if I couldn't read the black print, I recognized the end of the object. A wooden baseball bat, a.k.a. a Louisville slugger. It had to be the same assailant. There was no way in hell a random mugger happened to target two different neighborhoods and two random men who both connected to me and this case. This was intentional.

When morning came, I hoped I had dreamt the second assault. However, the SD card remained beside my computer. This wasn't a dream, only a nightmare.

I arrived at the office with a million new tasks to add to the list of things I already hoped to accomplish. First and foremost, I had to find out who was behind these assaults. I was halfway through dialing Detective Taylor when the elevator doors opened.

"Lucien," Justin drew my attention away from the phone before I could place the call, "Mr. Steed is here to see you."

Charlie Steed was sitting in our break room. He had a croissant on the plate in front of him and something in a cup that he was sipping with a straw. The man was lucky his jaw wasn't wired shut.

"He showed up on his own," Justin said when I got closer. "He asked to speak to you. Given the footage you sent last night, I assumed you wanted to talk to him."

"I do."

Justin glanced into the executive kitchen. "Let me know if you need anything."

I handed him the messenger bag I'd been carrying before making my way into the break room. "Hey," I said.

Steed looked up, his face still swollen, the cuts barely concealed beneath band-aids. "You didn't tell me this would happen." His words came out a little mumbled. I wasn't sure if that was due to the swelling or if his jaw was fractured or sore.

"I didn't know." I opened the freezer and pulled out an ice pack. After sliding it to him, I poured a cup of coffee and sat down. "Do you want to tell me what happened?"

"I was late leaving work. As soon as I locked up, this guy jumps me. He was all in black. He had a bat or club, something like that. I don't know."

"Did he say anything? Make any threats?" I'd seen the footage. Steed spoke to him.

"He wanted my phone and wallet. After I gave them to him, he beat the shit out of me."

"What else did he say?"

"That I should mind my business if I knew what was good for me."

"That's it?"

Steed glared with his one good eye. "Isn't that enough?"

"A little clarification might have been nice."

"You're fucking kidding me with this." Steed sneered, which made him grimace. "Ow." He cradled the side of his face. Everything from his chin to his eye was bruised.

"I'm surprised the hospital released you."

"I didn't go to the hospital. Someone must have heard me screaming because the police showed up. They found me outside the store. They called the paramedics, but the deductible on my insurance is insane. I can't afford a ride in an ambulance, let alone what the emergency room would charge."

"Come on," I said, getting up.

"No. You've done more than enough."

"I have a medic on staff. Let him take a look at you. No hospital. No charges. Nothing. All right?"

Steed's one eye narrowed, which looked more like a twitch. The swelling made it impossible for him to look suspicious. "Who are you? I thought you worked for a law firm."

"I do sometimes, but Cross Security handles a lot of sensitive issues."

"Sensitive." Steed climbed out of the chair, the ring of keys hanging from his belt loop jingling. "You mean this could have happened because of something else?"

"No. This has everything to do with what we discussed." I remained beside him as we made our way to the elevator. Steed favored his right side, limping slightly. "Are you sure the assailant didn't say anything else to you?"

"That was it."

"Do you know who he is?"

Steed sighed as he stepped into the elevator. "He wore all black. It happened so fast."

"But you know," I said.

"I'm not sure. I told the police I wasn't sure. That I didn't get a good look. I don't want this to happen again."

"I can offer you protection."

Steed snorted, which made him wince. "Thanks, but no thanks. You've gotten me into enough trouble."

"The only way to ensure this doesn't happen again is by telling me who came after you."

"What happens if I tell you and then he gets released? What do you think will happen then?"

"I'll make sure he doesn't get released."

"What are you going to do, Mr. Cross? Kill him?"

I ignored the twitchy feeling as best I could. "No, but I won't divulge anything until I'm sure the police have a rock solid case."

"He could still get bail."

"Not if he's dangerous. I'd say two aggravated assaults says he's pretty damn dangerous."

"Like I said, I'm not certain who it was."

The doors opened on the floor below. I led Steed past the door to the computer lab and down the corridor which led to our medical wing. Right now, there wasn't much there but a medic, a portable x-ray machine, and the rudimentary materials needed to deal with basic emergencies.

"I'll investigate further," I promised as I helped the medic get Steed onto the exam table.

"That's how I got into this mess." Steed winced again.

"How did this happen?" the medic asked.

"I got mugged last night. The guy had a bat or something." Steed exhaled uneasily as the medic poked around. "It may have been Vincent. I'm not sure. Be careful. I don't need you causing more trouble for me."

"You have my word," I said. "Now, let the doc do his job. He'll get you patched up in no time."

The medic looked at me. "We'll talk later, Cross."

"I'm counting on it. Let me know when Mr. Steed is ready to leave."

By the time I made it upstairs, someone else was waiting for me.

"Not now, Ace." I pushed past him and went into my office. "I'm a little busy right now."

"I heard someone was beaten to a bloody pulp. Obviously, it wasn't you."

"How did you hear about that?"

"I have my ways."

I wasn't in the mood for this. "Answer the question."

"I heard building security talking about it when I got in. They said they weren't sure he'd make it out of the elevator with the way he looked. Who was it?"

Justin caught my eye from beyond the doorway. *Tell*

him, he mouthed.

"Charlie Steed."

Darrow pointed a finger emphatically in my direction. "I told you this has to do with that grocery store. And you were telling me all that research and effort was a waste. It's not a waste." He looked around. "Where is Steed? I'd like to ask him a few questions."

The bandage on Darrow's palm caught my eye. "What happened to your hand?"

He turned his right hand over and stared at it. "I cut it on the jagged edge of a crushed beer can."

"Let me see."

Darrow pulled his hand away. "No."

"Why not?"

"It's fine. I don't need you to kiss it and make it better."

I took a step toward Darrow. Justin took that as his cue, entered my office, and stepped between us.

"Hey, boss, you don't want to be late for your meeting." Justin jerked his chin toward the door. "I'll update Ace on the situation while you take care of business." His eyes told me he had this.

"Yeah, thanks."

THIRTY-FIVE

"What do we know?" I asked.

Justin swiveled in my chair. "The police report doesn't say much. Charlie Steed wasn't particularly forthcoming. He told them the same story he told you. He left work late. Someone jumped him, took his wallet and phone, knocked him around, and left."

"What else did he tell them?"

"That was it. They urged him to go to the emergency room, but he refused care. He signed a waiver and everything."

I sat in the client chair in front of my desk, feeling a little discombobulated by the change in perspective. "How did Taylor connect Steed to me?"

"Your card was in his wallet."

"But the attacker took his wallet."

"Officers found it tossed in a dumpster not far from the grocery store. The mugger took the cash. That was it."

"Not the credit cards?"

"No."

"That seems odd."

"He didn't want to get caught," Justin said. "That's how muggers usually get caught."

"Maybe." Except I didn't believe this was a mugging, and neither did Justin. "Have you gotten in touch with Nathan Boter?"

"He knows what happened. The police didn't question him, but they informed him of the attack when they asked for the security cam footage."

"Was that in the report?"

Justin nodded. "Sara says hi, by the way."

"Is that all she said?"

"You can use your imagination for the rest."

"I'd rather not." I checked my phone for messages. "I'm surprised Boter hasn't called. Doesn't he think the attack on his assistant manager could be connected to what happened to him?"

"Why would he think that? Steed wasn't scammed and isn't a gambler. From Boter's perspective, what would any of that have to do with this?"

"That tells me one very important thing."

"The guy's self-centered?"

"No," I said, "he doesn't owe money to any loan sharks. If he did, he would have feared someone was retaliating or got him and the assistant manager confused."

"They look nothing alike," Justin said.

"Not the point." My mind had gone to other places. The attacks didn't have to do with the money or scam. They had to do with the investigation. Boter spoke to me, as did Greene. Neither knew they could be in the crosshairs because of it. "Let's assign security teams to keep an eye on Greene and Boter in addition to the teams monitoring the Kershaws."

Justin reached for the phone. "Do you want me to let them know they could be in danger?"

"No."

My assistant wasn't expecting that answer. "Oh-kay. I'll tell the teams to monitor from a distance. Since we're a little short, will a two-man team be sufficient for each of them?"

"I hope so." I waited for Justin to make the arrangements. Once that was done, I asked, "What did you find out from Darrow?"

"Not much."

"Did you get a look at his hand?"

"No."

"Is he still insisting the grocery store is the key to this?"

"More than ever." Justin sensed my unease. "You think Darrow attacked Steed last night."

"I have no way of knowing for sure." I pulled out my phone. "I'm going to call Boter and see if he can help me with the security footage. Maybe there's a camera with a better angle the police didn't want me to see. I should have time to run by the grocery store before meeting Powers for lunch. Or I could postpone."

"Don't," Justin said. "We need to keep the lights on in here."

"It hasn't gotten that bad."

"It will if we start losing clients like Powers."

I grabbed my jacket and messenger bag. "Don't get too comfortable. This is still my office. My name is on the door."

"Yeah, but wouldn't you like something more spacious?" Justin asked. "My so-called office is massive compared to this. We could switch. Think about it."

I paused in the doorway. "Any word from Fox or Kincaid?"

"Do you really think they'd call the office?"

"That's a good point," I said.

"One of us has to make them on occasion."

Rolling my eyes, I headed for the elevator. By the time I reached the garage, I'd spoken to Nathan Boter who knew to expect me. Forgoing car service, I got behind the wheel of a company car, put my phone on speaker, and called Kincaid while I drove to the grocery store.

"Any updates on Tessa Gold?" I asked.

"If there was something you should know, Fox would have told you," Kincaid said.

"Someone else was attacked last night."

"Oh?" Kincaid normally didn't show much of an interest, which made his tone surprising.

"It wasn't someone who'd been scammed. It was someone I spoke to."

"You're bad luck, Lucien."

"Don't I know it?"

"Rest assured, if someone were to show up at my club to rough me up, he'd never be seen again."

That didn't make me feel better. "Do you know where Tessa Gold is now?"

"She's at the racetrack, probably picking out her next victim while half a dozen undercover officers keep tabs on her." Kincaid laughed. "I told you I could get you what you wanted."

"I'd prefer if you could tell me who's behind the assaults."

"I'm not a genie. You don't get three wishes. You get one. Now, we're done."

The line went dead.

Nathan Boter was waiting for me when I arrived. He led me to the back of the store, through the freezer and double doors, and past the break room where I'd chatted with Steed days before. He opened the door to his office, which housed several monitors and the security feeds.

"I gave the police everything I had. I don't want anyone getting hurt," he said. "The police said this appears to be a random mugging. I wasn't expecting you to call."

"I'm starting to think nothing is random anymore." I pointed to the monitors. "Are these all the cameras?"

"Everything from the exterior."

I leaned closer to the screens. "Charlie Steed was attacked at the side door. The footage I saw didn't get a look at the guy."

"Maybe the camera out front caught it." Boter pointed to footage from another camera. This one mainly covered the entrance, but the range caught almost the entire front of the building.

"Did you give this to the police too?" I asked.

"I gave them all the footage we had. Charlie's a good man. I want whoever did this to him caught."

I checked each camera. The one in front was my best bet, but I didn't see anything on the footage. I tried the cameras facing the parking lot, but they didn't show much either. "I'd like my techs to take a look at this."

"Why do you think someone attacked Charlie?" Boter asked. "For you to be asking these questions, it must connect to what happened to me."

"Another victim of the scam was assaulted a few days ago. I spoke to Charlie, thinking he may know something, and now this happened."

"What could my assistant manager possibly know about any of this?"

"I'm not entirely sure yet." Though I had my suspicions, just none I wanted to share.

"Do you think he had something to do with whoever wiped out my bank account?"

Darrow's words came to mind. For some reason, unbeknownst to me, I asked, "Does Charlie know Eloise?"

"Yes." Boter scratched the back of his head. "My daughter didn't steal from me. If she didn't want to give me money, she wouldn't. Why would she go through the trouble of creating this ruse to take the money back? That's ludicrous."

"I agree."

"Then why did you ask if she knows Charlie?"

"I was curious."

The color drained from Boter's face. "Do you think whoever attacked him will go after Eloise? Is he the reason this is happening?"

"What makes you say that? Does Charlie have a checkered past? Known enemies? Anything like that?"

Boter threw his hands in the air, exasperated. "Dammit, Mr. Cross, I'd like to know what the hell is going on."

"You really don't know?" I didn't think Boter was involved, but Darrow had crawled into my brain. I needed to knock those thoughts loose before they burrowed any deeper and made a nest. The fastest way to do that was to toss around a few suspicions and see if anything stuck.

His eyes went wide. "Do you?"

"Not yet, but I will get to the bottom of it. In the meantime, keep your eyes peeled for anything suspicious. If something doesn't feel right, call the police or me. Just call someone. Tell your daughter the same thing, and stay away from the tables and track until things get settled."

"How long will that take?"

"I'll let you know."

Running damage control was my least favorite part of this job. Yet, it may have been the most important. With the footage in hand, I returned to my car and headed for the Japanese steakhouse.

Arriving first, I brought my bag in with me and used the few moments I had alone to update Justin on the situation. Now that we had the raw footage and not just the carefully curated version Detective Taylor had handed me on a silver platter, we may be able to get a glimpse of this guy on one of the other feeds.

Kershaw and Steed had similar stories. Based on what they'd said, the attacker was male, broader than me, and possibly built like Vincent from Good Day Marketers. Steed said it could be Vincent, which meant he thought it was, but I'd need proof. Wondering what Vincent Lyman was up to, I performed an internet search.

Despite running online campaigns and having dozens of social media pages, Vincent didn't have any check-ins that I could directly link to him. I had no idea where he was or what he was doing, but given the time of day, he was probably at his office dungeon.

The bastard must have been working with Jasmine O'Neal. She'd been my prime suspect. But she wasn't behind the assaults, even if she had a penchant for disguises. The police had eyes on Tessa Gold, who also couldn't be responsible, given that she lacked the basic physical characteristics of the assailant, but it never hurt to have a few irrefutable facts to back things up.

"They're all in on it together," I surmised.

"Lucien?" Powers hovered above me.

I stood, extending my hand. "How long have you been standing there?"

"Long enough to realize you don't have time for a leisurely lunch."

"It's fine." I waved the thought away, tucked my computer into my bag, and placed it on the empty chair beside me. "It's better to be busy than bored."

"Given the way you get at the tables when you're bored,

I'd agree with that." He sat down beside me. "Did you order yet?"

"No."

"Let's get that out of the way so we can get down to business." Once that was done, we went over the outage and issues he'd had.

"It sounds like it should be a simple fix. It'll take some time to get everything updated, but I can probably get it done overnight. It'll keep your office from shutting down and cause minimal disruptions," I said.

"That's wonderful. It must be my lucky day."

"Given how your luck was the other night, I'd say it's your lucky week."

Powers grinned. "Possibly more than that."

"Oh yeah?" I asked. "How come?"

"I got a call, saying I won a sweepstakes."

"Did you enter a sweepstakes?"

"It was more of a raffle. I bought a ton of tickets for charity on the off chance of winning a luxury getaway. Really, I just needed the write-off."

"Did a woman contact you and say you'd receive an e-mail with further instructions in the next day or two?"

"How did you—"

"It's a scam," I said. "Contact your bank, make sure none of your information has been changed, and have them flag any unusual activity."

"I didn't give her any information. I just verified my contact information and date of birth." Powers froze. "Shit."

"Yeah, that's how they get you. It starts out sounding pretty basic and innocent." I waited for him to call his bank, accountant, and assistant. Once that was done, I asked, "Did you speak to the woman who'd been playing cards with us the other night?"

"Which woman?"

"She was the only one at the table."

"The one you knocked out of the game?"

"That's the one."

"Just basic pleasantries."

"Have you seen her before?"

"A few times. Why? You looking for an introduction or a date? Axel could help you with that."

"I think she's involved. Did she see you win a big hand?"

"Come to think of it, a few times. She spoke to me once afterward, congratulated me, and offered to buy me a drink. But I told her my wife wouldn't like that very much. She never spoke to me again after that." He glanced down at his naked ring finger. "Do you think she knew I was lying?"

"I'm not sure that would matter, but it may have saved you from getting scammed sooner."

Powers finished his lunch and wiped his mouth with the napkin. "It's a good thing she wasn't my type."

THIRTY-SIX

I didn't return to the office after lunch. Instead, I went to Jasmine O'Neal's apartment. The last time I was here, I had every intention of knocking, but Almeada had talked me out of it. Today, I wasn't calling him first. I needed answers. Either O'Neal would give them to me, or I'd find other doors to knock on.

The security at her apartment was no joke. There was no way in or out without getting spotted by at least one or two cameras. However, getting inside the building wasn't as difficult as getting into mine. The doorman didn't stop me. There was no code or requirement that a tenant let me inside.

Stupid mistake, I thought as I stepped out of the elevator. More cameras were in the hallway. A thief or killer could get inside without a problem, but there was no way they wouldn't be caught after the fact.

I stopped in front of her place and smiled at the doorbell camera. When she didn't answer, I banged against the thick wooden door. "Ms. O'Neal?"

I waited, listening. The light pattern beneath the door didn't change. Was anyone inside?

"Ms. O'Neal?" I tried again. "Your colleague, Vincent,

gave me your address. I want to discuss a marketing campaign with you." Even that didn't make her come to the door.

I took a step back. No signs of forced entry. No obvious scratches on the lock, so Darrow hadn't tried to break in. Casually, I tried the knob, but it was locked.

The elevator doors opened. I turned, expecting to see building security approaching. An elderly man emerged, carrying two brown paper bags. I made my way to him.

"You look like you could use a hand," I said.

"I got it, I think." He stopped at the apartment door two away from O'Neal's. He put one bag on the ground between his feet and the door while he shifted the other to the side while he rummaged in his pocket for his keys. An apple rolled out of the top, and I grabbed it before it hit the ground. "Nice catch. Hang on to that for a second." He unlocked the door and reached for the bag at his feet. He put his groceries down inside and turned to retrieve his apple. "Is there something I can do for you?"

I jerked my thumb in the direction of O'Neal's apartment. "I was wondering when you saw your neighbor last."

"Who are you looking for?"

"Jasmine O'Neal."

"She's an odd one," he said. "What do you want with her?"

"It's business."

He looked me up and down. "You seem like a nice guy, so word of advice, find somewhere else to go."

"Are you talking about her marketing?"

"If you want to call it that. I don't know much about her business, but there have been a lot of arguments lately. She likes to go for walks when she's talking on the phone. I'll hear her outside my door, having screaming matches with her clients, partner, someone. It's always about money and business. I shouldn't talk out of turn, but I don't think most people would want to get wrapped up in that drama."

"Thanks for warning me." I peered toward her door. "Do you know if she's home?"

"I haven't heard a peep out of her in days. The last time

was over the weekend. It was late. I'd already gone to bed. Her door slamming woke me up. I heard her yelling at someone."

"Did you hear anyone else?"

"She must have been on the phone, or she was screaming at one of the voices in her head."

"I do that sometimes," I said.

The guy laughed. "To each his own. If that's what you want to do," he gestured toward her door, "by all means, go ahead. I just thought I'd return the kindness you paid me. Go ahead. Knock yourself out."

Deciding to confide in him, I took out my private investigator's license. "If you have a few minutes, would you mind answering some questions?"

The guy took my credentials and examined them more closely. "Come on in. I'm sure I have stories for you."

Not needing to be told twice, I entered his apartment and closed the door behind me. The tiny voice in the back of my head warned that I better not be the common denominator in the attacks or this guy might not survive. But I brushed it aside. He didn't connect to anything. He should be safe. Still, I would suggest he give building security a heads-up to remain on alert.

He picked up one of the grocery bags and went into the kitchen. I grabbed the second bag and followed.

"What has she done to warrant the attention of a private detective poking around?" he asked.

"She may not have done anything. I'm just looking into things. There have been complaints." I didn't want to give too much away. For all I knew, this guy could be playing me.

"That would explain the screaming." He opened the cupboard and shoved the new container of oatmeal inside. "It's always about money."

"She wants more?"

"No, her customers want more. She's always saying none of this is a surefire thing, that there's no guarantee how much it'll pay or what the payoff will be." He put the box of Cheerios on top of the fridge and grabbed the jarred tomato sauce from the bag. "Whoever she's talking to doesn't take the hint. There have been three or four occasions where she's had the same conversation. Over and over. It's the same thing every week."

"She has the same conversation weekly?"

"Pretty much." He gestured with the tomato sauce as he crossed the kitchen to put it in the pantry. "I may be a little off on the timing, but there's always several days in between. You get the point."

"Are you sure she's talking to the same person every time?"

He snickered. "You think all her clients are disgruntled?"

"Possibly. Are you sure she's talking to a client and not a coworker?"

He picked up the empty paper bag and folded it. "I don't know."

"Has she ever mentioned any names?"

"I don't pay that much attention. I wouldn't pay any attention if she wasn't so damn loud."

"What about visitors? Has anyone stopped by her place lately?"

"There's a guy who drops by pretty often. Her boyfriend, maybe."

I palmed my phone. "Would you recognize him if you saw him?"

"I've never seen him. I hear them in the hallway on occasion, either when he's leaving or arriving. I'm not sure which."

"Do you think you'd recognize his voice?"

"He isn't a loudmouth like her. He seems soft-spoken. I just hear mumbles. Then again, my hearing isn't what it used to be either."

"But you hear Jasmine," I said.

"It's hard not to."

"Did you ever overhear her mention any companies?"

"I can't be sure. I do my best to tune her out. It doesn't always work."

Maybe those security cameras could be beneficial. "One final question. Do you have any idea when she'll be home?"

"She comes and goes at all hours. It's tough to say."

"All right. Thanks for your time." I pointed to the pint of ice cream he'd pulled out of the bag. "Enjoy that."

"I intend to."

After leaving my new friend, I strode past Jasmine O'Neal's apartment one more time. Breaking in would not go well. But if I happened to find a hidden key, I could argue I was doing a wellness check since her neighbor hadn't seen or heard from her in days. However, she didn't have a key hidden above the door or under the rug.

I had no reason to think she'd been harmed. More than likely, she was involved in the harming. Without reasonable suspicion, the police wouldn't enter her apartment without a warrant. And Detective Malloy told me they didn't have enough for that.

As I made my way back to the lobby, I considered my options. I could make an anonymous call and a phony report. But letting the cops snoop around inside her place wouldn't help me, and I doubted it'd result in the apprehension of the so-called mugger. Instead, I did the only thing left to do. I spoke to someone in building security who could conceivably get me access to the security cam footage. I wanted to know who'd been visiting O'Neal.

"Sir, if you leave now, I'll pretend this never happened. If you refuse or if I see you again, I'll let the authorities deal with you."

"I don't need copies. I just need to see the screen for a few seconds. I'm trying to identify someone."

"Sir," the security guard reached for the phone, "I won't tell you again."

I pulled out my wallet. "Obviously, two hundred isn't enough. What do you want? Five?"

He started dialing.

"Okay." I backed away from his desk, tucking my wallet into my pocket. "Forget I said anything." Why did I have to find the one guy who couldn't look the other way for a few seconds while I got what I needed? Damn that cosmic kick-me sign. Now I'd have to do things the hard way.

Back in the car, I scanned for networks, hoping to hack into the camera feed. Unfortunately, firewalls safeguarded the security system. I could get in, but it'd take time. Sitting here that long in broad daylight with an already suspicious security guard watching my every move wouldn't be wise. The police would come knocking, and I didn't want to have to explain this. I'd come back later or see if I could gain remote access to O'Neal's doorbell camera from the privacy of my office.

"Now what?" The nagging itch was back with a vengeance. I had to be in motion. "Go with your gut, Cross." So I drove back to Good Day Marketers.

From the outside, the place looked even more abandoned than last time. Was that even possible? I tried opening the door, but it was locked. Peering through the glass, I spotted Jeff behind the desk. His moppy, purple hair was on full display, no longer concealed beneath a hood.

"Hey," I yelled, knocking against the door, "are you closed?"

He didn't hear me on account of the headphones.

It took every ounce of self-restraint not to shoot out the glass and let myself inside. No wonder Justin worried when I got in these moods, but I could keep the destructive tendencies at bay for now. "Hey," I tried again, tugging more vehemently on the handle and making it rattle. When that didn't work, I found Vincent's number and dialed.

"Mr. Cross, it's nice to hear from you again. Have you made a decision?" he asked.

"I have a couple of questions. Can we discuss?"

"Absolutely. Fire away."

"I almost did."

"What?"

"Are you at the office?"

"Yes, but—"

"Great, I'm outside. Tell Jeff to let me in."

THIRTY-SEVEN

Vincent Lyman opened the door. "Mr. Cross, we're in the middle—"

I brushed past him, not sure what I hoped to find, but desperate to find something. "Where's Jasmine O'Neal?"

"She's out of the office."

"You said that last time. In fact, you got your story confused. I want to know where she is."

"Why do you care?" He followed behind me, unsure where we were going as I made my way past Jeff's desk and down the hallway. The offices I'd passed on my last visit remained empty.

"I have my reasons." I stopped at the conference room where we'd previously spoken. The only things inside were the table and chairs. I continued down the hallway.

"Look, Mr. Cross, I don't know what you think you're doing, but this is inappropriate behavior. I'll call security."

"I doubt you have security. They would have stopped me at the door. Though, I'd think a place like this would need it. You rip off the wrong person and there will be hell to pay." I pushed open the first door I found. Inside was a professional card table. "What's this?"

"Our recreational area."

I wasn't buying it. "Sure."

Vincent grabbed the back of my collar. I spun, pulling my arms up and into a guard position. Luckily for him, I didn't start swinging.

"Whoa," he held up his palms and stepped back, "take it easy. Why don't you tell me what's wrong?"

"Besides you and Jeff, is anyone else here?"

"No."

"What about Rita?"

Vincent looked increasingly uneasy. "Is that what this is about?"

"What do you think?" I'd hit on something, but I had no idea what that something was.

"That's proprietary. I won't discuss it."

"Didn't you tell me Rita was your assistant?"

"She is."

I let the words sink in. "She's not real."

"The word you're looking for is virtual," he said indignantly.

"Like Siri or Alexa?"

"The programming does more than that. It runs our entire marketing operation, analyzing trends and traffic." He stopped. "I said I wasn't discussing this."

"How does Jasmine feel about Rita?"

"Jazz does things her way, and I do them mine."

"Let me guess, Jazz is the velvet touch and you're the wooden bat?"

"What are you talking about?"

My questions confused him enough that he didn't notice I was moving backward down the hallway. The next door I happened upon was Jasmine O'Neal's office. A bamboo plant sat on the desk. Her workstation had dual monitors and three tablets charging. The only thing missing was the woman herself.

"You can't go in there," Vincent bellowed.

Ignoring him, I went behind her desk. Everything was neat and orderly. Her computer wasn't locked, so I opened her calendar. She didn't have any appointments or meetings this week. After clicking a few times, I found her client list. Tessa Gold was at the top.

"Jasmine O'Neal's working for Tessa Gold," I said. "Gold Gaming is one of your clients."

Vincent ripped the plug out of the wall, abruptly turning off the computer.

"You're a tech guy. You know better than to shut down like that. Now you're going to have to boot up in safe mode, and that's just a pain in the ass," I said.

Vincent wanted to kill me. Too bad he hadn't brought a baseball bat with him. "I have been very patient—"

"I thought that was because you were surprised. I caught you unaware." I put some distance between us, fearing he'd go for my throat.

"Jeff called the police. They're on the way. I suggest you leave before they arrive."

"More lies. Jesus. Did you and the truth have a nasty breakup?"

"I'm warning you. I will press charges."

"You didn't call the cops. You don't want them in here any more than you want me in here. You're afraid of what they'll find, which is why you and I are going to have a nice long conversation. Depending on how that goes will determine what happens to you."

"You're delusional. This is your last chance to leave without repercussions."

"Did you happen to look me up after our last meeting?"

"You run a security firm, so what?"

"You missed the investigation part of the name. Cross Security and Investigation. Everyone misses that. Maybe I should make the font bigger. You're in marketing. What do you think?"

"Why do I care?"

"Maybe you don't, but I was hired to investigate why someone's checking account was wiped and that led me to you."

"What are you talking about? That's ludicrous. You can tell it to the police."

"Cut the crap. We both know no one's coming. Well, not the police anyway." I pulled open a drawer, revealing a pile of hair. "Why is your partner hiding a tribble in her desk?"

Confused by the sudden shift in conversation, Vincent

peered into the open drawer. Picking up the frosted wig, he held it at arm's length as if it might be an alien creature.

"Smile." I snapped a photo with my phone and sent it to Justin.

Vincent tossed the wig onto the desk and stepped back. Whether he was more afraid of it or me was anyone's guess. "What do you want?"

Now we were getting somewhere. "Who's running the scam?"

"There is no scam."

"What do you call preying upon gamblers, offering to pay them their winnings, and then using that information to empty their checking accounts?"

"Gamblers?"

"Am I speaking Klingon?"

Vincent shook his head. "Jazz."

"Jasmine O'Neal is running the scam?"

I saw the guilt in his eyes. "I don't know what Jazz does. We manage our own clients. We don't collaborate."

"That wasn't what you said last time we spoke. I want the money back."

"I don't have it. I don't know anything about it."

"Right." I looked around the rest of the office, but I didn't see anything else. The wig alone would be enough for the police to get a search warrant. Making my way to the door, I peered into the hallway. Armed men weren't waiting for me. No one was. Not even Jeff.

"Mr. Cross, I can assure you, you have it wrong. I don't know anything about—"

I didn't wait. I left the office and opened the door across the hall. This had to be Vincent's. Framed posters of iconic, sci-fi sex symbols covered the walls. Could this guy be any more cliché?

Ignoring the Princess Leia begging me to get her out of those shackles, I focused on the desk. I only made it halfway around when I spotted the scarred wooden bat on the floor. I didn't touch it. Instead, I took a few more photos, sent them to Justin, and called Sara.

"Hey, I found your mugger."

Vincent stood in the doorway, horrified. Considering the

two violent attacks, I expected him to jump me. Instead, he made a run for it.

"Shit." Shoving my phone into my pocket, I chased after him. He was faster than I expected. He made it out the front door before I caught up.

"Lucien," Sara's voice beckoned from my shirt pocket, "answer me. What's going on?"

I turned, finding the front desk unmanned. Jeff had abandoned ship. His boss had done the same. And who knew where Jasmine O'Neal was hiding?

"The suspect is fleeing on foot." I gave her the address and cross street before describing what he was wearing. "See if you can catch him."

"Don't you dare go after him," she warned. "Stay put. I'll send units to you."

I glanced back at the office. "Tell them to focus on getting him. I'm not going anywhere." I had a search to conduct.

THIRTY-EIGHT

When the police arrived, they found me waiting outside. I kept my hands visible with my identification and credentials at the ready. But that wasn't necessary since Detective Taylor was the first to show. Sara must have tipped her. If not, I'd be identifying myself to a patrol officer who'd ask if I was *that* Lucien Cross.

"I thought I told you to call me," she said.

"The more you say it, the more it sounds like you're looking for a date."

"The answer's no."

"I wasn't asking."

"What am I looking at, Lucien?"

"An abandoned office," I said.

"No shit."

"Then why did you ask?"

"Don't be cute."

"So you think I'm cute." Maybe I should react the same way Justin had.

She peered through the door. "Did you break anything?"

"No."

"But you were trespassing."

"Vincent's a marketing manager. He let me inside. After

that, things took a turn."

She pulled open the door. "Walk me through that."

"I asked about his associate, Jasmine O'Neal. When he didn't know where she was, I went to see if I could find her myself. I found her office. She wasn't there. Instead, I found a hairpiece you may find interesting." I pointed to the desk where Vincent had left the wig. "That's when I got suspicious."

"Right. That's when it happened."

I shrugged. "Since he and O'Neal are the only two marketing managers who work out of this office, I figured he might be involved too. He was cagey and refused to answer my questions, so I thought we should continue that conversation somewhere more private, where he'd be comfortable."

"Uh-huh." Taylor wasn't buying it, but that didn't matter. She wanted to know what I found, not what led to me finding it.

I took her to his open office door. "So we came in here. Well, I came in here. Apparently, Vincent thought we should continue the conversation elsewhere. I assumed it was because he was embarrassed by the décor." I pointed to the framed posters. "And that's when I spotted it." I indicated the bat.

"Did you touch it?"

"No."

She gave me a look.

"I didn't," I said. "I know better than that."

She pulled on a pair of gloves and picked it up. "That looks like blood."

"And paint transfer." I crouched beside her, indicating the dark-colored streaks scarred into the wood. "That could be from Kershaw's car."

She looked around. "What else did you find?"

"That was it."

"Right."

"When I spotted the bat, Vincent took off. I'm assuming the guy who works the front desk, Jeff something, must be involved since he took off before his boss did."

"Maybe it's Jeff's bat."

"Could be, but why would Vincent run?"

"They could be in on it together."

"All three?"

"Why not?" she asked. "What else do I need to see?"

"I don't know. I followed Vincent out and waited for help to arrive."

"Sure, you did." She didn't open any desk drawers or touch anything. She'd wait for a warrant and do things by the book, which was why she wanted me to do the dirty work for her. "Let's say you're clairvoyant and have some sixth sense ESP thing going on. Where should I focus my attention?"

"Besides finding out where Jasmine O'Neal is, I'm not really sure what to tell you."

"You don't know where she is?"

"She's not at home, and she's not here. Tessa Gold is one of her clients. Perhaps she knows where O'Neal went."

"Are you thinking foul play?"

"I wasn't until you said it."

"A smart guy like you? I'd think that'd be the first thought you had."

"O'Neal's skittish, according to Detective Malloy. She takes precautions. However, if I were you, I'd have a conversation with her neighbor and see what he has to say. Also," I headed toward the front entrance, "I'd put a unit on the building in case she returns or in case someone else stops by, looking to cause trouble."

"You think someone's out to get Jasmine?"

"Two people who've cooperated with this investigation were brutally attacked. I don't want some old guy to get his head bashed in because I told you to talk to him."

"I'll keep him safe," Taylor promised. "Which neighbor is it?"

"I didn't get a name, but he lives two doors down."

"Okay."

I pulled open my car door. "Next time, how about you find a lead and give me a call?"

"I have no interest in asking you out," she said.

"Keep telling yourself that."

* * *

Justin stood beside me. "Is that everything you found?"

"It's everything I had time to find. Whatever else we need, I'll have to get from the police."

"I didn't realize we were working with them."

"We're not. Not really. But I can't do anything to stop a mugger. Well, anything legal. Cross Security is meant to privatize policing, but we have no authority to make arrests. Violent crimes are something I've always tried to shy away from."

"You're not doing a great job, boss."

"Tell me about it."

Amir examined the photos I'd taken of the bat. "Without physical evidence, I can't do much with this. That looks like blood. That looks like paint, and that looks like damage from making contact with asphalt." He indicated sections of the photo. "But without the object to analyze, those are nothing more than guesses."

"How about the security footage from O'Neal's apartment building?" I asked.

Amir indicated the screen where numbers were populating at record speed to circumvent the system and grant us entry. "I'm still working on getting a hold of that. Whoever designed their security system knew what they were doing."

"Too bad it wasn't us," I said.

"That would have made it easy, boss," Justin said. "You know we don't do easy around here."

I glanced behind me, but the door to the lab was closed. "Have you found anything indicating Darrow is involved?"

"Besides the files he hid from us, I haven't found anything conclusive," Amir said. He pointed to the photo of the bat. "If that smear is blood, it would be in the right place for someone who cut his palm to leave a trail."

"We'll need to get a DNA sample from the crime lab. Do you have any friends who owe you favors?"

"Why don't we let them run Darrow against what they have and save us the work?" Amir asked.

"However you want to do it is fine, but I need to know if

Darrow's behind the assaults."

Justin studied the screens and made a face. "Don't you think Vincent's behind the attacks? Steed IDed him. He ran. The weapon was found in his office. He and O'Neal work together, which means Tessa Gold hired the firm to conduct her research. It all connects in a weird, twisty way."

"I don't know. We have too many questions and not enough answers, but we tossed around the theory Darrow could be working for whoever emptied Kershaw's account, which means Darrow could be playing for their team," I said. "I don't know how likely that is. It doesn't feel right, but nothing about Darrow feels right."

"You shouldn't have hired him," Justin said.

"Yeah, I know. Dumb move. I got the memo."

Justin held up his hands and backed away. "What do you want us to do to fix this?"

"There's nothing you can do except continue running everything down. We need to figure out who the players are and where they are. If they have any other targets in mind, whether financial or physical, we need to get ahead of this," I said.

"Do we alert the police?" Amir asked.

"Alert me first."

Amir nodded. "Besides pulling the apartment footage, I'll see if I can get into Good Day Marketers' security system. That should tell us who's been to that office."

"I don't think they have a security system. I didn't notice any cameras while I was there."

"Maybe outside," Amir said. "If not, I'll check for nearby CCTVs."

"I'll pull the profile we made on Vincent and get a timeline together to see if he can alibi out for either of the assaults," Justin said.

"Did you pull anything from the grocery store footage?" I asked Amir.

"The attacker doesn't appear on any of the footage. There must be a blind spot between the two cameras, but I don't know where it is. All I know is we have nothing."

"Thanks for trying." Several thoughts came to mind. But

I couldn't move on them at once, not until Amir figured out how to clone me or created a time machine.

Darrow could be working for the enemy or deliberately sabotaging me. Regardless, I wanted his input. With any luck, I'd catch him in a lie or get the answers I needed.

I knocked on his open door. "I need your help."

"You do?" Darrow suspected this was a trap. "I'm already following leads."

"I know. The grocery store. You believe that's how the scammer is picking out his targets. How much research have you done on the store?"

"I told you how many varieties of frozen pizza they sell."

"What about their security protocols?"

"Pretty basic stuff. They have the typical credit card encryption for taking payments. The cash is taken to a safe."

"I'm not looking to knock the place over," I said.

"Then what do you want to know?"

"Security cameras. Inside. Outside. Wouldn't they have caught our scammer and his victims at some point?"

"Sure."

"What about yesterday's assault? It occurred outside. I collected the raw footage, but the assailant isn't anywhere to be seen. The guy's invisible."

"That's not possible," Darrow said.

"Amir said there must be a blind spot."

"I don't see how. The side camera covers where deliveries are brought in. It shows the trucks that arrive and any employees who are tasked with unloading. There are actually two cameras that cover the side."

"Two?"

"You didn't get footage from the second camera?" Darrow asked.

"I didn't see a second camera."

Darrow grinned. "That's because it's not on the side of the building. It's on the front."

"Yeah, I got that. But it doesn't show anything either."

"Are you sure?" Darrow gave me a look. "That should cover everything from the corner to the front door. It won't show the loading and unloading, but it will show any employee who exits out the side."

"There's a blind spot."

"No, there isn't."

"Then the attacker is invisible."

"What about the camera at the rear? Maybe the guy snuck out the back."

"Is that possible without being spotted on the side camera?" I asked.

Darrow thought about it. "Maybe." He grabbed a pencil and drew something on the back of a printout. "If he gave the camera a wide enough berth, maybe he could have slipped past." Darrow squinted at the drawing. "Still, if he went that far over, the front camera may have spotted him. I'll need the rear camera footage to be sure."

"I didn't get it."

"Lucien, always get all the camera footage there is. You never know what you might need." He palmed his keys to the company car. "I'll go get it since I can't trust you not to botch it."

"All right, you do that."

He clapped me on the shoulder. "It's about time you started trusting me."

THIRTY-NINE

I didn't trust him. I called Boter and had him send me the files from the relevant timestamp. The footage didn't show anything useful. If it had, I would have discovered if Darrow was hiding evidence. But lack of evidence didn't exonerate him either. He may have been responsible, knew he hadn't been spotted, and told me about the third camera to appear helpful.

While he was gone, I went through his research. I didn't find anything on Tessa Gold. No hidden files. No photos. No leads.

Darrow had covered the wall of his office with photos and locations for Nathan Boter and his daughter. He'd placed pins and overlaid red yarn on top, connecting those locations to the other points of interest. A few made sense, like Eric Greene delivering to the grocery store. But some, like Kershaw's alleged mugging, had nothing but a sticky note with a question mark hanging beneath the string. Studying this for too long would give me a headache.

Instead, I returned to my office to do my own research before setting out to locate Jasmine O'Neal. Vincent was in the wind. The police were looking for him. By now, an all points would have been issued.

I rifled through the papers on my desk, looking for Detective Malloy's number. He had Tessa Gold under surveillance. Surely, he picked her up now that Vincent was under suspicion and she was a known client of the marketing company.

"Mr. Cross." The medic stood in my doorway.

A millisecond later, the intercom beeped. "Lucien, the doc's here to see you."

"Thanks, Justin," I yelled as I gestured for the medic to enter. "How's the patient?"

"He's resting downstairs. The bruises on his chest and arms are superficial. No broken ribs or anything like that."

"Alan Kershaw wasn't that lucky."

"I was surprised it wasn't worse. Charlie Steed said the attacker hit him with a club or bat."

"The footage showed the edge of a bat."

The medic made a face. "I'm no expert, but the injuries sustained aren't consistent with being struck by a club-like weapon."

"You think the attacker used his fists?"

"I'm not sure. The injuries to Steed's face are the most severe. Almost as if he'd been hit with a broader object. Something flat. Maybe a two by four."

"Not a bat?"

"It's unlikely. When a cylinder impacts, the rounded edge would land with the greatest force. I'm not seeing that. Instead, the highest points on Steed's face took the most damage."

"Couldn't that be where the bat landed?"

"Then it struck the ridge of his cheekbone and his brow at their highest points. Given the angle of the attack, the injuries couldn't have happened during the same swing. And neither of those swings caused any additional damage to Steed's face."

"I saw the video footage. He was hit multiple times."

"I've seen the footage too. Yet, not a single blow was captured on screen."

"What are you saying?" I asked.

"I don't know. But it looks more like Steed was hit with a wooden plank or a slab of concrete than a bat or club."

He showed me an x-ray indicating a fractured cheekbone. "There should be spiderweb cracks emanating outward from the impact point. That doesn't happen here."

"What do you think caused that?"

"I'm not sure, but the attacker must have had a different weapon."

"So you're sure he didn't use a bat?"

"I'd be surprised if he did."

The blind spot didn't help matters. I brought up the footage and froze the screen when the end of what I assumed was a bat came into view. "That's what the attacker used to hit Charlie Steed."

The medic squinted at the image. "Let me run some simulations and see if I can figure anything out."

"Did you ask Steed about it?"

"You heard what he said."

"Since he's still here, maybe he can help us figure this out."

"I gave him something for the pain which put him out like a light, but you can wake him up and talk to him if you want."

"Let me take care of something else first."

"All right. I'll be downstairs, whenever you're ready."

I called Detective Malloy. "Have you arrested Tessa Gold yet?"

"On what grounds? Did you find something?" Malloy asked.

"She's one of Good Day Marketers' clients."

"I already suspected that," Malloy said. "Remember, I told you about her."

"She may know where Jasmine O'Neal is. We need to find her."

"I asked. Gold says she hasn't spoken to O'Neal in over a week. I can't prove otherwise. I haven't seen them together. Surveillance hasn't seen them together. And even if we had, it wouldn't do us much good."

"Have you been listening to radio chatter? Vincent's suspected of committing two assaults. Those assaults connect to the scam which connects to the marketing agency—"

"Can you prove that?"

"Bring Gold in," I said.

"I will when your father calls with the same request."

The pencil in my hand snapped in half. "At the very least, she should be a person of interest."

"Yeah, I know."

"Then—"

"Don't tell me how to do my job. I don't tell you how to do yours." Malloy sighed. "We'll be keeping tabs on her. With any luck, Vincent Lyman or Jasmine O'Neal will go to her, or she'll go to them. Unless you got any idea where Vincent might have gone?"

"He wasn't apprehended?"

"Not unless you know something I don't."

"Plenty, just not that."

Malloy hung up.

Since Jasmine O'Neal was in the wind, maybe Vincent joined her. Unless he'd done something to her. Taylor's question about foul play nagged at me. Two people had been attacked. Neither assault made much sense. I couldn't figure out the purpose of either, other than confusing me.

Charlie Steed better have something insightful to share that wouldn't lead to more questions because I had reached my limit.

I found him asleep on the cot. The medic said the pain pills knocked him out, but my guess would be that was a result of being up all night.

"Charlie," I said loud enough to cause him to open his eyes, "we need to talk."

"I told you what I remember. It all happened fast."

"Are you sure this guy came at you with a bat?"

"It could have been a club. It could have been anything. I just remember seeing something swinging at me and trying to get away."

"What do you remember about your attacker?"

"I didn't get a look at him. Big guy. Broader than you. That was about it. I'm pretty sure it was Vincent. He was built like Vincent. He sounded like Vincent."

"Lyman?"

"Yeah."

"Why would he want to hurt you?"

"I don't know. You asked me questions about him, about Good Day Marketers, and the next thing I know someone's trying to knock my block off. Shouldn't you have some idea why that would happen?"

"You weren't happy with the way Good Day Marketers conducts business. You said they punished you. I'm assuming that's why you changed paths and got out of marketing and went to work as an assistant manager. You know things about them, damning things."

"I learned my lesson. I'm not saying another word. You want Vincent, you figure out how to get him."

I thought about what Steed said. "Is it possible it could have been someone else?"

"I guess." But he didn't look convinced.

"Tell me about the attacker. Did he have any discernible traits? Eye color? Hair color? Tattoos?"

"He was covered."

"Did he wear gloves?"

"I don't know."

"Did you see his car?"

"The attacker didn't drive."

"Where did he go afterward?"

"I don't know. He just walked away," Steed said.

"What about the weapon he had?"

"He took it with him."

"So some guy walks down the street holding a bloody weapon and no one notices."

"It was the middle of the fucking night, and it's the city. People do all kinds of shit. Everyone knows it's best to mind their own business."

"Yeah." But someone should have seen something. Before I could say as much, my phone rang. *Darrow.* "What is it?" I asked.

"Lucien, I checked the other camera footage, but there's nothing to see. I don't know how this guy did it, but he pulled an Invisible Man when it came to conducting the assault. That tells me one thing. It should tell you the same thing." Darrow waited.

"I'm not in the mood for a pop quiz. Spit it out."

"The guy must have intimate knowledge of the security cams. That indicates it's someone who works here, but before you tell me I'm wrong again, it could be someone who shops at the store a lot and pays attention. Since I'm already here, I had loyalty card records pulled. I have a list of every card that was scanned around closing time, figuring the assailant may have been scoping things out while he planned his attack. It's what I'd do."

"Did you scan your loyalty card?" I asked.

"I wasn't here," Darrow said, "but that reminds me I should get some pizzas since I didn't get a chance the other day. However, that wasn't what I was going to say."

"I would hope not."

"What I was going to say," Darrow said pointedly, "is Vincent Lyman scanned his card at 10:47 last night. The store closes at eleven. Do you want to know what he bought?"

"Don't say pizza."

"He bought a large wooden cutting board."

"How large?" I asked.

Darrow said something to someone that I didn't hear. "Hang on, I'll look for a tape measure."

"Buy the damn thing. I'll reimburse you."

I could hear the grin when Darrow said, "In other words, I did good?"

"We'll see."

"Are you going to cover my pizzas too?"

"Fine. Whatever." I hung up, finding Steed staring expectantly at me. "Could the man who attacked you have been wielding a wooden cutting board?" That didn't go along with the footage I'd seen, but it wouldn't hurt to ask.

"I thought it was a bat, but I guess if it was one of those big ones turned sideways, I may not have noticed the difference. We sell some at the store that are more like serving trays or miniature paddles. They have a built-in handle. It could have been that. Like I said, I didn't get a good look. My back was turned, and then it all happened so quickly." Steed's good eye twitched. "There's something else. What is it?"

"Vincent was at the store last night."

Steed nodded, the facts combining to tell the narrative. "He bought the cutting board and waited for me to leave."

"Is that what happened?" I asked.

"It makes sense."

"How?"

"I told you everyone at Good Day Marketers was up to no good. He knew I never cared for the way they conducted business. He must have found out I talked to you and came to shut me up or scare me off."

"How do you think he found out? Have you spoken to him or Jasmine?"

"Not recently," Steed said. "Maybe someone was following you."

FORTY

I wasn't buying it. Vincent didn't tail me to the grocery store. I would have noticed. Hell, Darrow would have noticed. Was that how Vincent knew I'd spoken to Steed? Did Darrow tip him?

My associate's phone records didn't indicate he'd made contact. Nothing did. Darrow looked clean. The only indication he was going behind my back was the blackmail and our history.

Frustrated, I continued my search. I pulled bank records, phone records, and anything else I thought might be of use to track down Jasmine O'Neal. Everything indicated she had dropped off the face of the earth. Had she gone into hiding, or had someone hidden her body?

Calling her family and friends could lead to something, but the police should be doing that if they were serious about locating her. Instead, I called every host and dealer I knew.

O'Neal had been infiltrating illegal games. According to the files I'd copied from her computer, she hadn't had a gambling problem prior to taking Tessa Gold on as a client. In fact, O'Neal had never played a single online poker game before beginning her research for Gold's campaign. Maybe O'Neal was still researching, or she'd developed a habit she couldn't quite shake. However, no one had seen her or any newcomer in disguise at any games in the last week.

Justin's voice came over the intercom in a whisper. "Darrow's here."

A moment later, he appeared in my doorway. "I dropped the cutting board off with your team. The medic thinks that may explain the injuries. He said it's more reasonable than a bat."

I nodded, remembering I hadn't told him not to speak to Darrow. "Okay."

Darrow took a seat on the couch. "I found a few points of interest when going over the loyalty card scans."

"Oh yeah?"

"Vincent made purchases on days that coincided with incidents. The night Boter met Jasmine at the poker game, Vincent had been at the store. I took the liberty of pulling some camera footage and I even spotted the two of them conversing." He held out a tablet. "Do you want to see?" Crooking my finger, I waited for him to bring me the device. After a battle of wills, he climbed off the couch and ambled toward me. "I asked Boter what they discussed, but he didn't remember. I think he told Vincent about the game."

"You think that's how Jasmine O'Neal heard about it?"

"I do."

I watched the interaction. It occurred between the front door and the customer service desk. Vincent had his receipt in his hand, which he was showing Boter. Since Boter was the store manager, that didn't surprise me, but Darrow could be on to something. "What else do you have?"

"We aren't cops, Lucien. Do I need to remind you we don't need hard evidence?"

"What else do you have?" I repeated.

"Like I said, Vincent was at the store when the other incidents occurred. You know he was there last night before the assault happened. He was even there before Greene was arrested."

"Greene didn't work that night," I said.

"Not that night. The day before."

"Greene delivered after the store closed. There's no way Vincent would have had any interaction with him or known his whereabouts."

"I'm telling you he was at the store. He was always there. Always shopping. Look at these scans." Darrow opened a tab, showing a long list of times and dates. "No one shops this much."

"He probably stops on his way to or from work to get whatever he needs that day. Can you track his purchases?"

"Yeah." Darrow clicked something else. "That doesn't prove anything."

I was right, but unlike Darrow, I didn't feel the need to say it. "Unless Vincent bought a baseball bat or made an overt threat, this doesn't tell us anything."

"It tells us everything. I've been saying the store is where the scammer is selecting his targets. This proves it."

"You also said Boter was behind this."

"That was a theory. It was disproven."

"You thought Eloise stole from her father."

"That was another theory."

"What you're telling me now is also a theory."

"Okay, smart guy. You tell me what's going on here."

I tilted my head from side to side, the itch back, the familiar tingles going through me. Now wasn't the time to throw a grenade into the mix, but maybe shaking things up would get me answers. It couldn't make things worse.

"Do you really want to know what I think?"

Darrow took a step back, a little afraid. "Uh...yeah."

"You're sure?" It sounded like a challenge. A glimpse at the mirror showed how deranged I looked. If I were Darrow, I would have run. But he didn't. "Because I don't think you'll like it very much."

"What are you thinking?"

"I'm thinking Good Day Marketers ripped off Alan Kershaw, Nathan Boter, and Eric Greene. Based on what the police have said, those aren't the only victims. I don't know how they stumbled upon their targets. My guess is these were crimes of opportunity. The targets weren't selected for any other reason than being in the wrong place at the wrong time."

"But the grocery store—"

I held up my finger, silencing Darrow. "I don't know if Tessa Gold put the marketing team up to this or if they came up with the plan on their own. I'm not even sure what their goal is. Motivation appears financial. The risk would be minimal if they had no real interaction or overlap with the victims, which is why we haven't found much of anything." I moved closer and poked Darrow in the chest. "Except you found something."

"The grocery store?"

"No. You figured out who masterminded this scam. I don't know how, but you found out, just like how you found all that shit you're hiding from me."

"I'm not—"

"Don't fucking lie. I've seen the files you have hidden. The videos. The photos. What are you planning on doing with them? Are you going to blackmail Kershaw, or are you going to sell them to someone else who plans on blackmailing him?"

"Lucien—"

"Is this because the scammer didn't take enough when he emptied Kershaw's checking account? You ran a profile. You know exactly how much our client is worth and the liquid assets he's amassed. Is that why you want to exploit him?"

"I never—"

"Oh, you never?" The ringing phone didn't distract me. I moved closer to Darrow, backing him against the wall. "You never what?"

"You had no right to access my files."

I found myself with a twisted smile on my face. "That's what you have to say? How do you think I felt when you breached my system?"

"So that's what this is about. You wanted to get payback to show me how it feels."

"Why do you have those files? To whom are you feeding this information?"

"No one."

"So you're going to use it yourself?"

"I didn't—"

"Lucien," Justin's sharp tone made me look in his direction, "you have a call."

"Take a message."

"Boss, this can't wait."

Neither could this. I stared at Darrow. "Tell me who's behind this. Is it Vincent or Jasmine?"

"I don't know."

"You expect me to believe you haven't been sharing our progress with the party responsible? Because that's the only explanation I can come up with as to why Kershaw and Steed were attacked. No one should have known I spoke to Steed. He wasn't a victim. He was nothing. Why would anyone go after him?"

"Because this all links to the grocery store."

I shoved Darrow hard, but he was already against the wall, so it didn't do much except make the art rattle.

"Lucien," Justin snapped, "phone. Now."

I took a step back. Darrow hadn't offered any real explanation. He didn't even cough up an excuse. I wasn't sure what to make of it. I pinned him to the wall with my stare. "Don't go anywhere." I turned to Justin. "Keep an eye on him." Then I went to my desk and picked up the phone.

"Line two," Justin said, blocking the door while he gave Darrow the quick once-over.

"Cross," I answered, the rage seething beneath the surface.

"I know where Jasmine O'Neal is," Axel Kincaid said. "I need you to do something about it. If not, I will."

FORTY-ONE

The address Kincaid had given me was in the middle of nowhere. We weren't even in city limits. This looked more country. Visions from *Deliverance* came to mind. Thankfully, I hadn't been traveling south. Instead, I worried I might be facing some *Amityville Horror*.

However, after taking another turn, I found myself on the main thoroughfare in a tiny town. Exotic sports cars lined the streets. I recognized half of them from the alley beside Spark. Engines revved. Silver, red, and yellow blurs zipped along my periphery. This was a car race, possibly illegal, definitely one of Spark's off property events.

Finding a place to park, I got out of my car and approached the crowd. I recognized several of my clients, both from my Wall Street days and the present. Kincaid remained in the background. Fox was beside him.

I kept my head on a swivel as I approached, but I didn't see Jasmine O'Neal anywhere. "What is this?" I asked.

"An event." Kincaid cast his gaze across the expanse. "O'Neal's on the other side. She's been chatting up the winner. I'm assuming she's hoping to make him her next victim. Handle this, or I will."

The woman he indicated didn't look anything like the

versions of O'Neal that I'd seen. She had neon pink hair tied back in pigtails. She wore a mini skirt and cropped top with thick suspenders. I'd seen something similar in a movie and wondered if that was her inspiration. Maybe she was into cosplay.

"Who's the man she's speaking to?"

"That doesn't matter," Kincaid said.

I moved through the crowd. O'Neal hadn't spotted me. Even if she had, I wasn't sure she had any clue who I was. Every time I'd come knocking, she'd supposedly been out. Once I was close enough, I hooked my arm around her waist, expecting to take an elbow to the stomach or jaw.

But she didn't hit me or jerk away. Instead, she turned, a little confused but still in character.

"I've been looking everywhere for you." I smiled at the man she'd been questioning. "Do you mind if I borrow her for a minute? This won't take long."

"Not a problem. I need to get a drink." He headed in the direction of the walk-up bar.

The structure looked like a converted gazebo. I wondered if Kincaid had put that there for this purpose, or if he'd asked the town if he could borrow it. In fact, I wondered if he had permission to do any of this.

"I'm sorry," O'Neal said, "but you have me confused with someone else."

"I don't think so."

She squinted. "Do I know you?"

"You should. I'm Lucien Cross."

Her face gave nothing away. "Again, I think you have me confused with someone else."

"Jasmine O'Neal," I said. "You work for Good Day Marketers. Tessa Gold hired you to research area gambling. Since then, you've approached several men who had their bank accounts emptied after they were scammed."

"You have me confused with someone else."

"Fine. How about I share that information with these nice people and see what they think?"

She scowled. "Don't you dare."

"Axel Kincaid told you to stay away. You didn't listen.

You really should have."

She pulled away from me but didn't try to run. Looking me up and down, she said, "You're the muscle?"

"Do I look like muscle?"

"What do you want?"

"So many things. For starters, how about you give Alan Kershaw his money back, and while you're at it, call off whoever's behind the attacks."

"Attacks?" The question sounded sincere.

"The alleged muggings. Your accomplice put Kershaw in the hospital."

"I had nothing to do with that."

I wasn't sure why, but I believed her. Darrow would disagree. He'd tell me I was wrong. "In that case, you're going to need my help. The police have issued a warrant for your arrest. They could push for conspiracy to commit unless you name names."

"You're a cop?"

"No. Do you think Kincaid would allow a cop at his events?"

"You work for him?"

"I'm here, aren't I?"

She considered what I said. "Why would you help me?"

"I promised Alan Kershaw I'd find the person who attacked him. Money can be repaid. Violence is a different story. You're the lesser of two evils."

"But you can fix this?"

"Only if you tell me what there is to fix." I kept one hand near her back and gestured toward my car with the other. "Let's take a ride. You answer my questions truthfully, and I'll do what I can to get you out of trouble." That wasn't exactly a lie. If she stayed here, there was a good chance no one would ever see her again. "I know about Atlantic City," I said. "I have friends there. Kincaid has friends there." I wasn't sure what mafia movie I was channeling or exactly what kind of threat that was, but I went all in with the bluff. "It'd be better if you told me your side of things. Maybe I have some of it wrong. Maybe someone else is responsible. Vincent said this was all you."

"He's such a fucking liar." She glanced nervously in

Kincaid's direction. "I hoped he wouldn't recognize me. We needed one big score to get out. I didn't know where else to go."

"I would have thought you'd be smarter. Axel's annoyed you defied him by showing up. He warned you to stay away. Either I handle this, or he will. I'm a teddy bear compared to him. But it's your choice."

She looked at me again. "Let's take a ride."

"After you."

Once we made it to the car, I took her purse. She didn't have any weapons on her. The cell phone she carried was turned off. I pocketed it and handed her back her bag before opening the rear door. This wasn't a cop car, but the child safety locks worked the same. She wouldn't be able to get out unless someone on the outside opened the door for her.

"You're making me ride in back?" she asked.

"It's either this or the trunk. You pick."

She got in without another word.

Once we were on our way back to my office, I said, "How about you start at the beginning?"

"You know the beginning."

"Pretend I don't."

She stared out the window, her jaw clenched.

"How long has Good Day Marketers been scamming people? Did it start with Tessa Gold, or was this going on before that?" I asked.

She didn't answer.

"Do you want me to bring you back to Kincaid?"

"No."

"I can always take you to the closest police station instead."

"We'd been pulling credit card numbers, but that didn't work. The accounts would get flagged. No large purchases or cash transfers could be made. The concept was good, but the execution was flawed. I thought he'd give up. We'd worked on so many projects together. Legitimate projects. We didn't need the cash. Our business was starting to turn a profit. It took a long time. Years, but we were starting to make it." She sighed. "Except things were changing. So we took on more projects and more clients, hoping to get ahead, to figure things out. When Tessa approached, wanting research on gambling institutions, legal and illegal, that's when the pieces came together." She eyed me through the rearview mirror. "The people we targeted were gamblers. They were used to losing money. Most of them were doing illegal things anyway. They couldn't report us. They wouldn't even know who did it or how it happened."

"Is Tessa part of it?"

"She wasn't supposed to know, but when we were going over the research, I stepped out for a minute, and she saw some things she wasn't supposed to see. I told her she had it wrong. She didn't believe me."

"You paid her off," I said.

"I returned her money and told her to forget all about Good Day Marketers. She wanted my research, so I gave her that too, hoping she wouldn't go to the cops."

"Instead, she went to Kincaid."

"She did more than that." O'Neal sighed. "She wanted in on the scam. She figured she could run the same game at the casino she planned to open. He thought that would be great. Once it was off the ground, we'd have an endless supply of marks, so he cut her in on the deal."

"Vincent?"

"I'm not saying a word. He'll kill me if I give him up."

"You're talking about your partner?"

"We were supposed to be partners. But he made the decision to bring Tessa in, and he decided to scare off anyone who was willing to talk to the cops. That wasn't me. I never wanted anyone to get hurt."

"You have to come forward."

"What part of he'll kill me don't you understand?"

"I can protect you."

She snorted derisively. "Why should I believe that? I'm not convinced Kincaid didn't ask you to take me somewhere to kill me."

"I'm not going to kill you."

"Yeah, sure."

"I'm not."

"The look on your face says otherwise."

"For someone who's been grifting and gambling, you need more practice reading people."

"You said you were going to put me in the trunk. That you take care of Kincaid's problems."

"I'm private security." I tossed her my card. "I'm also a private investigator. Alan Kershaw hired me. He didn't like that you took his money. We have all the proof we need to bury you for the theft. We know you played online poker with him, that you were behind the phone call and e-mail. We have recordings. The bank has additional proof of the transfer. All that connects to you. We know the assault was committed by a masked man, but that happened because you wanted to scare Kershaw off. None of this looks good for you. You could go down for all of it, if you don't cooperate."

"I told you that wasn't my idea."

"Someone else has already come forward. What's the harm in verifying it?"

"You're lying."

"I'm not."

"Who told you Vincent's behind this?"

I wasn't going to fall for that. "Nope. That's not how this works."

"You don't have shit," she said.

"We have the bat used in the assault. The crime lab has already established it was used to harm Alan Kershaw. Do you want to know where I found it? In Vincent Lyman's office, your partner's office."

"It doesn't sound like you need me for anything. Pick him up."

"Tell me where he is."

"I don't know."

"Did you miss the part where I said I would protect you?"

"You're one cocky bastard." She rolled her eyes. "You don't know who you're dealing with. When he puts his mind to something, he's an irresistible force. He finds a way to get exactly what he wants. He'll find a way to kill me."

"No one's been killed yet."

She let out a bitter laugh. "You saw what he did. That was a warning. Next time, someone's brains are getting splattered on the pavement. Like I said, irresistible force."

"In that case, it's a good thing I'm an immovable object."

"Sinatra? Really?"

"You started it."

FORTY-TWO

I wanted to question Jasmine O'Neal further, but she'd gone mute and wouldn't talk to me. Despite her stubbornness, her eyes showed fear. She believed her accomplice would kill her, which was why she was taking her chances instead of naming names.

That left me with little choice but to hand her over to the police. The things she had said would be enough for the police to bring in everyone assumed to be involved. Hopefully, Tessa Gold would be more willing to cooperate.

Detective Taylor grinned as she read the statement I provided and listened to the recording I'd made in the car. Of course, I had edited it down to the few relevant lines. The police didn't need to hear the entire conversation.

"I thought you didn't want to do my job for me," she said.

"Someone had to."

"Where did you find her?"

"Out of town."

"That's not an answer."

"Ask her."

"She won't talk without a lawyer."

"In that case, have fun." I grabbed my jacket off the

chair and slipped it on. "She won't name her accomplice either, but she called him her partner. She said they worked on legitimate business, not just scams. The context clues should be enough."

"She's talking about Vincent Lyman."

"That would make sense. Except, in my experience, cold-blooded killers don't usually run. They kill."

"Be glad he didn't have a spare bat in his hand when you went into his office," Taylor said.

"Did you get anything off the security feeds?"

"Good Day Marketers didn't have any interior cameras."

"What about Jeff? Have you found him? Maybe he'll talk to you."

"He left the office, headed straight to the bus station, and took off. He's on his way to Minneapolis. Once he arrives, the locals will pick him up."

"That's a long ride."

"Yeah," she said.

I tried to reason through what I'd learned. "Does Vincent have a record?"

Taylor shook her head. "The smart ones usually don't."

"Most criminals aren't that smart, and even if they are, they didn't start that way. There is a learning curve involved in committing crime."

"How steep is it?"

I smiled. "I'm not a criminal, Detective."

"Maybe I'll call you when we bring him in."

"I thought you didn't want to call me."

"You would have made a good cop, Cross."

I continued out the door, hoping to force that thought aside. For a vice detective, Taylor had been unnaturally adept at getting in my head, and I couldn't afford that right now. I still had the Darrow situation to deal with. Justin and a few members of my security teams were keeping him detained until I returned.

Back at the office, I found Darrow sitting at the conference table, his arms folded across his chest. He glared at me. "Keeping me here is illegal, Lucien."

"People in glass houses."

"I thought you were Mr. Sanctimonious."

"Jasmine O'Neal's in police custody," I said, taking a seat across from him. "She and her partner started scamming people. First, it was credit card numbers, but that didn't work out, so they expanded. Are you working for them?"

"Lucien—"

"Answer me."

"No."

"Is that why you kept insisting the grocery store was where we should focus our attention? You didn't want me to poke around into the marketing agency's practices."

"That's not what this is." Darrow sighed. "You're mad. I get it. But the files I have on Kershaw are for your own good."

"My own good? Explain that to me."

"Kershaw was targeted once. Twice, if you count the assault. Sure, he comes off clean. But his family has secrets. Everyone has secrets or things they wouldn't want coming to light. We dig up dirt, present it, and offer protection."

"Protection? What mafia movies have you been watching?" I hoped it wasn't the same one I'd been reenacting most of the day.

"Not like that. We offer to keep an eye out, an ear to the ground. We do a wipe. Eliminate all of that from the internet. Clean things. Make them sparkle, and we keep a list of people who know about this stuff, so if a problem pops up in the future, we know where to begin."

"That's your plan?"

Darrow shrugged. "It's how you keep clients."

"That's extortion."

"It's not."

"It is, and Cross Security will have no part of it. You were contracted to work for me. You do not conduct yourself like this. There was a morals clause when you signed on the dotted line."

"It's not unethical. It's practical. Worst case, you have something to use against your client if things take a turn."

The way he said that made me wonder how much he knew about my past. "Again, that's extortion."

"It's a safety net. A kill switch." He held up his hands.

"Do what you want. But that's how I conduct business. It's always how I conduct business. You have to be smart and careful. No one else has your back in this profession, so you always cover your ass."

"You expect me to believe that's all it is?"

"That's all it is," Darrow said.

"How did you cut your hand?"

He glanced down at his palm. "On a can. Didn't I say that?"

"Kershaw identified you as the man who attacked him."

Darrow chuckled. "That's a bald-faced lie if I've ever heard one. We both know it's not true. You wanna know how I know that? Because I didn't attack Kershaw. I wasn't anywhere near him when it happened. But I'm sure you already know that. You must have run the GPS in my car and pinged my phone. Why are you playing this game, Lucien? What are you hoping to accomplish?"

"Why the grocery store?"

"It connects."

"How?"

"I don't know yet. You said something about credit cards being scammed. Maybe there's something to that."

I got up, unsure if I was being gaslighted or edging closer to certifiable. "Tell me one thing and answer honestly. Do you have an axe to grind with me?"

The tiny muscles around his eyes tensed. "I'm trying to let that go."

"But you've thought about sabotaging me."

He didn't say anything.

"That's the reason I can't believe what you say."

"Well, that's kind of a you problem, isn't it? I told you the truth. Now, I'm going home." He stood. "I'll see you tomorrow, unless you fire me."

I waited until he was in the elevator before I told two members of the security team to keep an eye on him. I didn't know what to believe. All I knew was this was a giant mess. Instead of being relieved to have caught the woman responsible for stealing Kershaw's money, I couldn't help but think this wasn't over yet. There was more work to be done. Until the police had Vincent Lyman in custody and a confession, I wouldn't be satisfied.

*   *   *

Sometime during the night, Vincent Lyman was arrested at a local motel. Taylor didn't call me, which was for the best. A call that late could easily be misconstrued as something it wasn't. Instead, I found out the next morning when Almeada phoned to tell me Detective Malloy presented Kershaw with a six-pack. Kershaw couldn't identify the assailant from the lineup. But I knew Charlie Steed could.

"Didn't I tell you I didn't want to see you again?" Malloy asked.

"I heard about the arrest." I took a seat in the chair beside his desk and studied the file which was splayed open. "Did you get a confession?"

"What do you think? Vincent Lyman denies everything. He said he had nothing to do with the scam or the assault."

"What about Tessa Gold? Did she say anything useful?"

"Nope."

"What about Jasmine O'Neal?"

"What do you think?"

"Did you try telling Vincent that Jasmine O'Neal's in custody? If he thinks she's cooperating, he may change his tune." I reached for a crime scene photo. "Where was this taken?"

"That's from Lyman's apartment."

"I thought he was apprehended at a motel."

"You're not a cop. None of this is your business. You're interfering. I could arrest you."

"Think about your future career, Jeremy. Do you want to risk it?"

"Your father had you kicked out of the academy. I doubt he'd care if we tossed you in a cell for a few hours."

"What about our night together? We exchanged information. I made you coffee. Doesn't that mean anything to you?"

A few nearby cops heard what I said and gave Malloy curious looks. He scowled at me. "We executed a search warrant after he was arrested."

I put the photo down. "Is your case airtight?"

"Are you looking for a thank you?"

"No." I studied the photos and reports.

The bat found in Vincent's office had Kershaw's blood on it and paint transfer from his car. It didn't have Steed's blood or Vincent's fingerprints. The computers found at the marketing office were being analyzed, but there should be proof on them that they were used to execute the scam. Banking information and transfers should be hidden somewhere on those drives.

The search of Vincent's apartment didn't reveal much except a pair of shoes with blood spatter. The spatter wasn't a match to Alan Kershaw. A more thorough analysis was needed, but the blood type found on the shoes matched Charlie Steed, according to the records I had.

"What did Vincent say when you confronted him about his bloody shoes?" I asked.

"He said they weren't his." Malloy got up from his chair, uncomfortable discussing this with me but unsure how to get out of it. "Just so you know, I told him we had his partner in custody. He said he knew Jazz was doing something illegal and feared whoever she ripped off was coming for him. That's supposedly why he fled when you showed up at his office. He thought you were a knee-breaker. Other than that, he's claiming he's innocent."

"At least someone got my mafia references."

"You told him you were in the mafia?"

"I told him I was a private investigator. I went to him under the guise of prospective client. He had no reason to fear me."

"Regardless, he says he fled because you are one scary son of a bitch obsessed with Jazz. He figured you were there to get payback because she ripped someone off. Other than that, he says he doesn't know any of the specifics of what she was doing and made it a point not to know."

"What about Tessa Gold?"

"I'm not an information booth." Malloy jerked his chin toward the other end of the bullpen. "You want to know anything else, go talk to someone who doesn't despise you."

"You don't despise me, Jeremy. That's just jealousy." I clapped him on the shoulder and headed for the door.

Being in the precinct too long would lead to trouble. More than likely, I'd find myself on the wrong side of the bars. That's why I always thought it best to avoid the place. Yet, this case required a level of cooperation with which I wasn't entirely comfortable. But I'd been trying to make the best of it.

On my way out, I stopped to see my favorite desk sergeant.

Sara sighed dramatically. "Now what did you do?"

"I heard more arrests were made. Y'know, I helped with one yesterday."

"I should have stopped at the store on my way here and bought stickers, knowing you'd want a gold star."

"Maybe I could get a consolation prize instead. How about a copy of the Jasmine O'Neal file?"

"Lucien, you know I can't give you that."

"What about Tessa Gold's file?"

"I can't give you that either."

"But she's in custody?"

Sara entered something into the computer. "Yes, and that's all you're getting out of me."

I'd have to get the reports and transcripts myself. "You can't blame a guy for trying."

She pointed at me. "Go away. And stay out of trouble."

"Yes, ma'am."

FORTY-THREE

The police reports left a lot to be desired. The physical evidence from the assaults connected to Vincent Lyman. The bat used against Kershaw was found in his office. Shoes with blood spatter which I suspected matched Steed had been found in his closet at home. The weird thing about that was Vincent Lyman denied those were his shoes. But he lived alone, and no one else had access to his place.

"You should have come up with a better excuse," I said to my computer screen.

Amir had phoned the crime lab and called in a favor to get a sample of the spatter found on the shoe. Cross Security could run the test faster. We didn't have a backlog. We had one case. And since we'd already offered them a previous comparison, it was only fair that they share with us. I wasn't sure who Amir knew or how much clout he had, but there was no reason to look a gift-horse in the mouth.

Jasmine O'Neal hadn't said much since being taken into custody. She'd copped to the things she'd admitted to me that had been on the recording I supplied to the police. Other than that, she kept her mouth shut.

Tessa Gold had been apprehended. At the present, she

was denying her involvement. The police were focused on the wrong things. They shouldn't be concerned if she was involved. They should have been pushing her to give up the people who masterminded the whole thing.

Could Tessa Gold be behind this? I ran a hand over my face and dug into the files I'd copied from Good Day Marketers. The scams I knew about occurred after Gold hired the marketing firm. Could she be the one Jasmine feared? Maybe that's why she didn't provide a third name, but I didn't think Tessa Gold identified as he/him, and O'Neal had always referred to her partner as he. That supported Vincent as the muscle and possibly the mastermind. So why was I questioning his involvement?

"Fucking Darrow," I muttered.

The intercom beeped. "Did you say something, boss?" Justin asked.

"Is Darrow here?"

"I don't think you should talk to him. It's not good for your blood pressure. That vein at the side of your head might explode."

"I don't want to talk to him. I want to know if he showed up to work."

"He's downstairs in his office."

"Justin," I called, not bothering to press the button on the intercom, "you don't have to walk on eggshells. I'm not going to do anything crazy."

He rolled in front of the open doorway. "You mean like put a Darrow size hole in the wall?"

"I wasn't going to hurt him yesterday."

"Are you trying to convince me or yourself?"

"I wasn't," I said. "He just gets under my skin. Even now, I keep wondering what if he's right. What if I'm missing something? Do you think the grocery store is relevant?"

"It could be a coincidence."

"That's what I think. It happens to be a hotspot in the neighborhood. It could have easily been a liquor store or a gas station. Some place people often go."

"Right."

I raised an eyebrow. "That sounded the tiniest bit

patronizing. You don't think it's a coincidence, do you?"

"It could be."

"Justin, what do you think?"

"Law enforcement doesn't teach coincidences. Two could be a coincidence, but this is what five or six?"

"It's four. Vincent Lyman shopped there. Charlie Steed and Nathan Boter work as management, and Eric Greene delivered there."

"When you put it that way, it could be a coincidence."

"Damn Darrow for getting in my head."

"I thought Jasmine O'Neal confessed to ripping off people. You have footage of her doing it."

"Yes, which is what Kershaw wanted. But Tessa Gold was at Spark. She knew me, and I'm pretty sure she intended to rip off Dennis Powers had I not stopped it. That confuses matters."

"Powers should thank you for saving him."

"He did." I wagged my finger in the air a few times while I thought. "Do me a favor and call him. Let's make sure his funds are secure."

"Will do." Justin rolled back to his desk.

While I waited for the verdict, I pulled up phone records and internet logs. There was no absence of communication between Jasmine O'Neal and Vincent Lyman or between Jasmine and Tessa. However, there wasn't a single call between Tessa and Vincent. The few e-mails that had been exchanged were basic intake and welcome information that was sent to every marketing client.

"Powers said his money is locked up tight. No one has even tried to touch it," Justin called.

"At least I did that much right."

"You thought the women were both grifting." Justin entered my office and made himself comfortable on the couch. "That goes along with what Jasmine told you when you confronted her."

"I don't have a problem with any of that. What I don't get is why she didn't name their third. She referred to him as her partner. The logical assumption is Vincent Lyman. For all intents and purposes, he is her partner. They work together. They worked on legitimate projects together, but she's afraid of him, afraid of what he'll do to her if she gives him up."

"Right…"

"But by calling him her partner and giving us those context clues, isn't she doing exactly that?"

Justin stretched out and yawned. "Maybe that's the work of her subconscious. If her story is to be believed, she didn't want to do these things. She said she needed one big score to get out. That's why she went to the car race. That may be why Tessa zeroed in on Powers. The ladies could have been looking for a way out."

"Or to cut him out."

"Also possible," Justin said. "Perhaps O'Neal wanted Vincent to get caught because she wants to do the right thing. You said you believed her when she said she didn't know anyone had gotten hurt. This could be her way of making amends without putting herself at risk."

"I guess it's up to the police to sort out the rest."

"That's a very enlightened view you have, boss. Since when do you say things like that?"

"Since I'm not sure what else to do."

Justin closed his eyes. "Y'know, I totally get why you nap on this couch."

"It'll kill your back."

"I'll take my chances."

"Don't you have phones to man and work to do?"

Justin opened one eye and looked at me. "Not really. Your first meeting isn't until lunchtime. We basically have the morning off."

"Shouldn't you prepare for the meeting?"

"It's not my meeting. I'll be right here if you need help with anything. We both know you can't function without me."

"How did Tessa Gold know who I was?"

Justin opened his eyes. "What?"

"When she saw me at Spark, she knew my name. I hadn't gone to Good Day Marketers yet. Maybe there is something to the grocery store." O'Neal's words about the credit card scam came to mind. Most people paid for their groceries using plastic. Could that be the connection?

I had to keep digging. Every time I missed something, the results were catastrophic. I wanted to avoid that this time.

I looked again at the crime scene photos taken inside Vincent Lyman's apartment. The bloody shoes were the only evidence found. They'd been in his closet with the rest of his shoes. The only oddity, they were half a size larger. I checked the brand, which was known to run small. That didn't tell me anything. Nothing did.

Between meetings, I went over everything I had on O'Neal, Lyman, and Gold. Unfortunately, I didn't have much. The police database hadn't been updated, or they hadn't made any progress either. Was this case even a priority? When Kershaw went to them for help, they sent him away.

I tapped Agent Olsen's card on my desk. I could call him, but I didn't want to. When I couldn't take it anymore, I went downstairs to Darrow's office. He glanced up when I entered.

"Are you bringing me my walking papers?" he asked.

"Not yet." Turning my back to him, I stood in front of the wall that he'd turned into a house cat's wet dream. Hooking my finger around a piece of red yarn, I followed the path it took.

"Can I help you with something?"

"I'm just looking."

"I didn't realize this was a shopping trip. Can I offer you something in a different color or size?"

"How does Jasmine O'Neal connect to the grocery store?" I couldn't believe I was playing six degrees with Darrow, but I hadn't come up with a connection. Since he'd been obsessed, he must know something.

"She approached Boter at Chelsea's Bar and Grill. As you know, her fellow marketing manager frequents that store. Her intern/personal assistant gave up a budding career in marketing and business to be an assistant manager at that store. She has plenty of connections to it."

I followed the string. "Is that it?"

"She has a loyalty card. She hasn't been in the store recently, not since any of this started."

"When's the last time she was there?" I asked.

"Um..." Darrow rifled through the records. "She hasn't scanned her card in that store since Charlie Steed started working there. I'd say things didn't end on the best of terms between them."

"What makes you say that?"

"The conversation you had with him for one."

"Anything else?"

"She hasn't gone inside the store now that he works there."

"But Vincent goes all the time."

"Yeah, but Charlie Steed wasn't Vincent's intern. He was O'Neal's intern."

I let that simmer. "What about Tessa Gold?"

"She's not local. No loyalty card."

"Is it necessary to be a member to shop at the store?"

"No."

I gave him a sideways look. "Did you get a card when you bought the pizzas and cutting board?"

"With the things I've found out about that store, do you think I'd want to give anyone my personal information?"

"But you still got a discount?"

"I asked the person behind me in line if I could use their card. Most people don't mind, if you're nice." Darrow eyed me. "I could see why that might be a problem for you."

Letting that go, I couldn't help but think I was no closer now than I'd been before I made the trek downstairs. "When you were shopping, did anyone from customer service insist you sign up for a card?"

"No."

"I must have found the only pushy clerk in the place."

"Or someone in that store really wanted your information and thought that'd be the easiest way to get it." Darrow grinned. "I wonder if any of those questions are useful when emptying out bank accounts. I bet they are."

"What about credit card scams? Does anything connect to the grocery store?"

"People get scammed all the time. As far as I know, their system was never breached. They have the recommended encryption in place."

"But only large-scale breaches would be made known. If one or two people got their credit card numbers stolen, there'd be no way of knowing where that happened."

"What are you thinking?" Darrow asked.

"I don't know yet." I rubbed my lip. "Jasmine O'Neal confessed. She said she and her partner were running scams. No one at—" I froze. "Shit."

"What is it?" Darrow asked.

"I need to check something."

"You figured something out. What is it?"

Ignoring him, I headed to the door.

"You couldn't have done it without me," he called to my retreating back.

FORTY-FOUR

"Twice in two days. You can't get enough, can you?" Detective Taylor asked.

"Did you get the footage from Jasmine O'Neal's apartment building?"

Taylor indicated the empty chair beside her. "I've gone over this with a fine-tooth comb, but there's nothing here that I can use against Vincent Lyman. He went to her place a few times, usually with takeout, and he'd leave a few hours later." She glanced at me. "Do you think they're dating?"

"My guess would be those are working dinners. The body language doesn't indicate a sexual interest."

"I wasn't sure you were capable of picking up on such things."

"I'm a trained investigator." Reaching for the mouse, I checked the relevant timestamps. "Do you have audio?"

"No."

For such an advanced security system, I would have thought the apartment building would have splurged with their recording equipment. "What about her phone records? Do you know who she was having those conversations with while she paced up and down the hallway?"

"The timestamps don't coincide with the records we have."

"She has a second phone."

"Brilliant deduction, Columbo."

"Did you find it when you searched her place?"

Taylor shook her head. "We thought the phone you took off her would have matched, but that was her regular phone."

I already knew that. I'd checked it and downloaded the data before handing it over. "What about her other visitors? You know that's why I'm here."

"I thought this was an excuse to see me." She smacked my hand and took control of the mouse. "Tessa Gold never went to her place, so don't bother asking."

"I'm not looking for Tessa."

"Who are you looking for?"

"Charlie Steed."

Taylor consulted her notes.

"He was there, wasn't he?" I asked.

"Several times. He used to go by her place a lot more frequently. He stopped showing up so much. I figured he was an ex-boyfriend or they had an arrangement."

"An arrangement?"

"Friends with benefits, two a.m. booty calls, whatever you want to call it."

"Did he ever show up at her place at two a.m.?"

"A time or two." She found footage from more than six months ago. Steed wore a dark hoodie. He tried not to get spotted, but when he exited the apartment, the camera always caught sight of his face before he could step out of view. He hadn't been to her place since. "I recognize him now. He was the second mugging victim."

"Yeah."

"You think O'Neal sent the same goon after her ex?"

"I don't think Steed's her ex."

"C'mon," she indicated the screen, "they look cozy."

"According to Steed, he couldn't stand O'Neal or the things the marketing agency was doing. He worked as an intern and had some very unflattering things to say about her."

"My gut says spurned lover. O'Neal must have gotten revenge." Taylor made some notes and printed a still from the footage. "Thanks for the heads-up. Now I'm going to have a chat with O'Neal. We'll see what she says and bring Steed in for a follow-up now that we have some idea who may have been responsible for his assault."

I stared at the screen. The pieces were falling into place, except for the assault. That I still couldn't explain. "Do you have security cam footage from Vincent Lyman's apartment building?"

"Why would I need that?"

"Do you have it?" I asked.

"We pulled it when we were hoping to track his whereabouts. No one had been to his place except him."

"What about after he went MIA? Have you watched the footage since?"

"Why would we? A patrol unit was keeping watch out front. He never showed."

"Yeah, okay." I gave the screen another look.

"If you ask nicely, I'll let you watch me interrogate O'Neal."

"I have more pressing things to do."

Leaving the confused vice detective behind, I headed to Vincent Lyman's apartment. Thankfully, building security had no problem showing me the surveillance footage for a price.

A man in a dark hoodie had entered Vincent's apartment after I confronted him at Good Day Marketers. The man didn't break in. He used a key, but it wasn't Vincent. They had similar builds, but the hanging keyring gave him away.

After getting back in the car, I considered my options. Everything I had was flimsy. The assault served as the perfect alibi, but I still had no idea how he pulled it off.

"Justin," I said when he answered, "has the lab run the comparison yet?"

"Amir just sent the results. They're on your desk."

"What do they say?"

"The blood on the shoes is a match to Charlie Steed."

"Did Amir ever figure out how the assailant wasn't seen on the cameras?"

"That remains a mystery."

"Not so much," I said.

"You figured it out?" Justin asked.

"Only if the wounds could have been self-inflicted."

Justin laughed, thinking I was making a joke, but when I didn't crack, he said, "You're serious? How could someone inflict that much damage? You said he took a beating. His cheekbone was fractured."

"He made it look like he took a beating."

"But you saw his face. We have the medical report."

"Ask the experts if those injuries could have been self-inflicted." The medic's warning about the weapon not being a bat came to mind. "I'm thinking he slammed his face into the wall when he was out of camera range. There is a blind spot, but it's tiny. Only big enough for someone to stand straight up. If he tried to leave, he'd get spotted, but Steed wasn't going anywhere. He had to make himself look like a victim."

"Are you sure about this?"

"I don't know. Taylor said she's going to bring him in for a follow-up. I'm heading to his place to see what I can find. In the meantime, I'm sending you footage from Vincent Lyman's apartment building. See if you can enhance it. I want to know if the keyring in the video is the same as the one Steed wears."

"You want to make an ID based on a guy's keyring?"

"Unless you or Amir comes up with something better, that's all we can do. Also, check whatever footage we have from outside Good Day Marketers. Charlie Steed used to work there. He knows how to get in and out of the building. Hell, he probably has a key." That may have also explained how he had a key to Vincent's place. "See if you spot anyone sneaking in with a bat or a bag big enough to conceal a bat."

"You think he planted the weapon in Vincent's office?"

"That would make sense."

"How could he have had time? Wouldn't Vincent have noticed it?"

"Not if he knew Vincent had other plans that morning and encouraged me to confront him. He must have figured I'd find it."

"That's a gamble. That only works if everything goes perfectly. If not, Vincent finds it and gets rid of it."

"Unless he didn't know what to do with it...or unless Charlie got Jeff to help him with that. That would explain why the current intern ran for the hills when I showed up the second time."

"All right. I'm on it, boss. Should I notify Almeada to be on standby in case you get arrested for B&E?"

"Use your best judgment."

Normally, Charlie Steed would be at work, but since he was recovering from the alleged assault, he had taken the day off.

My gut said the bastard had played me. He'd been damn convincing too. Our first conversation indicated he wasn't a suspect, but since he was on my radar, he must have figured staging the assault would turn my attention away from him.

The sight of a silver sedan parked near the building made me do a double-take. That was one of my cars. What was Darrow doing here? Did he show up to warn Steed? Was that who he'd been feeding our intel to? All the pieces fit. Darrow's obsession with the grocery store. Steed showing up at Cross Security to tell me what happened. But Darrow had said to my face he didn't know who was behind this, and I didn't think he was a good enough liar to pull that off. I was the poker player. He wasn't. Could that have been a bluff?

After parking across the street, I hurried up the steps. If Darrow hadn't shown up to warn Steed, then he was here to show me up.

The door to Steed's apartment had been jimmied open. The sloppy scrapes told me Darrow was already inside. For a professional, he should have been better at picking locks.

Entering, I looked around. The place was clean. Darrow hadn't made his usual mess.

Voices froze me in place. The man speaking was clearly Darrow. The other sounded like Steed.

"I told you I dropped by to see if you were okay," Darrow said. "This is a courtesy call. When you didn't come to the door, I got freaked out."

"That's why I found you trying to break into my computer?" Steed asked.

Shit. The police were supposed to have picked Steed up. Darrow must have realized what I figured out and came straight here instead of verifying the facts first.

"I wasn't. I...wanted to check my e-mail."

"Use your fucking phone," Steed said.

"I...uh..."

Steed snorted. "How did you figure it out?"

"Figure what out?" Darrow asked. "I told you I came here to check on you. What are you talking about?"

The bad acting was how I knew Darrow hadn't lied to me. No wonder he wore strange outfits. The distraction kept people from noticing the over-the-top lies.

"How much do you know?" Steed asked.

"Know what?"

A sharp bang came from the bedroom, followed by a surprised whimper. The whimper was Darrow. I wasn't sure what made the bang.

"Do the police know?" Steed asked.

"No one knows anything."

"What about your boss?"

"Lucien isn't my boss. We're associates," Darrow insisted.

I had to do something before he got himself killed. Luckily for Darrow, I had no interest in taking a play from his book. Running for help wasn't in my nature. Instead, I removed the gun from my holster, took the safety off, and made my way to the bedroom.

FORTY-FIVE

Charlie Steed had his back to me. Sneaking up on him would have been the easy play. A gun to the back would force him to comply. Then I'd put him in cuffs and wait for the police to arrive. That would be two arrests in one week, thanks to me. At this rate, they'd have to give me a badge.

However, Darrow spotted me first. The sudden relief on his face tipped off Steed, who moved faster than any marketing exec or grocery store manager should. He spun around Darrow, wrapping one arm around his clavicle while pulling the boxcutter from his pocket and sliding the blade above the guard. Steed pressed it against Darrow's throat before the private eye could think to do anything.

"Charlie," I said, entering the room, gun aimed, "it's over."

Steed stepped backward, urging Darrow to move with him. A tiny trickle of blood ran down Darrow's neck. "How did you figure it out?"

"The faked mugging. The scammer had no reason to go after you. You weren't a victim. You had nothing to do with anything," I said.

"That was it?"

"Our medic said your wounds weren't consistent with

- 293 -

your story. You smashed in your own face," Darrow said.

I gave Darrow a look, hoping he'd get the message and knock the back of his head into Steed's face, but Darrow didn't move. The boxcutter to the carotid held him in place.

"He figured that out from x-rays?" Steed asked.

"The people I hire are that good," I said. "Also, you spent a lot of time at Jasmine O'Neal's place, especially for someone who despised the woman." I glanced around the room, realizing Steed was hoping to escape through the window. It must have led to a balcony and exterior stairs which would take him to safety. "Did she know you planned to sell her out? After all, you're the reason she was arrested."

"She deserves it. I wasn't lying when I told you what they do at Good Day Marketers. It's so damn frustrating. Do you have any idea what it's like to spend years learning and studying only to find out you're gonna get replaced by a fucking machine before you even got your shot? It's happening everywhere. The way they run their campaigns is only making it worse. Everything is automated. Good Day Marketers are literally putting themselves out of business."

"Someone has to push the buttons," I said.

"They weren't even doing that. That's what Vincent designed Rita to do." He dug the blade in deeper, making Darrow squeal.

"Lucien, now's not the time," Darrow choked out. "How about you try not to piss people off for once in your life?"

"So that was it? You didn't like how they conducted business so you decided to take them down?" I asked.

Steed took another step backward. "Not exactly. Jasmine and I had a conversation. We needed to find other sources of revenue. The marketing firm was drowning before any of this came about. Sure, they were finally making ends meet, but that would dry up once the inevitable happens, which it will."

"That's how the scams started," I said.

"We figured if we got caught, we'd blame good ol' Vinnie. After all, this was his fault."

"What about the people you ripped off?" I asked. "What

did they do to deserve it?"

"They deserved it. The wealthy always have more, and gamblers, shit, they would spend it anyway, regardless of if it was their last dime. I saw no reason why I shouldn't put it to better use."

"You found out about the games from your boss," Darrow said. "Nathan Boter likes to gamble. He would have known about all the underground establishments."

"Too bad you're not going to be around to tell anyone about that," Steed said.

"Whoa," I held up my free hand, steadying my aim with the other, "time out. Even if you kill Darrow, that won't make this go away."

"Maybe not, but it'll buy me time to get away." Steed gave me a satisfied smirk, like he'd thought through everything and realized he was still the smartest person in the room. "I slice his throat open, and you have to stay here to save him. That gives me time to escape."

I snorted. "Go ahead and kill him. I don't care. Frankly, you'd be saving me the trouble. I've been driving around all week with a machete and shovel in my trunk."

"You what?" Darrow asked.

"You're lying," Steed said.

"Only one way to find out, Charlie. Go ahead." I gripped the gun in both hands. "But keep in mind, the second he goes down, you won't have him to use as a shield. I can shoot you."

"You're not that fast. He won't drop right away. I'll have time." Steed pulled Darrow a little closer to the window.

"You still have to get it open. I hope it doesn't stick," I said.

"Lucien—" Darrow began.

"Shut up." I scratched my head with the barrel of my gun, like a crazy person. "Actually, y'know, I've come up with a better plan. I shoot him. Then I shoot you. They call that friendly fire, and if he dies, oh well. Two birds, one stone."

Steed eyed me. "You're not a killer."

My eyes grew dark. "Do you wanna bet?"

In that moment, Steed saw it. "Fuck." He shoved

Darrow toward me, knocking us both to the ground. That bought him enough time to pull open the window and climb onto the balcony.

"You good?" I asked, pushing Darrow aside and pausing long enough to make sure he hadn't been sliced and diced.

He gave me a thumbs up, clutching his throat. "Good."

I went out the window after Steed. He was almost at the bottom when two patrol officers came around the side of the building. Seeing Steed fleeing, they pulled their weapons and hurried to meet him. Steed tried to reverse course, but I caught him from behind, gun aimed. Hopefully, the cops didn't plan on shooting me.

"Where do you think you're going?" I asked.

One officer came up the steps while the other remained on the ground. I didn't put my piece away. Instead, I told him who I was.

Once Steed was cuffed, I put the safety on and holstered my weapon. Detective Taylor appeared on the balcony above me.

"You should have called me," she said.

"Maybe next time."

"You mean we're doing this again?"

"God, I hope not."

*　　*　　*

Darrow knocked on my open door. Justin had gone home an hour ago, or he would have alerted me to Darrow's presence. But I knew Darrow was on his way. Gloria had texted to tell me.

I put the phone down, shaking my head while I reached for my drink. "It looks like case closed."

"You saved me," Darrow said.

I swallowed another gulp. "I thought you were going to accuse me of wanting you dead."

"I knew you were bluffing."

I fixed him with my piercing stare. "Was I?"

"Don't play like that." Darrow sunk into the chair across from me. "I'm waiting for you to say it?"

"Say what?"

"I was right about the grocery store."

"You weren't."

"I was a little." He reached for the bottle, looking around for a clean glass. "If it hadn't been for my research, you wouldn't have figured out Steed was responsible."

"Whatever you want to tell yourself."

Darrow grumbled, getting up to get a glass from the bar cart before making himself a drink. "You realize this makes us even. I saved you. You saved me. We're back on solid ground. No reason for any more distrust. No more grudges. We're good now." He sat back down. "What do you think about keeping me on?"

"Full-time?" I eyed the glass in his hand. "How many of those did you have before you came up here?"

"None."

"Did they dope you up with something at the ER?"

"Lucien, I'm serious."

I knew he was. He also made a fair point. "What did you do with the blackmail you have on Kershaw?"

"I deleted it. You can check." His eyes narrowed. "You already did."

"Are those your only copies?" I saw it on his face. They weren't. He had hard copies stashed somewhere. Probably at his place. "Show me where you're keeping the rest and destroy them, then we'll talk."

"Really?"

"I said we'd talk. But you can't do that again. If you do, we're done. Extorting our clients is not how I do business."

He snorted and took another sip. "Yeah, sure."

"Anyway," I said, making a note to search Darrow's place for whatever he had on Kershaw and me, "Detective Taylor said they were able to trace the stolen funds to an offshore account Steed had set up. It'll take some work, but everyone who was scammed will get their money back eventually."

"Mr. Kershaw must be thrilled."

"He's more relieved we found the person who assaulted him."

"Do we know why Steed did that?" Darrow asked.

"He knew we were investigating. The police were closing

in. It was meant to be a misdirect. He wanted to pin everything on Vincent. Jasmine and Tessa were looking for that big score so they could get out of town and open that casino. Different state, different jurisdiction. They thought that would put them in the clear."

"You're sure?"

"That's what Tessa Gold said in a statement she provided. Unlike O'Neal, she had no problem turning on Steed. She said he was behind everything, that he manipulated her into helping, that she never wanted to have anything to do with any of it, but he forced her into it."

"Do you think that's true?"

"No. O'Neal gave her an envelope full of cash. That was meant to be a signing bonus to encourage her to go after the big fish at Spark. Since O'Neal was banned, Gold had to do it herself, but she needed a little encouragement."

"A preview of the kind of money she stood to make if she could pull it off," Darrow said.

"Pretty much."

Darrow cocked his head to the side. "Axel Kincaid is another of your clients. Was that a freebie, or does he get billed for the assistance you provided?"

"It was a favor."

"Which he'll repay."

"How do you know I wasn't repaying him?"

Darrow shrugged. "You don't extort clients, but you trade in favors. That makes sense."

"Y'know what, I changed my mind. I don't want you anywhere near my business."

"But you already made me an offer."

"That wasn't an offer."

"It sounded like an offer."

"It wasn't."

"I think it was." Darrow grinned. "Face it. You're going to give in because you're afraid I have something that can bury you."

"You've got it wrong. You should be afraid I plan on burying you." I winked at him. "Just FYI, I wasn't kidding about that shovel."

LOOK OUT FOR KNIFE'S EDGE, THE FIFTH
BOOK IN THE CROSS SECURITY
INVESTIGATION SERIES.

AND FOR MORE LUCIEN CROSS, CHECK
OUT *ON TILT (ALEXIS PARKER #14)*
NOW AVAILABLE AS AN E-BOOK AND IN
PAPERBACK

ABOUT THE AUTHOR

G.K. Parks is the author of the Alexis Parker series. The first novel, *Likely Suspects,* tells the story of Alexis' first foray into the private sector.

G.K. Parks received a Bachelor of Arts in Political Science and History. After spending some time in law school, G.K. changed paths and earned a Master of Arts in Criminology/Criminal Justice. Now all that education is being put to use creating a fictional world based upon years of study and research.

You can find additional information on G.K. Parks and the Alexis Parker series by visiting our website at
www.alexisparkerseries.com